THEY SAY HE FLIES AT NIGHT

AMY MATAYO

They Say He Flies at Night

by

Amy Matayo

Two things I am most attracted to: the human soul, and a work of art. Funny how sometimes they can be one and the same.

So, this is to the artists out there. Keep using your gifts to change the world.

Xo, Amy

PROLOGUE

Present Day

The leaves rustled underfoot despite last night's rain, a dead giveaway to the boys' location. They muttered amongst themselves, each worried for their lives but too far gone and curious to turn back. Once you're halfway through the middle of downtown, it's too late to change your mind, especially when the sun is down, and a possible Santa sighting is involved. Sure, a Santa sighting on a mid-October Arkansas night might be odd to some, but obviously, the man they came to spy on couldn't live in Christmas Land all the time. Rumor had it among the fourth-grade crowd that Santa relocated here from the North Pole eleven months out of the year to shake people off his scent. Who would think to look for him at an antique store in Silver Bell, Arkansas, anyway? No one, that's who.

No one except three nine-year-old boys already late for dinner and shushing one another way too loudly to stay anonymous.

"Ow! You stepped on my foot," Tim O'Brien said, gripping his barely injured right foot with his hand while hopping dramatically on his left one. Dried leaves crunched all around them as they scattered, the sound mixing with Tim's cries and echoing in the air for the whole town to hear.

"Quiet, O'Brien. You're gonna get us killed," said Bobby McGooden, poking Tim on the side with a stern pointer finger. Tim yelped so loud that an interior light switched on above Miss Berry's hair salon next door. All three boys ducked under a broken streetlamp, deep in the shadows and away from prying eyes, specifically hers. Miss Berry lived on the second floor above her store and oversaw everything that happened in this town, nosy as she was. She stood in the window and looked left to right and back again. Bored with obvious inactivity, her light turned off a few seconds later.

"Santa doesn't kill people," said J.D. James, his voice steely with disgust. "Now, would you both shut up and be still? If Mr. Lorry is who we think he is, we're never gonna find out with all the racket you two are making. He'll just gather up all his reindeer and fly away, and it'll be all your fault. Then we'll be on his bad list for sure."

As for J.D., he wasn't sure he even believed in Santa Claus anymore, but on the off-chance Santa lived here like everyone at school suspected... Well, you can't just go denying the existence of someone who brings you gifts once a year, can you? That'd be stupid. J.D. might have a failing grade in multiplying fractions thanks to his terrible teacher Mr. Foster, but J.D. was smart enough to put two and two together. And two plus two did not equal exposing Santa as the owner of their local antique store, not if he wanted gifts to appear under his Christmas tree. For now, he just wanted to see the man for himself, then go home and eat chili and Fritos before bed. Maybe watch a rerun of *Friends* with his older brother. Even at nine years old, J.D. had a thing for Rachel Green.

All arguing ceased when the front door of the antique shop opened, and the man called Mr. Lorry stepped outside. All three boys sucked in a collective breath when the old man appeared, looking like he had the ultimate power to add their names to the naughty list.

A sudden breeze lifted the old man's long scraggly beard and ruffled the dullish white hair that grew past his collar, both in serious need of a good combing. The wind chimes hanging across the front of his store took off, playing an odd symphony, like cymbals clashing together, out of sync and tune. Mr. Lorry's belly wasn't as big as they imagined Santa's to be, though they supposed he'd had ten months off eating cookies and was bound to lose a little weight. He was a small man, no taller than Tim's dad, and Mr. O'Brien was practically the shortest man in town, but that might be because Mr. Lorry was old and stooped over at the shoulders. He had a limp, too—a step, hop, drag that was tiring to watch, so it had to be hard to do. J.D.'s dad said the man was nearly seventy—and wasn't everyone bent over and draggy at least a little at that age? Mr. Lorry wore cream-colored long johns instead of a red suit— kinda disappointing—but they supposed the man had to do laundry occasionally.

If Mr. Lorry wasn't Santa Claus, he could pass for his brother for sure. His slower and shorter and weirder brother, but still.

All three boys stared wide-eyed from their hiding spot as Mr. Lorry unfolded a cot, all at once realizing the other rumor about the old man was true. Not about him being Santa, but about the odd way the man slept. He had a perfectly good house next door—a white, two-story clapboard with gas lanterns burning on both sides of the front entry and a lamp shining through a big picture window.

According to J.D.'s mother, the house had three bedrooms—a big one downstairs and two smaller ones up.

Yet the man slept on his front porch.

The boys watched as he looked around, up one side of the street and down the other, then lowered himself on the worst bed they'd ever seen. A military cot is what his dad called it. The green kind with a thick layer of tarp, light to carry but sturdy for sleeping. Mr. Lorry stood up again and dragged the cot closer to the antique shop entry, close enough to reach out and touch the front bell, an alarm of sorts, should he need one. Then he lay back down, spread a thin green blanket across his chest, tucked both arms under his head, and stared at the sky. It was only seven o'clock in the evening, but the whole town knew the man turned in early.

They just didn't know why he slept outside.

Of course, everyone had their theories.

"My dad said he fought in the war and can't sleep unless he's outside with his boots on." The absence of boots on Mr. Lorry's feet made this a questionable claim, but the explanation came from Tim, and his mother knew everything about everyone, just like Miss Berry, so there had to be some truth to the theory. Tim spoke in a whisper so low the others could barely hear him. On the porch, Mr. Lorry raised his head like maybe he had, so the boys

moved farther into the woods, deeper into the shadows. Mr. Lorry settled back down. "My dad also says
he was friends with the President. Not the one now,
but from a long time ago. I think his name was Ford,
like the truck or something."

"I heard he's an artist," said Bobby, not wanting
to be left out of the information-sharing. "And that
he has a bunch of paintings hanging in some
museum in New York City or London or somewhere.
Either that, or he's a writer or something. He has
books somewhere, maybe at the library. At least
that's what Mrs. Johnson said." Mrs. Johnson was the
boys' art teacher at school, a much nicer teacher
than Mr. Foster. But this explanation didn't make her
sound too bright. I mean, just look at Mr. Lorry. He
had old-people hands. And they shook. Tim could
see them wobbling back and forth from here.

"There's no way that's true. How could he paint
or write anything with those hands?" Tim argued.
"He can hardly hold them straight, and they're all
shaky."

He was right, they were shaky, but Bobby shoved
him a little anyways. "He could use a computer to
write books. Besides, I didn't say he did it yesterday.
A long time ago. Back before we was born. I doubt
his hands were all bent back then." Tim shoved
Bobby back, and the scuffling went on for a minute
until a twig snapped. That's when they both noticed

that J.D. wasn't saying a word, not even bothering to scold them, just staring at the old man with a strange look in his eyes.

"What is it, J.D.?" Bobby said, the wonder of wanting to impress his older-by-six-months friend evident in his voice. "What'd we miss?" Both boys quieted down.

J.D. remained silent, so silent both boys began to shift in place. J.D. was a thinker, and his thoughts often went places they didn't like to go. Monsters in the closet, axe murderers in the bushes, shadows that doubled as evil spirits climbing up the walls. He was good at telling ghost stories—too good. And as for believing in the boogie man, J.D. could have you convinced such a person existed in only a few seconds' time. It was the way he threw his voice, high pitched and excited one second, dark and low the next. A killer's voice in the minute before he lures his victim into a windowless white van.

"J.D.?" Tim and Bobby both blinked at him.

J.D. didn't look at them when he answered, his voice low and pinched. "When he shifted on his cot just now, I think I saw his wings."

Both boys frowned, first at J.D., then at each other, then at the old man. He looked the same as he did before. *Wings?*

Only Bobby dared to speak up. "Wh...why would he have wings?"

"Well, I don't see any reindeer anywhere," J.D. said. "Do you?"

All three heads swung left and right, looking for some.

But J.D. was right. They were in the middle of town with pavement all around—no grass or pasture or nothing. There weren't any reindeer here, and wouldn't there need to be if Mr. Lorry were Santa? Bobby looked behind him, just in case. "It's true. I don't see any reindeer nowhere."

"Then, of course, he would need to have wings," J.D. said it like it all made sense.

It didn't. Not at all.

"But...what for?" Tim said.

J.D. exhaled, exasperated. "Because." He said the one word like a full sentence, but just when the boys thought he was done with explanations, he dropped his voice to an even lower whisper, almost like he was talking to himself. "They say he flies at night. That's why he goes to sleep so early. So, he can fly later while we're all sleeping."

Two pairs of eyes blinked at him until Bobby spoke up. "But why would he need to fly? It's only October. It's nowhere near Christmas."

J.D. looked at him, pity in his eyes at the boy's obvious ignorance.

"Don't you know anything about jobs, Bobby? If Mr. Lorry is Santa, he'd need wings in the off-season to practice. He can't expect the reindeer to work all year long for no reason, can he?"

Bobby visibly mulled that thought over by scrunching his eyebrows and gnawing his lower lip, then settled his gaze back on the man that no one ever spoke to. Even though the sun had barely set in the sky, the man still lay on his back, but now his eyes looked closed. His chest rose and fell on steady, deep breaths. Five hours. That's how long Mr. Lorry had until midnight. Maybe he was resting up now to practice flying around their town later.

There was no telling the secrets the old man lived with. You can't really know someone just because you're watching them, right? For all this town knew, Mr. Lorry was a simple man whose real life took place among fables and whispered retellings. He never spoke to anyone, not even his customers, as he scratched out receipts and sent them on their way.

But the rumor mill...

Just like the local townsfolk, the rumor mill spun loudly with tales, gathering information all over Silver Bell even as the old man slept soundly outside on his porch.

PART I

1

TWO WEEKS LATER

Piper

The sun is just beginning to set over Lake Wedington, the same location as our first meeting. That night, we went paddle boating with a group of fellow honors students from three neighboring high schools in our county—a trip sponsored by local small-town bigwigs as one last hurrah before graduation. A *do your town proud* initiative that actually paid off. Not your typical outlet for connecting with what might turn out to be the love of your life, but it worked for Bryant and me. Seeing as we planned to attend the same state university—me to major in photography, Bryant in political science—from that point on, we moved from friends who dated other people to lovers who dated exclusively to debatable soulmates in nearly thirteen years. Not love at first sight, obviously—my mother fell in love with Bryant before I did—but a slow burn trumps instant connection anyway. All the experts say so. We're the stuff dreams are made of. The Hallmark Channel makes movies about couples like us and turns those stories into big business at Christmastime. So does Harlequin and every other big-name book publisher, for that matter.

Plus, we both turned thirty-one earlier this year —Bryant in January and me in April. If ever an internal clock could be heard ticking, mine is advancing to time bomb status with each spin of the dial. Not very modern-day feminist of me to feel that way, but I can admit it to myself, and Bryant can recognize it too. He wants two kids by the time he's thirty-five, so we need to get started right after the wedding. We already promised his parents.

But that's enough about kids.

Tonight's orange and bronze-lit setting is picturesque and perfect, film worthy and epic. It would jump right off the pages of a bestselling romance novel, sending pulses skyrocketing and heartbeats aflutter with anticipation. Just like I planned it. Just like *we* planned it.

Even though she's been gone for years now, I know my mom would be proud.

"Well done, Piper. Bryant is a good man."

I imagine the longed-for words of my mother,

her soothing voice still vivid in my mind even though seven years have passed since I last heard her speak. The memory settles over my spirit, a balm to my tired, questioning soul. Until I feel the pinprick of tears that threaten to well in my eyes and quickly shake my head, determined to find only the positives in this moment, resolved not to cry. Even the freckles I feel creeping up on my nose won't ruin this night. I slathered them in foundation to be sure. Red hair and ivory skin are the curse Ann Shirley made them out to be.

I've waited my whole life for this. Dreamed about it. Made image boards around it. I have written the Instagram caption in my mind, mentally eliminating every adverb from the witty, emotionally driven, poetic, condensed-to-two-hundred sixty-two words. I've imagined the perfect photo taken from the perfect angle. The perfect lighting. Perfect outfit. Perfect sparkly heels. Perfect surprised look on my face. Perfect friends smiling adoringly in the background at the virtual fairy tale happening right before their eyes. *Can you believe it?* A perfect ice-rink-sized diamond perched inside a tiny blue box, the perfect fiancé on one knee holding it open.

My mind snags on that last one because it's the only thing not going as perfectly as I imagined. A penny drops in my chest as I take in my camera and tripod set up by the water, and the many iPhones aimed in our direction. What is the matter with me? We *talked* about this. Planned for it. Decided this was the best thing that could happen to me years ago. Half the plan fell apart when my mom got sick, making it much more important to keep the rest of the plan together. My mother isn't here, so I need to be present for both of us. I give myself a three-second pep talk so as not to get caught frowning in a candid photo and straighten my shoulders.

It's time. You can't date someone for the better part of a decade without eventually making a decision. After this long, you've got to commit. We're both thirty-one. People keep asking. We've both tried dating other people and keep drifting back together. Of course, it's time.

I focus on Bryant. Pluck a wayward strand of long, wavy red hair—mine, of course, because I shed like a snake slithering into winter—off his collar and drop it on the ground. Audibly gasp when my gaze catches the diamond. Widen my eyes to feign surprise and muster a tear or two, telling myself I'm fine. It's just nerves. Or I'm coming down with a cold or an ill-timed case of seasonal allergies. Maybe a touch of a stomach bug. It's the only explanation for my hesitation when Bryant finally pops the question he already knows the answer to.

"Will you marry me?"

I imagine my mother smiling down on us. "Can't you

just see it, Piper? A member of the Ratliff family, like a dream."

"Yes!" I cry out, overcome with emotion that has nothing to do with the question Bryant just asked. I wish my mom were here. Sadness always tends to hit at the worst time. I force a wide smile, taking an extra second to fluff my hair before throwing my arms around his neck. "Of course, I'll marry you! It's about time you asked me."

Bryant pulls back and looks at me with a frown. "October was your idea, remember? If it had been up to me, I would have proposed on Valentine's Day."

The comment stings, but only because he's technically right. I did say I wanted an October proposal, but what I really wanted was a proposal as far away from Valentine's Day as I could get.

I hate Valentine's Day. It's a made-up holiday, and a proposal centered around it would have been the worst sort of cliché, not to mention paper hearts and stamped chalky candy are a cheap insult to lovers everywhere. That's the best idea corporate marketers of romance could come up with? No wonder fifty percent of marriages end in divorce.

I waive off his comment and bury my face in his neck. "I remember. But you have to admit, late autumn is much better. Just look at the trees. Think of the pictures!" At Bryant's appreciative hum, I know it's the right thing to say.

"Autumn. When the leaves flutter aimlessly, and Earth's colors are the prettiest."

My voice is muffled enough to hide the overwhelming emotion that always surfaces with memories of my mother. I swallow, get ahold of myself, and pull back to look at my hand. The giant pear-shaped diamond with sapphire baguettes on each side glitters back at me. It's honestly a little heavy.

"This ring is beautiful!" I say, injecting an exaggerated dose of enthusiasm into my words. Who cares how much the ring weighs? My hand is bound to get used to it eventually.

"I know how to pick them, even though I still think we should have gone with the larger cut." Bryant's voice has an edge like he's worried someone will comment that the ring was bought on a budget. It wasn't, and the larger one was pretty, but I preferred this one. How many times does a girl get married? Plus, this one reminded me of my mother's wedding ring. The longing to see her only intensifies.

"I love this one, and it looks amazing. Quick, let's take a selfie so we never forget this moment." I dig through my bag for my iPhone, my new two-carat diamond ring snagging on a loose string hanging from my wallet. I yank it free along with my phone, then frame our faces and quickly touch the screen with my outstretched left hand. The sun dips lower into the horizon behind us, a single ray of blood-red light catching on my diamond and sending a streak of crimson as bright as our smiles straight across the screen.

A perfect photo, just like I wanted.

All around us, our friends rush forward to squeal at the ring, at the picture, at us. It is remarkable. Perfectly perfect in every way, just as an engagement photo should be.

You can't even tell my smile is fake.

"WE FINALLY GET TO PLAN A WEDDING!" Andrea, my best friend since childhood, grasps my wrist and jostles it a little as she jumps up and down. There's no question that she'll be my maid of honor. We planned that detail during an eleventh-grade sleepover and sealed the deal with two kisses on Justin Bieber's concert poster from his Never Say Never tour. The poster still hangs in my bedroom at my aunt's house above my cast iron bed with its pink paisley comforter. Some things never change. Not my love for my friend Annie or my status as a die-hard Belieber—both of which are the foundation for my existence and have been since early last decade.

We've dreamed of planning each other's weddings for as long as I can remember. Now it has become a reality.

"Can you believe it!" I shout back at her, my voice rising an extra decibel or two, not to be outdone on the enthusiasm meter. We each squeal at my diamond as it blinds us momentarily. The sheer weight of it is giving me a slight headache.

"Would you look at the size of that thing?" Annie brings my hand closer to her face and shakes her head. "You know how to pick them, Pipeline. Boyfriends and rings. Your mom would be so proud."

The smile slides from my face before I remember not to let it. I force the corners of my lips upward, waving off the look of concern Andrea gives me.

"Fiancés," I teasingly correct her, hoping she won't ask questions and ignoring the use of her childhood nickname for me. We both grew up three towns over, so no one but Annie knows me as anything but Piper in this group. I reach up to rub my suddenly dry throat, then turn the dial up on my smile and flash my ring to all who want to see, which is pretty much everyone here. At least ten people grab for my hand all at once. We have great friends, Bryant and I. Made up of doctors and law students, and real estate developers that Bryant went to school with, they're the most supportive group of friends a person could ask for. I have no doubt that each of them will show up for us at any given point as we plan what will likely be the wedding of the century in this town. I mean, everyone who's anyone knows Bryant's parents. They've been in the local newspaper dozens of times. I'm the luckiest girl alive for getting to join their family. Me. A small business owner who photographs puppies, babies, and ninetieth birthday parties for a living. Happy photos, with pinks and purples and bright shades of blue mixed in to keep the vibe upbeat. I love everything about photography so long as I'm not required to think too much about it. The simpler, the better. Backlights shining so brightly that the shadows don't stand a chance.

I glance at my new fiancé before looking around our wide circle, encouraging myself to muster up the will to at least look enthusiastic. Mind over matter, as they say. But try as I might, I can't quite convince myself to feel anything but a bit lost.

Thoughts of Bryant's upper-crust family only make me wish harder for the ordinary one I no longer have.

~

"A TOAST TO THE HAPPY COUPLE." Bryant's father, Ben, holds up a champagne flute, his gaze sweeping the room. It's the night following our engagement, and we're having a celebratory dinner at the only country club in town, and all eyes are on him. Engagement party notwithstanding, most public functions thrust Ben Ratliff in the spotlight—by happy accident or force of will. The rest of us have learned to smile in the background. His magnetic personality commands attention, not to mention he owns the place.

The forty-seven people in attendance raise a glass; oddly, not one is looking in our direction. Irritation ripples down my spine because *can't this one thing be about us?* But I blink and force a soft smile at my future father-in-law, mimicking how Bryant is doing it. If I'm going to be an official member of this family, I need to learn to adapt. And adapting here means fitting in, accepting life relegated to the background. Basically, learning to live the way I used to, save for the last few years. I'm no stranger to the back row. Once you live in the cheap seats, you never fully emerge from them, not even when the well-heeled welcome you forward to sit with them at the head table.

"Hear, hear!" A man shouts from the back of the room, and a collective chorus of voices echoes him. Glasses go up, a clash of tinkling clinks play music like a bell choir, and people sip champagne. The expensive stuff because nothing is too good for

Bryant Ratliff, son of Ben and Julia, founders of Ratliff Masonry—the biggest manufacturing plant in the tri-state area if you don't count Walmart. Which none of us do because no company will ever compete, not even outside our southern region. Maybe not even outside the United States. It's a losing battle, no matter what side you're fighting for.

I take a sip of champagne and look adoringly at Bryant, suddenly feeling a few eyes on us. Mrs. Brewer is in the back of the room, and the lady who owns the hair salon in downtown Silver Bell is sitting next to her; both are town gossips to hear Bryant tell it. They're whispering to each other now, and my spine prickles. It's been a decade since the first day I met Bryant's parents, but that doesn't mean everyone has accepted me.

Not one of us, they quip.

Went to college on a government grant, they whisper.

No trust fund to speak of, they say.

As if I haven't heard it all and more.

I reach into my Marc Jacobs clutch—a birthday gift from my soon-to-be mother-in-law because it's "never too late to learn class," a backhanded compliment directed straight toward me if I ever heard one —snatch a mint, and pop it into my mouth, sucking slowly to keep myself focused on something besides the gossipy women behind me. There. Now I feel better. *Did she just call me a gold digger?* I look halfway over my shoulder before turning back around for appearance's sake, but I do give in to an eye roll. The only one digging anything around here is her shoveling the proverbial grave I'll put her in once I become an official member of the Ratliff family. *This is the last social function you'll be invited to, lady.*

I sigh and try to get ahold of my anger. Keeping everyone happy is a full-time job with absolutely no benefits, but at least Bryant's family has come to accept me. I set my glass down and sit back for more of Ben's speech, which will undoubtedly continue for a while. Twenty minutes, to be exact. I know this because at precisely seven o'clock—one hour after the dinner began—Ben's mother, Julia, leans in to fill me in on her plans for the wedding. I wondered how long it would take.

I wonder how well she'll accept the news that the plans have already been made...were made years ago, before we even met.

THERE ARE two main problems with Julia Ratliff's wedding plans. One, her budget is astronomically larger than mine. She's talking about Italian silk and gold-plated flatware and actual pearl buttons instead of the costume kind. Her ideas are a lot, but nothing compares to the outrageous request she just dropped like a hot rock on a sweltering July afternoon. Completely unwelcome and insane. Get it away from me.

She wants fairies. Not fairy lights strung around the room like many brides before me have used and wanted. But two dozen eight-feet-tall stone statue fairies holding strings of light in all corners of the room, along with Grecian marble columns flanking both sides of the altar. After fifteen minutes of listening to her overly dramatized and unrealistic views of modern-day weddings, this has come to light as my future mother-in-law's most desired wish for our wedding. This as though Bryant and I are Athens' nobility instead of merely Silver Bell marginally recognizable. I listen to her ramblings and will myself not to burst out laughing.

She's kidding, right?

If I had it my way, we'd get married in Bryant's backyard with only our closest friends and family in attendance and spend most of our money on the honeymoon, but I'm marrying a Ratliff. I knew the wedding would be high-profile the moment I agreed to a first date. Still, stone fairy statues and Grecian columns have never been on my radar, and I'd like to send them both plummeting toward a crash landing on the concrete.

"Um..." is all I say before Bryant swoops in and

declares his mother's idea brilliant. "Inspired" is his bonus word of choice, to which I'd like to respond with a few choice words myself. I wisely keep them inside my head, though I foolishly don't stay silent. "I'm not sure about the columns. I was thinking more along the lines of a wooden trellis with Clematis or..."

From the steely smile crossing Julia's face, it's the wrong thing to say.

"Not?" I finish and swallow.

"Clematis? You can't be serious, Piper."

Clematis is a happy flower. Clematis was my mother's favorite flower, so I am serious. "Well, actually I—"

But Bryant steps in with a laugh. "Of course, she's kidding, Mother. At the very least, we would need roses or some other sort of...flower?" Bryant looks to me to rescue him but seeing as he's just thrown me under the bus, I'm having trouble finding the desire to help. A glare seems to be slightly more effective. "Unless you don't want roses, darling."

Ah, the fun game of playing both sides. Why do men ever think it works?

"Honestly, son," Julia says. "I told you I wanted columns months ago, and you agreed. What's changed?"

I cross my arms over my waist, positioning myself in a defensive, "yeah, what's changed?"

stance. Unlike the playing both sides thing, coming at him straight-on always works.

"What are we talking about?" Bryant's father chooses this moment to join the conversation, a white-toothed smile on his face as though he's completely oblivious to the fact that hostility stands like a fifth person in the middle of this four-ring circus.

"We're talking about the wedding, Ben," Julia says with a flip of her wrist my direction. "But Piper is being unreasonable."

I'm being unreasonable?

Ten-foot-tall columns. Eight-foot fairies. I look at her. I look at Ben. I look at Bryant. I look at the wedding guests for help, but of course, no one is paying attention now that the free food and booze has stopped flowing. Every single person is reaching for their coats.

"All I said is that I wanted Clematis in my bouquet," I say.

We're all greeted with a loud "Ha!" as though I just stated I wanted giant poodles dressed in tuxes to serve as groomsmen. Which, come to think of it, is still a better idea than Julia's. At least poodles would entertain the crowd.

But I don't finish that thought. I'm too busy gaping at the backside of Bryant's mother as she bursts into tears and flees the room. Of course, the guests are paying attention now. One woman, two, then four, race after her, all groveling to be the one to comfort Julia first. Misery loves company in the same way small-town socialites love to be in the know.

Even Bryant moves to follow her before he stops to look at me, visibly torn on which side to take. I turn away with a sigh, catching the pointed stare of Mr. Ratliff a second too late. I'm judging his wife harshly, and he can tell. My heart skips a beat, then two, because despite his obvious charm and charisma, the man is quite intimidating. The kind of man who might technically be my father-in-law one day but doesn't have one bit of "fatherly" air about him.

Surprisingly though, he smirks.

"Told you about the fairy sculptures, did she?"

I look at him, my mouth opening and closing, wanting to both speak and shut up in case this is a trap. Surely, he knows the fairy thing is silly.

"It's silly. I know it is," he says, reading my mind. "And I told her so myself, but she won't listen." He crosses his arms and taps his lower lip with his thumb. "But this isn't about fairies, *really*, you know."

I stay silent because I don't know. I'm completely clueless. If someone would like to fill me in, that'd be great. I wait. No one does.

"My wife always wanted a little girl, but we

couldn't have more kids after Bryant arrived. We got lucky with him—she'll tell you that, too—but a wedding. She's always wanted to plan one, and I suppose she sees this as her shot."

I understand, I do. But I want to say that it's my shot too, my one chance to feel close to the plans made years ago, back when—

But I don't get the opportunity because Mr. Ratliff isn't finished.

"She'll be okay. I'll tell her we're scrapping the fairies, and that will be the end of it." He takes a deep breath, pauses, and then looks at me. I start to nod in relief, but there's more. I can feel it. What he says next doesn't surprise me in the slightest.

"Unless you would at least consider her ideas? I mean, it's only a wedding, and all she's asking for is a little give and take." He crosses one arm over another and leans in to give me the look. You know the one—the *"Consider me your closest ally, but also, I can make or break your future with my son if you attempt to make life difficult for me"*—look. I stop short of a glare and inwardly bristle.

That's what people rarely remember about magnetic personalities: in the same way they attract people, they repel others. *It's only a wedding.* My mother would scratch his smirk off. Sadly, she isn't here.

I sigh. "I suppose I could—"

Julia reappears like a phantom in human form, with no entrance or warning, taking over the reins of conversation once again. "I have a different proposal for you," she says, inserting so much determination into her voice that I already know I won't be able to turn her down. "Would you consider trading the fairies for handwritten wedding invitations?"

"Julia, please..." Ben says, exasperated.

I admit I share the feeling. I didn't see this request coming, nor do I understand it. Bryant, however, steps in closer to me, yet the move somehow seems like a silent nudge in his mother's direction. I start to respond, but Bryant beats me to it.

"Oh, Mother, that subject again? Luck isn't found in handwriting, no matter who made you believe it."

Clearly, I've missed something. The conversation is jumping around like a dozen hungry fleas looking for a landing spot, and I'm the one getting bitten. I scratch a phantom itch on my neck. Then again, breaking out in hives is a real possibility.

"What are you talking about? What luck?"

Bryant rolls his eyes. "My mother believes that if we don't use some old guy to write our wedding invitations, we'll start our marriage off like any other couple, and considering the divorce rate nowadays, the consequences could be disastrous." When I don't say anything, he keeps going. "You know—something borrowed, something blue, something old..." He waves a hand. "My grandmother once told her you have to add 'something no one else has done before to the list' or it's bad luck. And since no one our age has ever had that old man design their wedding invitations..." My speechlessness somehow gets interpreted as skepticism in Bryant's brain, and he sighs. "Just so you know, I think it's a ridiculous notion. Marriage is a crapshoot at best, no matter how unique the wedding might be. Plus, I guess the guy hasn't designed anything in years, which makes Mother want his work even more."

I blink at his flippancy, both baffled and irritated. First, marriage might be a crapshoot, but I'd rather not go into one with such a pessimistic groom. Second, why is everyone speaking in riddles? What old guy, what handwriting, and what luck? But first things first.

"Thanks for describing our future marriage as a 'crapshoot.' Maybe you could add that phrase to our wedding vows." I don't even want to hear his take on happy ever afters.

Bryant huffs. "You know what I mean. This whole idea is silly."

I'm not sure more romantic words have ever been said. Bryant should consider a career in greeting card writing. There's a company just up the road; maybe they could hire him.

Ben Ratliff clears his throat. "I have to say that I agree with Bryant on this. There's no sense in bothering a half-crazy old man just to ask for something he doesn't even do anymore. That'd be like asking me to take on a late-night shift in the warehouse." He laughs like warehouses are beneath him and not the backbone of his entire corporation. But there's something about his laugh that feels forced. Tense. His mouth presses into a straight line. "Besides, they say he's dangerous. That maybe he robbed a bank or even killed a man in a different state."

"Who's dangerous?" I ask, growing more confused by the second.

"The old man," Bryant and his dad say in unison as if annoyed I haven't caught on. Ben's eyes narrow at his wife. She waves him off.

"All of that is nonsense. Otherwise, he would be in jail," Julia says, dismissing her husband. "Son, just listen to me on this, will you?" She and Bryant have had this conversation a few times; that much is clear. What isn't clear is why no one thought to have it with me. "His work is stunning. Valuable. To have even one copy of something he's created just for you is a feat no one has attained in at least two decades, maybe more. If you could see his creations with your own eyes..."

"Julia, stop badgering Bryant and let it go," Ben shocks me by saying. I've never heard him or Bryant cut Julia off, not once since I met them. Not when she wanted to redecorate the house, not when she deemed her brand-new Lexus "undrivable" and traded it for a Range Rover less than two months later, and not when her four-carat wedding ring was suddenly upgraded to six carats. So, to hear Ben cut her off over some old guy's handwriting is... confusing at best. Five seconds ago, he was begging me to consider her ideas.

"Handwritten...how?" I ask, intrigued. Or maybe I'm just in the mood to make Ben Ratliff uncomfortable. Julia is spoiled, but he made her that way. And I'm personally not a fan of women being publicly scolded. "Why wouldn't we just order invitations online?" All the ones I've researched can be ordered in bulk and shipped in two days. What kind of person makes invitations by hand nowadays?

"I guess the guy does fancy calligraphy," Bryant says *calligraphy* like other people might say "nude selfies." Like it's a cheap imitation of art, low class and crass.

But Julia barely notices. "He does unbelievable calligraphy, art so beautiful his letters barely look like they belong to the alphabet. He used to, anyway. Other than the statues, it's the thing I've wanted most since Bryant turned twenty, and the idea of a wedding began to be within reach. Rumor has it he was once very popular in Hollywood; all the famous celebrities acquired his work. If you would agree to have the wedding invitations handmade by him, I can promise you I won't ask for anything else. It's the last you'll ever hear about the fairies."

Because I like the sound of that, I find myself agreeing to this request. Even hearing that the guy might be a murderer, even as Bryant offers an incredulous laugh next to me, and even as Ben begins to glare. I ignore them both and focus on making my future mother-in-law happy. Hand-written invitations, I guess that's what we're doing. Sounds easy enough, painless, and simple.

That's what I'm thinking when Julia drops one last thought.

"Of course, first, we have to convince that crazy man to do them. And that will take some work. It might be easier to haul in the fairies when it's all said and done. Living ones, at that." Julia laughs to herself, but I'm stuck on something she said.

That crazy man.

Who is this guy she's talking about?

And more concerning...did he really kill someone?

2

Piper

News travels a wide arc among the gossip crowd—meaning small-town wanna-be socialites who plan debutant balls and country club fetes like they're stars on Real House-wives of Beverly Hills and *not* living in Silver Bell, Arkansas. So even though I didn't grow up in this town, it turned out that I had heard of the old man with the great handwriting in a second-hand sort of way. Fuzzy on the details and sagging in the middle, the way you hear of local legends from thirty miles away. Likely twisted in the retellings and heavy on the rumors, but everything I heard added up to nothing good. Even though I was half certain that not all details were true, the possibility was enough to scare me away. Dirty, disfigured, mute, standoffish, angry. One arm missing from a bar fight gone horribly wrong—or was it one eye? No teeth, slurred his words, walked with a limp, and hurled sharp objects at anyone who came too close. I was terrified to approach him before I left the house.

This begged the question: why was I leaving the house when none of this was my idea? Which in turn begged the answer: the Ratliffs are too important to beg anyone in this town for anything. Apparently, I am not.

I'm unprepared for what greets me the moment I step my black Birkenstocks out of my newish black Toyota Camry onto the pocked pavement in front of Walter C. Lorry's antique store. If you can call this dump an antique store. The vibe is more incense and séance mixed with cobwebs, spiders, dust, and body odor. Decidedly not happy, and not my usual place to shop. I clear my throat and recite an internal pep talk that goes something like, *"You can do this, Piper. The odds of being murdered in broad daylight are very low."*

Not zero, but low.

I close the car door and sag against it to gather myself and think about how I'll approach the old man. I've never met him, so walking in to say, *"Even though you never speak to anyone and the whole town is afraid of you, I've heard you have great penmanship and are a whiz at calligraphy. So, can you do me a solid and scratch out some wedding invitations real quick to get me on my mother-in-law's good side?"* seems overzealous.

But it's the only reason I'm here, so what's the point in pretending?

I cannot—will not—have stone fairies at my wedding.

Even if getting murdered is a real possibility.

When I agreed to the idea of handwritten invitations at the reception, Julia's face transformed into a delighted smile. *"So, you'll walk into his store and ask him?"* she asked me as though it were the only clear option. I answered with more reservations than an Olive Garden restaurant on Valentine's Day. *"Um...I guess?"* Not a wholehearted agreement, but she took it that way. She clapped and squealed and added on a suffocating hug for good measure. I can't remember another time one of Julia Ratliff's hugs wasn't perfunctory.

For his part, Bryant was skeptical, eyeing me up and down before his gaze came to rest on my face. *"You're going to be the one to go talk to that crazy old man? You? You're a hundred twenty pounds dripping wet."* A bit harsh and not entirely true—I'm one twenty-five on a scorching hot day—but when I responded that he could come with me for moral support, he quickly backtracked. *"You've got this. Men are more likely to help out brides anyway."* A cop-out, though not a completely unfounded claim. All was forgotten the moment his mother began instructing me to, *"Do this...say this..."* convinced that even a recluse like Walter Lorry couldn't refuse her request —*my* request—if the words were spoken in some magical, mythical order. The subject of stone fairies wasn't mentioned again. Forgotten, just like Julia promised they would be. For that, I was relieved.

Until Ben managed to bring them up once more. "Are you sure all the stonework you want wouldn't be easier?" he asked again, uncharacteristically biting a thumbnail before she reached out to lower his hand. Manicures are expensive when you get them once a week, so it was mildly shocking to see him ruining one.

She assured him they would not be easier and encouraged me to go see Mr. Lorry the following Monday.

It's now Monday, and I'm not so relieved anymore. Irritated, honestly. Bryant should have come with me. But I'm on my own, so I take a step toward the front door of the antique store, then another, my feet encased in lead or concrete or whatever substance makes them feel weighted with dread. They say the best way around a problem is through the middle of it; hard to do when your limbs feel too heavy to move. But move them, I do; it's now or decidedly never.

Weeds line both sides of the sidewalk that leads

to the house, their spindly vines brushing against my calves as I walk, sticky and itchy, a perfect hiding place for snakes and spiders and other critters that would result in my immediate demise if I were to spot them crawling in front of me. I walk faster in case one decides to slither out onto the pavement and ascend the first step.

A single wooden step groans underfoot like my five-foot six-inch frame is nearly unbearable to support, so I make a note to lose a couple more pounds before the engagement photos are taken.

"Jerk," I mutter to it. It's a little embarrassing to feel insulted by an inanimate object, but here we are.

To my left is a large hand-painted sign that reads simply, "W.C. LORRY" in all caps, a visual reminder to all who pass just whose building this belongs to... as though anyone else would want it. Above the sign, a help wanted banner sways from a thin length of heavily rusted chain, painted in a similar style to a federal "Wanted" poster—intentional or not. Oddly enough, the smallest sign on the premises is the "Antique" sign sitting alone on the right. Without it, passersby might think this place nothing more than a run-down shack whose owner collects junk like toilets, old tires, and claw-foot bathtubs, all of which sit on the sparse grass out front, some with dead plants housed inside.

This place is gross. Also, it scares me.

Movement rattles the corner of my eye, and I whip my head around in self-preservation, holding my chest and breathing a rushing sigh of relief when it turns out not to be a serial killer wielding a chainsaw. It's just a boy. Eight years old. Maybe nine. Dressed in black sweatpants and a dark grey sweatshirt with a peanut butter stain on his sleeve from this morning's breakfast, he has dark brown hair—almost black—a pale tan birthmark between his eyebrows. His eyes are ringed in pale freckles that must not come and go with the sun like mine do. He looks wholesome, like a '50s sitcom; stares back at me like he's fresh out of Mayberry—a fictional town I remember from a show I used to watch when I was young. All the kid is missing is a fishing pole and a soft-spoken, whistling father. Where are this kid's parents, anyway? The child peers around the corner of the building at me, eyes wide like saucers, gaze darting back and forth between me and the building like one of us is insane. Considering I'm the only non-inanimate object between the two options, I'm guessing he means me.

"You gonna go inside and see that man?" His words are choked, clogged with terror.

Join the club, kid.

I drop the hand still pressed against my heart. "I planned to if I don't die of a heart attack first. I need to ask him a question."

The boy slowly shakes his head. "But he don't talk to nobody. Not anyone ever, not even his customers. They say he's Santa Claus just hiding out here until Christmas, and that's why. He's gotta stay a secret."

"Who says that?"

"The kids at my school," he says with a shrug.

So far, the old man is supposedly a bank robber, an artist, a murderer, a world-famous calligrapher, and now he's...Santa Claus?

I blink at the ridiculousness of this town but say nothing else. There's not much scarier to a small boy than a mute old man, and he can't help what the adults say about him. But as a grown woman, I can think of a few things a lot more frightening: a pap smear, being sneezed on during a raging pandemic, sitting next to an over-sharer on a cross-country flight, checking out at the market with a full cart but forgetting your debit card, being catcalled on your way to the car. Silence isn't golden to a kid. I guess when you're eight years old, you look for any reason to explain it away, though calling the man Santa incognito is a strange explanation to land on. I take another step toward the door.

"Well, he's going to talk to me. I'm not going to give him a choice." Brave words, but even I can hear the fear in my tone. What if Mr. Lorry doesn't want to talk? What if he can't or won't? What if the old man shoves me out the front door and locks it behind him? Worse, what if he just ignores me, and the only thing I accomplish today is chatting up an old hairbrush on sale for a dollar ninety-nine? Just before I reach the door, the kid slinks further behind the building in case he needs to make a quick escape.

"Mind if I stay here and watch through the window?" he whispers. What an odd request, I think, until I spot a lunch box, a backpack, and a tattered gray blanket. This kid has been here a while, maybe even more times than just today. Maybe he didn't eat breakfast at home this morning. "I promise not to make any noises or nothing."

I stare, trying to size up the reason for a small child to set up camp out here by himself. There's no threat that I see. It doesn't appear he's been kidnapped. No ropes, no chains, no electric fence surrounding the property. The boy could run away if he wanted to.

I shrug. "Suit yourself. But...what's your name? In case I need to find you after?"

He blinks at me, then raises his chin as though trying to summon his own bravado. I recognize the gesture because I'm mentally doing the same thing. Is it possible to be kindred spirits with a second grader?

"My name's J.D.," he says.

"Okay, J.D., I'll let you know how it goes," I say, reaching for the door handle.

"Let me know if you see his wings," he whispers quickly, and I look over at him again.

"His what?" *Did he say wings?*

I'm met with a solemn stare. "He's got 'em. Saw both of 'em myself just last night."

I stare, waiting for him to go on, my mind jabbing holes in his theory. Why in the world would a supposed Santa Claus also have wings when he has eight perfectly good reindeer ready to fly for him? Leave it to a kid to come up with a story like that. It takes work to keep a straight face.

"I'll be sure to let you know if I see anything." I would bet the last five dollars in my purse that the kid is long gone by the time I leave. No matter, he isn't my problem. On to business.

A ripped and rickety screen door groans when I pull it open. Inside my mind, the soft strains of horror music begin to play—ominous, dark, like surely there's a knife-wielding killer tucked away just waiting to slice me up. This definitely isn't Mayberry. For one brief second, I consider bolting but stay put. I have a future mother-in-law to please and one fairy fantasy to kill before it kills me. Though frankly, if I can't get Mr. Lorry to agree to this, something tells me Julia Ratliff won't be too sad to hear of my demise. This is a win for her either way.

The front door groans against its own weight and then slams behind me before I can catch it. I jump. The store is dark, and it takes a minute for my eyes to adjust to the dimness. My lungs are working over-time to adjust to the dust float-ing in the air around me, so I stay put,

breathing and trying not to cough. I'm a big believer in shopping local, but this place might be taking things too far. Surely there's a nicer antique store up the road, one with a cute coffee bar and blueberry scones, even. One that doesn't have talis-mans and windchimes and birdfeeders hanging from every possible surface as though to collectively ward off all the town's evil spirits. All of them clatter together at once, adding to the store's eeriness.

I clear my throat only to have it seize up again when a small man shuffles in from the back, one foot dragging behind him as he dries his hands with a paper towel and uses it to mop his face. Both hands, by the way. The loss of an arm was clearly just a rumor.

My breath catches. He isn't what I expected, but exactly how J.D. described. I'm struck with an odd urge to snap his picture; a first impression, an awkward meeting, confusion on my part, a memento to remember him by. His wiry white hair and long white beard do, in fact, give him the appearance of a miniature Santa Claus. His overalls and red long-john top only complement the image. Saint Nick could be his half-brother; his stooped stance makes him a distant relative to Ebeneezer Scrooge—stereotyping the man on both ends of the Christmas spectrum. He stops walking when he sees me, locking his eyes with mine in a Grinch-like stare-down. And now all the Christmas bases are effectively covered. Against my will, I find myself glancing at his shoulders. Not a wing in sight. *Sorry, J.D.*

Wariness clouds the man's expression as he takes me in, an odd way to greet a customer. But then I remember they say he doesn't speak to anyone, so I clear my throat again and brace myself for a one-sided conversation.

"H...hello," I say. "My name is Piper, and I—"

A harsh grunt stops me cold like he's disgusted with the mere sound of my name. Usually, people say my name is cool, hip, unique. Never has anyone scoffed at it. Not going to lie; I'm kind of offended, even more so when the man turns his back on me and walks away. Whatever they say about aging gracefully, this man is doing the opposite. Not sure I've ever met a ruder individual.

"Is there something wrong with my name?" I ask him with my back pressed against the door, but the man has already begun straightening a stack of haphazardly discarded books halfway across the store, ignoring me. His hands are rather agile, considering the state of the rest of his body. Long straight fingers make quick use of his work, albeit with a little shake. Still, he's a terrible businessman. I would leave now if I weren't hell-bent on groveling for my future mother-in-law's approval. Why am I like this? Why can't I just tell her to order invitations online? I'm a coward when it comes to her, that's why, and I know it. So, I take a couple of steps into the store and pretend to browse while sizing up a better approach that might make the man agree to help me.

Junk is everywhere, so much junk that the slightest movement finds me bumping into more junk. A spinning rack of postcards teeters behind me; I turn to straighten it but succeed only in knocking into a crystal jelly dish like one my grand-mother used to own. It slides to the edge of an antique school desk; I catch the dish and set it to rights before it crashes to the ground. When I straighten, a wooden broom falls to the floor with a loud thwack, dirt and grime puffing up and outward in its wake. I accidentally kick the handle before setting it upright again. This room is a China closet, and I am the bull; me, who didn't even want to be here in the first place.

I cover my eyes with my hands and take a deep

breath, only to have a speck of dust land on my eyeball, blurring my vision and causing my eyes to swim. I gently rub the spot until a stab of pain shoots from behind my eye. Just what I need, to be unable to see while in the presence of a man everyone says is nuts. Why do bad things always happen to good people? Now I can't even see to defend myself. After a few panicked blinks, things start to shift into focus. Mr. Lorry is now folding a stack of yellowed handkerchiefs, completely ignoring the drama that is me.

I wordlessly walk the store's perimeter, at a loss for how to broach the subject of invitations. Silence has never been my friend, and it sure isn't now. So, I start talking.

"How long have you owned this store?"

Not a sound out of the old man, not even an annoyed grumble.

"It's pretty," I add. The silence is so loud that even I hear the lie. "Interesting and unique." I should become more acquainted with the art of not talking. Alas, I failed art in school. "A bit dusty, maybe. Kind of cluttered." I reach for a stack of old magazines on the table in front of me that have cover models dressed in sixties attire, like Twiggy. "Maybe if we moved these—"

"Don't touch them." At the sound of his gravelly words, I snatch my hands back and nearly stumble. His voice slurred and raspy from disuse, like cranking up a grandfather clock that's been left in storage for years. Forgotten, rusty, out of practice, and weak, the sort of sound a man might make if he went days and days without using his voice and tried only after downing a bottle of merlot.

Still, there's a big difference between rarely talking and never talking. Turns out the rumor mill really does spin lies. The man isn't mute after all.

"I'm sorry, I'll leave them right here." I take a step away from the stack of magazines as my heartbeat fills my ears. Adrenaline courses through my veins, racing side by side against my pulse to see who'll come out as the winner. Right now, it's anyone's guess. I'll consider today a victory if I don't pass out from fear. "I wondered if I could ask you a favor?" The words come out as a question, timid and meek, so unlike the plans I made in the car driving over.

Go in. State what I need. Get the man to agree. Get out of there, hopefully with a handwriting sample of Mr. Lorry's to show Julia and make her happy. All business. Thank you very much.

Nope, this isn't going as I planned at all.

He doesn't acknowledge me. Doesn't look in my direction to indicate he heard anything I said. I realize some people don't like to socialize, but this is a terrible way to treat a customer. It's a wonder the man is even in business. No surprise that I'm the only person here.

"Excuse me?" I try again. "Did you hear me? I wondered if you could—"

I stop talking when he looks up and stares like my constant chatter is wearing him out. I can tell that a thousand things are going through his mind, but not one seems pleasant. His eyelids droop like he's tired, though I suspect it is a permanent feature. His stance is defeat, begging me not to make the request again. For one second, I'm tempted to surrender—that split second where my compassion overrides my temper—but alas, I swallow, clench my back teeth, and turn away to work out my next argument. I'll say what I have to say to convince him because I can't—*cannot!*—have giant fairy sculptures at my wedding, stone ones or otherwise. This isn't what my mother wanted at all.

I've just about decided what to say when I see it.

There. On the back wall.

Smack in the middle of a dozen paintings.

It's hanging in an outdated sixteen by twenty gold frame with a black mat that takes up most of the space. But it's the brochure-sized, white interior that draws me. From here, I can only make out two words written in the middle, both of which cause me to inch closer. Up close is the only way to prove this *can't* be right. I knock into an old wagon wheel on my way to the picture and stop to set it upright, my left thigh throbbing from the hard contact.

Antique stores contain a lot of things no one needs.

But I was wrong because there they were—the words. My eyes weren't deceiving me after all.

"White House." Preceded by the words, "You are cordially invited to attend the sixty-third birthday celebration of President Gerald Ford" in handwriting so beautifully styled and artistic that my breath catches in my throat. My eyes scan the length of the invitation, yellowed and worn with age, with a history surpassing anything I've ever experienced up close and in person. And at the bottom, in the tiniest print a microscope might have trouble finding, are three sharp letters. WCL. It's all I can do to keep from whipping my head around to look at the man —this store's odd-looking, slightly-deformed owner.

Walter Coleman Lorry. He had to have created this, just like Julia claimed. I'm staring at a handwriting sample right now, and I get it, the reason Julia wants handwritten invitations that look like this. His penmanship is impeccably gorgeous, with scrollwork so intricate it takes on a fine-art-like quality that computers can't generate. The "Sixty Third" alone takes up three inches of space to wrap around the bottom of the invitation. If my invitations looked like this, I would hang them in every room of our house as a reminder that...

My.

Wedding.

Was.

Fabulous.

In our theoretical house, that is. Right now, I live in a studio apartment above an Italian restaurant downtown, much to my future mother-in-law's horror. *"You practically have strangers milling around in your basement, Piper."* I've heard the words a dozen times in the year since moving in. Partly because she likes to hear herself talk, mostly because, with the strange exception of Saturday night's engagement party, Bryant has never spoken up to stop her. But I like where I live. In my estimation, it's better to have strangers in your basement than to be surrounded by no one. I've spent enough years on my own already.

Plus, my apartment smells like linguine and fresh baked bread one hundred percent of the time. Not an easy thing to walk away from.

But back to the subject of Mr. Lorry's artwork.

His calligraphy on the invitation is beautiful. Poetic. Artistic. And as I scan the room...I see it's used in several other paintings on display as well.

Above a portrait of a nude woman, with a title that simply reads, *"Sorrow."*

Below a field of flowers in a partially quoted Bible verse. *"Consider the lilies..."*

Sliced through the middle of what appears to be

a self-portrait entitled "*Torment.*" That last one has me turning around to glance at the tormented individual in question. That's when I notice he's staring back at me. I suppose the knowledge that I've discovered his art is the trigger that finally gets his attention.

"These are beautiful," I say, surprised by how much I mean the words.

A single nod is the response I get, curt and dismissive.

"Do you have any others I can see? In another room or somewhere else?" I ask, surprising myself. Wasn't it only a few seconds ago that I feared he might kill me? I'm getting dizzy, spinning inside my one-eighties, but I'm committed. Invitations aside, I want to see more pictures if he has them. Almost desperately so. The man's talent is remarkable.

"No." He speaks again, a word I don't like. I hesitate.

"Meaning you don't have any, or I can't see them?"

I'm met with silence; more frustrating, aggravating silence. I'll never get anywhere if I keep being dismissed. Mr. Lorry has already turned away, slowly shuffling toward the front of the store. At the lone picture window, cloudy and smudged from years of dirt, I can see two eyes peering inside. J.D. is watching us just like he said he would be. I would laugh if I weren't feeling so irritated.

I slide my phone from my skirt pocket and aim it at the White House frame, then turn on the flash for good measure.

"No photos."

My phone nearly falls from my hands.

"What do you mean, no photos? How can that hurt anything?"

"No photos and no phones," he barks again, each word missing the sharpness of proper pronunciation. There's a reason for the way he sounds, though I can't pinpoint exactly what that reason is. He isn't slow and he holds a conversation well, but he's somehow impaired. The one thing I now know for sure: the man isn't drunk.

I dejectedly return my phone to my pocket, disappointed at the lack of evidence I'll have for Julia. But then I remember I don't give up that easily. *Ask for what you want, and don't take no for an answer.* I remember reading that Tony Robbins quote once. Or maybe it was Oprah. Either way, wise advice.

"Well, can you please show me more samples of your writing? Specifically, what you can do for weddings." My feet start moving to catch up to the man. I follow him like an eager puppy, excitedly hoping for approval. *Watch me dance, see me perform, tell me I'm good and that you like me, show me more of your work.* "You see, I'm getting married in six months, and I wondered if I could pay you to—"

I stop babbling when Mr. Lorry opens the front door and points outside. The man is asking me to leave. Demanding it, in fact. His arm is held out in front of him as though to say, "Get out." Again, who runs a store like this?

"You want me to leave? You're not going to even listen to—"

I take a step outside, intending to turn and argue more. *I'm not leaving without a verbal agreement. I'm not leaving without a handwriting sample. I'm not leaving without—*

The heavy door slams in my face. Mr. Lorry walks to the picture window and makes a show of turning the wooden "Open" sign around, letting it slap against the glass as he walks out of sight.

Closed.

For business. To customers.

To me.

What in God's holy name just happened?

J.D. rushes up the porch to stand beside me. "Did you see them? Did you see his wings? Did he talk to you?"

"No kid, to everything," I say, moving past him. The man talked *at* me, hardly the same thing.

I didn't see the art, or the wings, or anything else I came here for. I'll be back, though. Tomorrow afternoon. Piper Moore doesn't take no for an answer, not if the alternative is her impending mother-in-law getting her stupid, idiotic way. If my mother were here, she would—

My shin connects with a cot on my way down the steps, stopping that thought cold.

Like everything else that happens in my life, it will leave an ugly mark.

3

Piper

    "He said no?" Bryant asks for what must be the tenth time in as many minutes. "Just like that? Does he not know who you are...who you're *marrying*?" The emphasis on his own wounded ego is something I try not to consider. He has a point, after all. The Ratliffs are to Silver Bell what the Kennedy family was to American politics. Fast forward a few decades and downscale the population by a few million, and you get the idea. The Ratliffs are important. They employ almost everyone in this town unless you count the Walton family and their little company, Walmart, with its headquarters three towns over. For Silver Bell's sake and the Ratliff family's ego's sake, we try not to think of them unless we're out of milk or bread. In that case, no one can deny they have the best prices in town.

Anyway, it's no surprise that Bryant is the humiliated one here.

"He said no, just like that," I say now, with zero inflection in my voice. I worked hard to let my offense die on the drive home and have no plans to let it resurrect itself now. Offense never got me anywhere. Determination, however. That's where my real power lies. At least, that's what I tell myself as I open Google and scan my laptop screen.

"What are you doing?" Bryant asks, even though I already told him my plan at dinner over an hour ago.

"I'm Googling him," I say.

"What for? You need to just drive back over there and tell him how it's going to be. He's going to do our invitations and make Mom happy. End of story."

I look up then and wonder if he has any idea how much of his whole family's decision-making is tied up in trying to keep his mother happy. I'm not sure this is normal for a grown man. Unless, of course, it's the only thing he's used to. Someone once told me that you should never live your life trying to make other people happy. That it's as fruitful as attempting to solve a termite infestation one slimy, wiggly pest at a time. The key is to douse the whole lot and forge ahead with a clean slate. Or home. In this case, I'm supposed to be the home. *His* home. My heart and head should be his home. And right now, nothing about what Bryant is saying is making me happy. If he wants to live in a termite-infested mind where his mother crawls all over it, that's his problem to deal with. I'm busy cyber-stalking a crazy old man.

I open a box of Cheez-its and fish a few crackers out.

"I'm not going to tell him 'how it's going to be.'" I say around a mouthful of crackers, using air quotes to emphasize just how much I'm not going to do it. "I'm going to convince him to do the invitations for me because he wants to. First, I just need to figure out how to make that happen."

"I think you're wasting your time," he says, kissing the top of my head. "But suit yourself, especially if we can avoid those ridiculous decorations. It's like my mother wants a wedding set inside *The Iliad* and *The Odyssey*. I'll see you later," Bryant walks out of the room and then my apartment. I wait until I hear the key turn in the lock, then resume my research.

"All right, Walter. Lorry. Let's see what we can find out, shall we?"

TWO HOURS LATER, I've eaten half a box of crackers and discovered too much about Walter Coleman Lorry. Pages and pages of fascinating information led me to conclude that there is no way I'll ever convince that man to do a favor for an insignificant, nameless me. Even the Ratliff name doesn't add any weight to my negotiations.

His life is far superior to anyone I've ever met.

At least it used to be.

His elaborate scrollwork is carved into the Guggenheim. He has personally designed invitations for not only former President Ford but also President Carter after him, nearly every member of the Rockefeller family, and the Queen of England. *Queen. Elizabeth.* I saw a picture of her standing next to him, chatting like old chums chugging beer at a rugby match, for heaven's sake. In most photos, he's dressed in high-end, three-piece suits and schmoozing with the well-heeled crowd. In one, he's standing solo, wearing head-to-toe armor, and holding a sword. There's no explanation accompanying the photo, so it's puzzling, to say the least. The young man in that last photo, dated three decades ago, cannot possibly be the same crotchety old man from the antique store earlier this morning.

For the next hour, I keep digging, clicking link after link after link, only to find more of the same. Mr. Walter Coleman Lorry with dignitaries. With state leaders. With Elizabeth Taylor and... and...*Michael Jackson*? It's the King of Pop himself, pre-plastic surgery, sequined glove, red leather jacket, and all. I can practically hear Thriller playing in the background as I scroll through more pictures.

And then the pictures stop.

Abruptly. Suddenly. A final photo shows Mr. Lorry chatting up Harrison Ford at a dinner party in the late nineties...and that's it. No mention of anything else. Like the man was zapped into thin air, all his tailored suits, crystal goblets, and fine art right along with him. The last article I stumbled across is a sort of "Where are they now?" type from five years later, but the article only references a wife, a son, a relocation away from the glitz and glamour of Hollywood, and nothing else.

With nothing else to look at, I sit back in my chair and eye the room, plotting...planning. Planning what exactly?

It's not like I can just march into his shop and demand an accounting for the last three decades. *You don't know me, but I'm a big fan of British royalty, and I've been stalking you online...*

There's also the very real issue that the man is a known recluse and rumored to be crazy, not to mention the stupid comment that kid named J.D. made about him being Santa Claus. How can so many rumors exist about the same man, yet no one actually knows anything about him? Wouldn't it just be easier to ask?

I lower my head to the desk and close my eyes.

I've spent the better part of my life burying my own truths, working to forget the pain of the past. It's easier than you think, pushing the hard things beneath the surface. Especially when most people just want you to smile, stay polite, and not speak of anything that makes them uncomfortable. Ironically, so many issues could be solved in people's hearts if just one person took the time to have an honest conversation, but most people would rather avoid them, including me.

So, this time, I won't.

I'll ask him.

But first, I have a plan, something I should have thought of first thing.

With that settled, I intend to stand up and get more coffee, a necessary ingredient for my plans to stay awake researching all night. Instead, I keep clicking new links until my eyes grow heavy and drift to a close. I fall asleep crafting an internal list of questions, numbering them one by one like counting sheep, one sliding over another until I'm no longer thinking anything, and the room slowly fades away.

4

P*iper*

You know what they say about best-laid plans, right? No matter how much you settle them in your mind, decide how things will be, and work out scenarios backwards and forwards until you can recite them word for word...they still tend to blow up in your face. My best-laid ones first blew up years ago. I'm watching it happen again, and I've only reached the bottom step of the antique store.

Mr. Lorry is right in front of me, doing the oddest thing. But rather than tiptoe quietly around the situation, I say the first thing that comes to me.

"Why are you sleeping on your porch?"

The words come out louder than I intended. Mr. Lorry opens his eyes and bolts to a sitting position, a scream bursting from his throat, the cot underneath him squeaking from the interruption. He squints at the world around him like God just tossed a bucket of ice water over his head and threw the empty container at his feet. A great big loud wake up from the sky, except I'm the one who just thunder-crashed through what might have been a very nice dream—a rude awakening for sure. Clutching my chest from the fright of his reaction, I nearly fall off the step.

I didn't mean to show up this early. The sun is just beginning to appear through the trees surrounding the Lorry property, the first sunrise I've seen in years because I am the opposite of a morning person. But I couldn't sleep. So, I went for a morning jog through town, something I had never done before because—like I said—I have a very close relationship with my bed. And now I'm here, dripping in sweat, probably smelling of burning sunshine and melting blacktop, rudely demanding answers from a half-asleep elderly man who looks scared out of his mind.

Not going to lie; I feel a little ashamed of myself. I'm the bully at the nursing home. Nurse Rachet, if you will. It's not my business where the man lays his head, odd as it seems. I take another step back to give him space and kick at a piece of loose gravel with my toe.

He sniffs, grasps his beard to give it a tug, looks

up at the sky like he's searching for a memory, and then gives an odd little salute. To the sun? To an airplane? To...God? I follow Mr. Lorry's gaze, but I only see a bird flapping its wings twenty feet up. By the time I connect with Mr. Lorry again, he's already up and limping toward the store. He looks over his shoulder briefly, the only invitation I'm going to get to join him. I follow him through the front door.

The antique store is as dusty and chaotic as I remember from yesterday, still smelling of old paper and musk, though I note with satisfaction that the stack of magazines has been moved. The man might not speak much, but it appears he listens. A good thing because I have a plan that will require some of that listening. Based on my shaky track record, the odds are not in my favor.

"So, I was thinking..." I start while side-stepping an old sled, then clear my throat. Turning on the charm isn't going to work with him, so I go for short and direct. "You look like you could use some help around here. Not that there's anything wrong with how you do business, but I thought I could help you organize the merchandise. I could talk to customers when you need me to. Clean up and straighten things a bit, maybe move some of the high dollar items to the front of the store and display them more efficiently to get more sales." *And get rid of the junk lying around outside, particularly those nasty toilets.* I keep that comment to myself. Offending the man won't get me anywhere. I wait for a response but get none, so I add, "You don't need to pay me."

I regret that statement for a moment.

Until I see the flicker of interest, the smallest second where we make eye contact before he looks away. I'm so encouraged that I dread bringing up the catch. Isn't there always one? I swallow. "There's just one thing... In exchange, do you think you could at least consider making my wedding invitations? It's important to me and my fiancé. To the entire Ratliff family, actually..."

I mumble that last part, so I'm surprised when I get a sharp scowl.

"Ratliff?" He barks the word in a curse like if he could chew it up and spit it out, he would. And then he does. He spits, right on the old wood floor, not three feet from my brand-new Brooks sneakers. I hop back to avoid getting them dirty.

I'm stunned. Confused at his reaction. Kind of disgusted, too, even though this is his store, and he spits where he wants. But seriously, besides their pretentious nature and high-rise-sized egos, what's wrong with my fiancé's family? I blink up at him.

"Yes, Ratliff? Do you have a problem with them?"

This time, I get nothing but a hard glare followed by loud footsteps as he shuffles away. Silence is not, in fact, golden. Although it doesn't escape my notice

that he's walking toward the back of the store, not
the front. This time at least, he isn't kicking me out. I
stand my ground in an internal debate, weighing the
benefits of following him against the drawbacks of
marching out the front door. He nearly ruined my
new shoes, and a large part of me is a small amount
offended.

Curiosity takes over, and I retrace his steps as
though I didn't know what my decision would be all
along. I need those invitations, but I'm careful to
keep my distance.

I find Mr. Lorry scooting backward out of a
closet, inexplicably holding a large, shrink-wrapped
litho. He props it against the wall opposite me,
giving me a clear view of the front as he deftly
unwraps it. It's a black and white photo of Bing
Crosby with the words "Mr. Christmas" emblazoned
across his face in red. The contrast in colors is striking, a piece that might sound simple when
describing it to someone but would knock you backward when you saw it in person. The penmanship
takes on a life of its own, the primary character
dancing across the photo in elegant swishes, twirls,
and dips. I squint a bit, and the letters seem to float.
It's unsettling, mesmerizing. How anyone could
create something so beautiful using only a pen and
paper is an impossible concept to grasp, at least for
me. Then again, I can barely draw a stick figure even

with a pattern right in front of me, so maybe a more talented person would get it.

I doubt a more talented person would get it.

"Wow." It's all I can manage because I'm too busy watching as he pulls out another frame and unwraps it, too. And another. And another until there's a deep stack of eleven all the same size, but each more astounding than the last. But the one that gets me the most is the photo of Madonna. Not Virgin Mary Madonna, but "Like a Virgin" Madonna, which seems sacrilegious in my mind but is absolutely holy to observe. This one is a photograph I've never seen before showcasing Madonna with her gapped front teeth and prominent dimples in a wedding veil and bustier. The lyrics to "Material Girl" are scrolled across her face in beautifully angry black ink, peaking at the top of the frame and dipping below her tiny lace-encased waist. My fingers itch with the urge to pull out my phone and snap photos, but I don't. Whatever spell that has Mr. Lorry pulling out these prints might become broken, and I can't risk that happening. Sometimes living in the moment needs to be enough.

"You know Madonna?" The question is barely a croak. I'm that awestruck. He shrugs in response.

Is that her name, Madonna? No big deal. So what? Oh, to be that blasé about a fabulous situation.

"Does she have her own copy?" The idea of

Madonna having her own copy of Mr. Lorry's work makes me dumbfounded. I'm unable to do anything but stare at the framed photo in front of me and wonder what life must be like not to be impressed by super stardom.

Whether he is or isn't, I may never know.

I move toward the stack for a closer look at the ones he didn't show me, flipping through them one-by-one like an oversized deck of cards. There's a litho of the Brooklyn Bridge, the phrase "Start Spreading the News" scrawled so elaborately over the image that it's difficult to decide which is more beautiful—the picture or the word picture.

There's a photo of a dog, possibly the one from that *Beethoven* movie? Another shot of an actor from *Star Wars* whose name I can't recall—I think he played C-3PO or Chewbacca or one of the more obscure characters I remember from my childhood.

I stop on a stunning photo of a small boy wearing a white t-shirt and navy shorts standing at the ocean's edge, his feet sinking into the sand until only his heels are visible. A smile overwhelms his features like the photo was snapped mid-laugh; possibly a first-time visit, and he's delighted with the discovery of sand and saltwater. I remember seeing the ocean for the first time as a child. The boy's face looks like my heart felt—in love with the wonder that the same body of water could stretch from my toes to the other side of the world. Unlike all the other designs containing graphic letters scrawled across the photos in Mr. Lorry's signature style, in this photo the words "Tiny Beach Boy" is painted in small but artistic letters across the bottom—as though this photo was too special to be covered up.

I agree. This one's a keeper.

The silence in the room catches up to me just as I notice Mr. Lorry has already moved to the front of the store. It's another minute before I'm able to pull myself free from my spot to join him. I locate him wiping a layer of dust off a gilded wall mirror tucked next to the equally dusty front window.

"But for real, you know Madonna?" I'm a fangirl who can't let it go, suddenly overcome with making it my mission to hear his answer. Maybe I can get an autograph—a signed picture of my own. Mr. Lorry answers by handing me a broom and dustpan. So much for answers, though I suppose it's still an answer of sorts.

It's confirmation that we do, indeed, have a deal.

LESSON NUMBER ONE: Never make a deal when you need a shower because you might find yourself stuck with the overwhelming smell of your own dried sweat without a deodorant stick in sight. Dirty skin and even dirtier conditions make the worst of combinations.

Lesson number two: Never make a deal with someone who won't verbalize it because the initial agreement might turn into more than you first bargained for. Take me right now, perched high on a twelve-foot ladder cleaning cobwebs off the exposed air conditioning duct all because Mr. Lorry pulled out the ladder from the back room, plunked it in front of me, handed me a rag and two packages of disinfectant wipes, and pointed up here. I didn't sign up for this, but no one seems to care. I sneeze for the fourth time in half as many minutes, and dust scatters. I sneeze again. And again. I sneeze so many times that I wind up half blind with watery eyes, all while twelve feet in the air.

Lesson number three: Never walk into an old antique store without doubling your dose of allergy medication. I feel a handkerchief land on my thigh and look down to see Mr. Lorry standing by the ladder, a concerned expression on his face. The man pays attention. I'm oddly touched, so I pick up the handkerchief and use it as quietly as possible. The last time I sneezed around Bryant, he complained that I might infect him with a virus and asked me to go to the other room.

I wipe my nose and look around the store beneath me, taking in all its chaos and messiness, wondering what I've gotten myself into. This isn't a two-day job; with luck, I'll finish in two weeks. Two months, more likely. I'm in the middle of an inward beatdown when I catch sight of them, two eyes blinking at me through a tiny front window. It was cute yesterday. Today, it's a swift reminder that four hands are better than two, and if you're going to hang out around here anyway, you might as well make yourself useful.

"You've got a lurker." I point out to Mr. Lorry, indicating toward the window and J.D.'s wide-as-saucer eyes. I nearly laugh when the boy's pupils visibly bounce left and right like a pinball stuck inside a tight corner, but the part of me still slightly afraid of Mr. Lorry feels sorry for the kid. He's caught, and he knows it. And seeing as I'm currently the misery part of this odd trio, personally, I wouldn't mind a little company. The kid should have hidden himself better.

Mr. Lorry scowls at the window, surprising me with a low but sharp, "blasted kid." The words are slightly slurred, but I'm starting to believe it has nothing to do with alcohol. I haven't seen a single bottle anywhere in this store. What is clear: little J.D. is a giant pain in the old man's backside.

Mr. Lorry flings the door open, and J.D. slides inside like a reluctant sloth—painfully slow and unable to run, back pressed against the wall like it might morph him to the other side. He appears almost desperate for it. Even with a curved spine, Mr. Lorry looms over the kid, a surprising feat since the old man is unusually short.

"What do you want this time?" No emphasis on consonants, each word blurring into the next. Still, I nearly fall off the ladder at Mr. Lorry's use of such a lengthy and complex sentence. J.D. shrinks into the wall looking flabbergasted, then glances my direction. The mute man speaks. Who knew?

"I just wondered what y'all was doing in here, that's all," J.D. delivers in a quivering voice. "You look busy. I ain't never seen you busy before."

"We're cleaning up the store. So, either grab a rag and help or get out. I'm tired of you always hanging around. Don't think I don't notice your face always pressed against these windows."

J.D. looks caught, terrified; a waste of energy since I'm scared enough for both of us. I can't believe the long string of forceful words that just came out of Mr. Lorry's mouth. Clearly, he's more perceptive than people give him credit for.

In a matter of seconds, J.D.'s fear morphs into another emotion entirely.

"You mean I can help?" he asks.

Mr. Lorry grunts in response, his word limit all used up for the day. J.D. looks at me for support, so I shrug and toss him my extra package of cleaning wipes.

"Here, start using these on anything covered with dust." Which encompasses the entire store. "You'll probably run out of wipes in ten minutes." When Mr. Lorry rolls his eyes heavenward in exasperation, I catch myself smiling. The state of this store is wide open for criticism. There isn't a speck of cleanliness anywhere unless you count the cobwebs I just cleaned off the ductwork. But you can't count them because they've merely been transplanted to a nasty pile on the floor for me to sweep up later. Except now that J.D.'s here...

"Find a broom and a dustpan, and you can start with that," I say, pointing to said pile from my high perch on the ladder. "There's a trash bag over by the bookcase."

The kid looks at them and then up at me. "Gross. Can't I just dust some tables or something?"

I shrug. "If you can find one empty enough to polish. You might need to clear them off first, in which case, use the wipes on the books and knick-knacks as you go. Everything needs to be cleaned around here. Everything." I return to work only to hear Mr. Lorry mutter, "Blasted kids," again from somewhere in the store. Apparently, J.D. and I now belong to the same club. Everyone must be a kid to a grumpy old man.

I HAVEN'T LOOKED in a mirror in hours, but when I walk into the kitchen at the Ratliff's house, it's clear that I should have stopped at my apartment to check out my reflection and shower before arriving. Instead, I relied on the contents of my gym bag to get me by and drove straight over.

Three sets of eyes ranging from mildly stunned to severely repulsed stare back at me, my fiancé being the unwise bearer of that last one. His lips are pursed like he's just sucked on a lemon, though I don't think he realizes it. Mainly because—when I shoot him a glare—he clears his throat and looks back at his laptop screen, quickly erasing the offending expression.

"Where have you been?" he asks without looking up again as if I didn't tell him when I left the house this morning. The good thing about getting engaged to someone you've dated for so many years is that you're entirely familiar with each other. The bad thing is...you're entirely comfortable, too. I plunk a hand on my hip and address the whole group.

"I've been at the antique store trying to get that man to design our wedding invitations. He said yes, by the way. You're welcome."

Julia gives an unusual-for-her squeal from her

spot at the giant mahogany table while Bryant's scowl returns.

Ben upends a mug of coffee, unusually silent for once.

"That took all day?" Bryant asks.

I open the refrigerator door to retrieve a water bottle. "His 'yes' came with a tiny condition." I twist off the cap and take a long drink to clear the dust from my throat.

"What condition?"

"I have to help him clean up his store."

He looks at me sidelong. "How much is he paying you?"

I swallow water. "Nothing. I'm doing it for free." It isn't like we need the money.

Clearly, that sentiment isn't shared by everyone. Enough silence descends around us to hold a Catholic wake. "*Free?* That store is a dump," Bryant says. "How much does he want you to clean?"

I wipe my mouth with the back of my hand. "All of it."

Ben Ratliff coughs like he's choking on air. "You can't be serious. That'll take years. Do yourself a favor, and tell the man no."

Julia scoffs her opposition but says nothing, so I take it upon myself to respond.

"I'm not telling him no, but it better not take more than a couple weeks, seeing as I have a job to get back to, and the wedding is in six months. I need to get the invitations out a couple of months early."

"Your job won't suffer that much," Bryant mutters. My temper shoots up like it's riding a rocket through space, but I refuse to respond. When Julia speaks up, I almost kiss her for the diversion.

"Was he scary?" she asks. The question catches me off guard. *Scary? Was he?*

"A little at first." It's true; he was. "But by the time I left, we had settled into a decent routine. He's not so much scary as extremely quiet. He seems to have some sort of speech impediment." Part of me wonders about an underlying cause, but I keep that information to myself.

Julia's mouth falls open in shock. "You heard him talk?"

"A couple of times, yes."

Ben gives a sharp huff. "I wouldn't get too friendly with him. I heard he murdered his wife and kid."

"I heard he embezzled money from some bank in New York." This from Bryant. "But he got off scot-free because he knew the president."

I wonder if he means the bank president or the President of the United States, but I don't ask because either is possible, and what difference does it make? Mr. Lorry is connected—or once was, anyway. I sigh.

"And J.D. thinks he's Santa Claus. There seem to be a lot of rumors flying around about Walter Lorry. It makes you wonder if any are true or just made up."

Bryant looks at me. "Who's J.D.?"

"Just a kid who helped out at the store today." For some reason, a protective feeling rises inside me, making me want to keep the boy's identity to myself.

"Well, you be careful working around that man," Bryant says. "I don't want you to go missing or get wrapped up in one of that crazy old man's scandals. Promise me you'll help out only long enough to get the invitations done, and then you'll get out."

It doesn't escape me that Bryant is worried enough to want me to be careful but not worried enough to tell me we don't need the invitations in the first place. His loyalty runs deep...to his mother. I try a small smile to mask my hurt.

"That's the plan. Once the invitations are finished, I'll leave."

He bends down to kiss me on the nose. "Good. Now go shower. You stink, and we have a thing to go to tonight. Jeff is throwing a World Series party, and I said we would come." He gives a love pat to my backside. "I can't have my fiancée looking anything but hot tonight. Got to impress the guys." I smile up at him, but inwardly I wilt.

I wish I didn't have to make an appearance. Or

keep up appearances. I wish appearances of all kinds weren't on my radar. I wish a lot of things, knowing my thoughts are pointless. An image comes with the last name Ratliff; I've always known that. My mother knew it too, and it's all she wanted for me.

But not for the first time, as I head for the upstairs bathroom covered in sweat and dust and decades-old grime from centuries-old, long-forgotten relics, I wonder how it might be to be liked for my mind, my heart, my personality, all the things about me that reside inside...

Instead of outside.

5

Piper

 I settle on an old pair of designer jeans and a Chicago Cubs t-shirt: I'm aware they aren't playing tonight but am rather fond of the year they won and wanted to honor the memory. The Cubs were my mother's favorite team and, by default, mine. Couple the shirt with the fact that I did my hair and make-up and made enough appetizers to feed a nineties youth group at church lock-in; the guys still aren't having it.

"The Cubs suck, plus they're poor sports when something goes wrong. Remember what they did to that fan a couple decades ago? They ran the guy into hiding, that's what. Now take off that shirt and put on a Cardinals one. Or leave it off completely, your choice." I roll my eyes at Jeff, Bryant's friend and host of the party, and possessor of a wall-sized framed photo of a faceless but fully topless woman hanging right above the sofa that I've been forced to stare at all evening. He calls the print "art," but it looks like a page ripped from a Playboy magazine cover, blown up ten sizes on a color copier, and shoved in a cheap dime-store frame. Nothing like the beautiful framed litho I discovered at Mr. Lorry's store. High five for bad taste, and so much for good examples.

Also, the media destroyed that fan's life, not the Cubs. But there's no sense in arguing with a half-drunk—or possibly fully drunk—egotistical jerk.

Bryant cackles at his friend's joke. So much for supportive fiancés.

Anger bubbles in my chest then fizzles when my gaze connects with a couple I've never met before cuddled close in a corner chair. She's on her phone, her denim-clad legs draped over his lap, and her black Converse sneakers are swinging carefree from side to side. She shows him something on the screen; he laughs and ruffles her hair, making it all messy, then leans in for a quick kiss before looking at the screen again. They stay that way as I study them for a long moment, too long. When the man looks up and catches me staring, I quickly look away, carefully squashing the pang of longing in my chest. Bryant hasn't ruffled my hair, not once, ever. I reach up and ruffle it myself just to see if anyone notices.

No one does. Too many interesting people in this house, I suppose.

Reaching for a glass, I pour myself some rosé, sit next to Bryant on the sofa, then check the screen to see the game is in the bottom of the fifth inning. Some guests are watching, most aren't, but Bryant is fully tuned in like a man who placed a bet and has everything riding on a win. I take a sip of wine and try to get into the game, but I'm distracted and tired. I lay my head back to study the ceiling, eyes growing heavy, thoughts drifting to Mr. Lorry and his store. There's still so much work to do before I can bring up my terms again, so much dust, disarray, and disorganization to wade through. Not to mention I still want to know his story. How does a person go from hobnobbing with dignitaries and politicians to sleeping on a porch outside a Silver Bell antique shop? It doesn't make sense. No one I know would trade that sort of former life for those present circumstances, not one person. Maybe the old man really is crazy.

Down deep, something makes me suspect he isn't.

I think of my mother's free spirit and the ease with which she moved from career to career from the sheer desire to learn something new. Hairdresser to interior designer to part-time teacher to caregiver of many. She once took in a newborn because she missed the smell of "baby" around the house. I was thirteen at the time. Some called her a hippy. Others called her a child of the Earth. I called her mom because she was the very best one.

My mother would have believed Mr. Lorry to be perfectly normal, despite his visible and internal flaws. She might have called him a kindred spirit because my mother found joy in life's oddities, especially when those oddities came in the form of human interaction. Recalling that unique-to-my-mother characteristic might be what draws me to the man in the first place.

I open my eyes and lean forward, a decision making itself for me.

"I think I'm going to go," I say more to myself than anyone.

Bryant half-glances my way, distracted by the television. "Go where?"

"Back to the antique shop. I should probably help out today."

"On a Sunday? The game isn't over yet." He chews a fingernail, focused on the game.

"I know, but I'm bored, and I want to get my hands on those invitations. The faster I get this job done, the faster I'll have them." That seems to satisfy him, and he reaches for his beer.

"All right, but don't have too much fun without me."

"Fun cleaning someone else's junk?"

Bryant doesn't hear the flippant comment, so I lean forward to kiss his cheek. I stand, preparing to say goodbye before he tugs on my hand. I look down and see him frowning up at me.

"What?"

Keeping one eye trained on the screen, he crooks a finger at me, and I bend down. My heart flutters to life when he reaches his hand toward my face but falls when he tugs at a piece of my wayward hair and settles it into place with a pat.

"Your hair was messed up," he says. "Now it's perfect, just as it should be." Bryant leans back to watch the ballgame.

I let myself out without saying another goodbye.

"WHAT ABOUT THIS?"

I hold up an old blue and white vase with a hairline crack down the middle for Mr. Lorry's inspection. Like everything else I've shown him this afternoon, he cuts off the question with a firm shake of his head and a deep scowl. Not a single word is spoken, but the answer is a clear no. Although it's unbelievably cluttered from top to bottom and side to side, there's no getting rid of anything in this store except dust and spiderwebs. It's a hard line for Mr.

Lorry, every item is considered too valuable to discard. I barely contain a longsuffering sigh. Aside from the frames he pulled from the closet, I only see junk surrounding us.

"Look, we can't organize this store if you're not willing to part with anything," I say for the dozenth time, turning the vase over in my hand. "Besides, this thing is broken. Do you see this crack?" I hold up the bottle as proof. "It couldn't even hold water. Put the wrong-sized stem inside, and the whole thing will break apart. A sunflower would kill it for sure." I might as well be talking to the bottle itself for the acknowledgment he gives my words, which is none. It's growing increasingly difficult to decide if the man is rude or simply living inside his own mind and not liking the conditions. I've lived inside my mind for years, so I know the quiet ways a person's thoughts can torment when played backward and forward and inside and out. Turn them upside down and play them again, and the process turns into an endless highlight reel that can drive a soul mad from constant analysis.

What if I had demanded my mother see a doctor the moment she felt the lump?

What if I hadn't laughed it off as dramatic paranoia?

Believe me; I get it. Maybe Mr. Lorry and I don't have much in common, but one person with a ransacked mind tends to gravitate toward the familiar chaos of another. It's human nature. Or maybe it's just how the "crazy" few wade through life. Resident crazy, at your service.

"Can I have that vase?" J.D. asks hopefully, shaking me free from my thoughts. I shrug. A broken vase will never sell anyway.

"Sure." I'm about to hand the vase to him when Mr. Lorry strides over in two steps, yanks it out of my hand, and then stalks toward the back. A child marching home with a ball and declaring "game over" might look more mature.

"It's a broken vase," I say, annoyed. "You're seriously not going to let J.D. have it?" I'm greeted with the slam of a door, followed by complete silence. I look at J.D.'s crestfallen face and wink. "I guess that vase means something to him." But I'm certain it doesn't. Walter Lorry is simply a hoarder. One glance around this store will tell you that much.

J.D. stares forlornly after Mr. Lorry. "My mama woulda liked that vase," he says, disappointment oozing from his tone. "She has a collection of pretty things that aren't perfect. She has a glass elephant with the trunk broken off and a glass monkey missing its tail. Bought 'em that way, even." An odd collection, one I've never heard of, so I glance around us, spotting at least a dozen other things just like that vase dotted throughout this store, all seemingly cheap and meaningless. Not to J.D.'s momma, it seems. Broken and still beautiful, it's quite a concept. Maybe we could all take a lesson from her.

I tilt my head at J.D. "Why don't you pick out something else, and I'll buy it for you?"

His face transforms so quickly you'd think I offered him a shiny new bike. It's cute, funny even… until I really look at the kid. At his tattered jeans that barely brushed his ankles, his shoes with a hole in the toes, once white but now a dusty shade of brown like they'd been scrubbed a few too many times. His ill-fitting shirt hugs his thin biceps instead of skirting his elbows like a correctly sized one might. And then I glance at my high-end yoga pants and two-hundred-dollar sneakers, neither of which my mother could have afforded when I was a kid. Funny the things you see when you stop looking out only for yourself. It's true that one person's junk is another person's treasure.

"Tell you what," I say, "I'll buy you two things if you want them for your mom. And if you work hard and help me out today, I might even throw in some money just for you. It'd be like earning your very own paycheck. How does that sound?"

If his face had transformed before, now it's like I'm looking at a whole different kid. I never knew a smile could stretch that big, from ear to ear, taking over his entire face. Paired with the freckles, the kid is so cute that I can almost hear my internal clock ticking. *You should have a baby, you really want a baby...*

I do not, under any circumstance in the next three to five years, want a baby. Clearly, my clock needs batteries. Maybe I should smash it with a hammer.

"That sounds good," J.D. says enthusiastically. "What do you want me to do?"

Give a kid some motivation, and suddenly work becomes fun.

This place is so chaotic that I have no concrete ideas, so I offer the easiest job I can think of. "Why don't you grab a broom and start sweeping?" The broom still sits where I put it yesterday after completing only half the store. "Maybe if the floors are clean, it might improve the whole look of this place."

J.D. grabs the broom and gets to work. Every time I glance at him over the next two hours, he never loses his smile.

SPOILER ALERT: sweeping a filthy antique store does not, in fact, make the filth look any less dirty. Especially when the person doing the sweeping only manages to spread the dirt around because he's too busy discovering treasures, pausing to pick them up and play, and therefore routinely forgetting what he was doing in the first place. J.D. spent all afternoon moving one pile of dirt into another pile of dirt and never swept any of it out the door like he was supposed to. Money well spent does not apply to this situation. Still, I hand J.D. twenty dollars anyway, wrap the things he picked out for his mother—a milk glass soap dish and, curiously, a matchbox car from 1994 still in the package—in a brown paper bag, and thank him for the help. He assures me he'll be back to help tomorrow. I would tell him not to bother, but I kind of liked the company. Plus, he never stopped talking. Not always to me, mostly to the objects around the store as he picked them up and examined each one—*"Where did you come from? I'll bet a pirate owned you a long time ago"*—but the chatter was nice when the only other alternative was a man who grumped or said nothing at all.

"Then I'll see you tomorrow," I say as he hops down the steps and runs toward home, waving to me as he goes. Cute kid. A talkative but distracted J.D. is better than an AWOL and unspeaking Mr. Lorry. Where did the old man wander off to anyway?

Wiping my hands on a cloth I'm fairly certain was used to clean the front window, I head for the back of the store, stopping to pick up a fallen price tag and a discarded book, returning them to their respective shelves as I go. After almost two days of straightening up this place, it still looks as bad as the moment I walked inside. Part of me—an increasingly large part—wonders if the tradeoff I've made is worth it. You can buy invitations for ten bucks a dozen on Amazon, so why all this fuss?

My mother-in-law and the whole Ratliff family at large, that's why. Bragging rights are a valuable commodity in Silver Bell, and I'll be able to cash these in for at least a couple of years. More if nothing particularly newsworthy happens to swing the gossip circle in a new direction.

I spot the blue vase sitting on top of an old wooden filing cabinet even before I dare to step into the back room. I haven't approached this part of the store before and am unsure if I should be doing it now. What if this is Mr. Lorry's home? What if this is where he hides the bodies? What if his mother's skeleton is strapped to a rocking chair next to an open back window and swaying softly in the breeze? What if I hear her say "Walter..." in a high-pitched voice as eerie background music begins to play? Worse, what if the back of the store is just an extension of the rest of the store, and I'm stuck cleaning this place for as long as I live? There are so many things that could go wrong here. All of them horrific.

Yet nothing—and everything—does.

Mr. Lorry is sound asleep on a cot, much like the one stashed on his front porch—the one I found him sleeping on yesterday. Military-grade but worse off, stretched and anchored on only three corners, the fourth frayed and sagging like it might snap at any moment and take his body with it. The sort of cot found in the corner of a second-hand shop where all the unwanted items go to collect dust and fill space reminiscent of ninety percent of the things in this place. He's on his side, knees bent forward like he planned to hug them but paused halfway there, clutching a stuffed eagle to his chest like a child holding a treasured toy in the throes of a dream. The skin is pinched between his eyebrows; maybe the dream is a nightmare. With him lying so still, I can see that his left foot bends at an unnaturally odd angle; he doesn't just walk with a limp; he walks physically impaired. His lower lip is curled inward in a permanent position, possibly the reason for his lisp and slurred words. A wayward strand of hair is caught between his lips, trailing into his mouth and disappearing into an abyss of tongue, teeth, and tonsils. So much of me wants to reach forward to drag the strand out gently, but I'm afraid of waking him. A midday nap seems essential for an older gentleman despite the oddness of the hour and the way it's being taken, like he stomped back here with that old vase and lay down in a fit of temper and petulance, only to fall asleep against his will. But here Mr. Lorry lies, and there the vase sits, and here I am...wondering what to do.

Dragging my eyes away from the man, I take in the rest of the room with its single lamp, bare walls, stacks of books and papers and dirty dishes scattered along every surface. The dingy toilet, sink, and pipes are hidden by a thin floral curtain draped over cable wire connected on opposites sides. There's an old brown oscillating fan swirling left to right in the corner of the room, background noise for a lack of activity coming from the store, drowning out my unsteady thoughts that I shouldn't be back here. But still, I study the place—really study it. It's like a jail cell in color and coldness, all gray and metal, sharp corners and jagged edges. It's a place a person might go to punish oneself. I know for a fact that Mr. Lorry owns the two-story house next door with its lanterns and wrap-around porch and fluttery white eyelet curtains hanging from front picture windows. So why on earth is he napping back here? Maybe punishment is exactly what he seeks.

It makes no sense. Unless the rumors are true, then maybe it does.

My eyes settle on an old shoebox on the floor by Mr. Lorry's hand, which lies limp as though he was leafing through the contents of the box right before falling asleep. His pointer finger is wedged between two papers, bookmarking a spot, keeping tabs for later. I glance at Mr. Lorry's face once more, unsure how to react, debating whether to wake him up or let him rest until I see them.

Tears. Dried and streaked on his cheeks like blurred chalk marks on summer pavement. Evidence of the sadness I'd sensed earlier, yet I'm uncertain what triggered it. I'm no stranger to memories creeping up unbidden at inopportune times, but he's been crying over a broken vase? A vase just like at least a dozen others on display in the other room. Why have it for sale if it means so much? The man is a puzzle with large sections of missing parts.

I'm in the middle of trying to solve him when he flips over to the other side, mumbling something on the way around, his back now to me and making it harder to hear. Leaning in closer, I hold my breath and wait for him to speak again—hopefully louder this time to give me a little more context—but there's nothing but steady breathing in and out for several long seconds. And then it happens, low and anguished.

"Scotty..."

The word sounds like "Scotty," though I suppose there could be a dozen more options or variables. *Snotty* or *spotty* or *sorry* or *get out of my freaking bedroom you nosy voyeur in the obscenely expensive yoga pants*—so many other things the man could have said or meant.

"Scotty..."

There it is again, clearer this time, that name. It means nothing to me, nothing at all, the puzzle surrendering yet another piece to the void of unanswered riddles. I turn to leave the man in solitary slumber when the rustling sound of crinkling paper stops me. As Mr. Lorry moves to get comfortable, a small, gray moleskin notebook slips from under his waist and falls to the floor. I stare in an internal debate, wondering if I should leave it there. Or pick it up. Or kick it under the bed, out of sight and mind. Or maybe I should return it to the box where it belongs. I should probably close it and not glance at any part of the handwritten inscription I see peeking out of one corner.

For sure, I shouldn't read it.

I bend down and snatch the notebook off the floor, knowing full well the moral debate I'm pretending to have with myself is just for show. Of course, I'm going to read it. With my conscience telling me to mind my business, put the box down, and leave the room, I do the opposite. The high road is not one I'm used to traveling on. I open it slowly, read the first two lines, then walk over to the wall and slide to the floor, knowing with everything in me that I'll be here a while.

A long while.

Dear Sarah,

I'm so sorry I failed you...

All at once, I know it won't just be a while. I'll likely be here all night.

PART II

6

26 YEARS EARLIER, SPRING 1996

W*alter*

His bowtie was crooked; the tilt irritated him like a sliver of wood under a fingernail, pulsing and stubborn in its refusal to quit. No matter how many times he fastened and refastened the small fabric, the tie declined to do anything but stubbornly sink to the left. This was what he deserved for buying a clip-on tie in the first place, but years of toying with formalwear had resulted in nothing but frustration and aching knuckles. Despite his diagnosis, he'd mastered the art of sought-after calligraphy well enough to scroll an entire wall with letters and poems in his sleep without a single hand cramp, but a three-inch strip of fancy fabric was his undoing. Pun intended.

He bought the clip-on last year, though it hadn't fixed the persistent problem of never hanging right. Blasted tie. Blasted Hollywood parties and their proclivity for high-end fashion. What he wouldn't give to be home in his studio in socked feet, wearing his favorite sweatshirt and worn in Levi's, surrounded by paper and ink. Instead, he was here among the well-heeled crowd, obscenely dressed in a wool Hugo Boss suit that itched around the wrists, accepting dozens of compliments like they mattered and offering twice as many stiff smiles like he meant them. They didn't. He didn't.

He needed a drink.

Walter wound his way past Burt Reynolds and Jane Seymour—*Doctor Quinn, Medicine Woman!* Okay, maybe he was slightly excited about her—and nearly slammed into Harrison Ford, a.k.a. Hans Solo himself, before making a sharp right toward the bar. Not without a backward glance, he was as big a Star Wars fan as anyone and would admit to being slightly starstruck, if only to himself.

Thank goodness his left foot wasn't giving him much trouble tonight. He'd struggled with it a little more lately, but with the physical therapy he'd endured all week, one would have to study him closely to suspect anything was off. Only his closest friends knew the bitter details of his life, a journey that had begun at age ten and had been blessedly slow to progress up to this point. If God kept smiling on him, his downward spiral would continue to be a slow swirl managed with medication. For that, he was grateful. He would be downright giddy if it weren't for tonight's gathering. An admitted blessing on all counts except one:

Walter hated crowds.

His pulse pounded between his ears as he approached the bar. These parties would give anyone anxiety but did a more impactful number on Walter for a few reasons. One, if his foot began to hurt it might fail him completely, resulting in a fall, and he couldn't have that happen around all these people. Two, if he found himself forced to shout over the noise, his speech impediment might become more pronounced, presenting itself like the slur of an inebriated man. Add extreme introvertedness and an aversion to public speaking to the mix, and nights like this made his anxiety skyrocket. Talking was not Walter's strong point, nor was being the center of attention. Most artists felt the same while knowing they needed to make appearances to keep the work coming. Ask a novelist if they like to promote their own books, and ninety-five percent of them will tell you no. The other five percent are either lying or they love the fame more than the writing. As for fellow calligraphy artists like himself, keeping a low profile was a way of life. Except on nights like tonight. And he knew full well he was the luckiest calligraphy artist who ever walked the face of modern-day Earth. Save for the lucky few; his chosen art form had withered in popularity years ago.

Walter slid onto a bar stool with a loud sigh.

"A scotch on the rocks," he said to no one in particular, relief overwhelming him like the stool was an island in the Maldives, and he'd spent the afternoon treading water a mile offshore. That's how Hollywood felt, exhilarating one second, lonely and suffocating the other fifty-nine. But even he had to admit that seeing Jane Seymour was a highlight.

A scotch appeared in front of him atop a paper napkin, three square ice cubes floating atop the amber liquid, the perfect antidote to his rapidly fraying nerves. Since he'd stopped moving, his left toe had developed a telltale twinge. Walter picked up the scotch and tossed it back in one swallow; too much, perhaps, but the warmth spreading through his bloodstream begged to differ. Suddenly his toe stopped demanding all the attention.

"Another, please," he said to the bartender without looking up, setting his empty tumbler on the counter in front of him and pushing it forward.

"Already done?" said a female voice, shocking him enough to look up. "You should try to taste the scotch instead of chugging it down in one swallow, especially when it's a Glenlivet."

Walter stared. A woman bartender, not that he'd never encountered one before. He had many times at one nightclub or another, at one function or another, at one party or another—most of which had been scantily dressed. It wasn't the woman part that rocked him.

It was the way this woman looked.

Her white button-up was tucked into low-slung black trousers, a matching black studded belt hugging her slim hips. Her hair fell in long chocolate ringlets loosely tied back on the sides. Eyelashes swept her upper lids when she blinked. Sea glass blue eyes so clear they were nearly translucent in color studied him. At the same time, her lips instantly ruined all thoughts of any other lips for the foreseeable future—maybe even forever because none would measure up. Jane Seymour, who? This woman winked at him in a way that zapped electric currents to every part of his body, causing him to shift on the stool. If he had to guess, he'd say she was thirty, thirty-two tops. Being newly forty himself, it wasn't an age difference that bothered him in the slightest.

Good God, had he ever seen anyone so beautiful? And this came from a man who'd rubbed shoulders with Hollywood starlets only minutes ago and had just been fantasizing about it.

"Fine, then give me another and I'll sip it."

"Promise?" she asked, drawing out the word in a dizzying Southern accent. Was she flirting? With his entire being, he hoped she was flirting.

"I promise."

Seemingly satisfied, she scooped out ice, unscrewed a bottle of the aforementioned amber Glenlivet Scotch, and slowly poured it in small swirling motions. The action alone was sexy, though maybe it was just him and his long dry spell talking. Walter hadn't been on a date in months. Twelve of them, if he was being honest. He had projects lined up that stretched for miles in front of him and behind him; there wasn't time for a social life, not even if he wanted one. There was also the fact that most women found him awkward once they got past the famous artist part. Good first impressions don't matter when the second one causes your flame to dim.

The bartender set the tumbler in front of him. Without breaking eye contact, he sipped the drink while she held the bottle and watched, an eyebrow raised in a "well?" Okay, fine. She was right. The scotch was delicious, and this was the first time he recalled noticing.

"Touché." He lowered the tumbler and dragged a

thumb over his bottom lip. "From now on, I'll pay more attention." To the drink and to her, but he kept that part to himself. Besides, what is the fantasy in talking a pretty girl up, asking her out, and taking her back to his hotel room if you speak about it? No longer a fantasy, that's what. He was scheduled to be in this room most of the night and on a flight first thing in the morning. Fantasy or not, he didn't have time for anything more than sitting on this stool and enjoying her company for another ten minutes or so. Long enough to be missed until the vultures descended again. If that made Harrison Ford a vulture...so be it.

"For the amount of money they've spent on this scotch," she said, "you should pay attention to it. When will you have an opportunity like this again?" *Tomorrow night in Chicago*, he thought to himself as she moved down the line to a woman sitting three stools away. "What'll you have?" she asked. The woman's answer was insignificant; Walter was too distracted trying to decipher the bartender's accent. Maybe from Tennessee. Kentucky? Walter was an Oregon man himself. Where he came from, they didn't have accents. At least none that he noticed.

"Where are you from?" he asked when she came back his way before considering maybe he shouldn't. What business was it of his where the lady lived when she worked here in Malibu? He expected her to answer as such, but she didn't. Just cleared her throat.

"Arkansas."

His head jerked back in surprise. Arkansas? The state where people went without shoes, wore nothing but overalls, and married their cousins? At least, that's what he remembered from the television shows he watched as a kid. She defied every stereotype in his brain and blew them to bits. She gave him another smile as she poured another customer a tall glass of merlot. She seemed to sense his gaze on her and glanced his way.

"What? Are you surprised to see me wearing shoes and talking halfway decent English? Please tell me you haven't been suckered into believing Hollywood's description of my home state."

Dang it, he hated being a cliché. He swallowed, not about to admit that was exactly where his mind had gone. "No...just..." It might help if he could form a full sentence, but his brain had melted a bit and traveled all the way to his toes. Useless, pointless, no good to him now. He took a deep breath and found his voice. "Okay, I'll admit I'm surprised. I've never met anyone from Arkansas before. Certainly, not anyone that looks like—"

He stopped talking, feeling his ears go red. A dead giveaway since childhood, a reaction he despised.

"Anyone that looks like...she could take down a womanizer with both hands tied behind her back and using nothing but her teeth?" she offered, that smile still playing on her lips. When her cheeks bloomed pink, he knew she hadn't intended the double entendre. Still, the thought of her teeth on him...

He mentally throttled the image with both fists.

"Not a womanizer, just a man who sometimes forgets to use the filter God wisely installed in his brain at birth. It seems that tonight, the switch on mine is broken. Sorry." He raised his glass in a salute, an apology. He needn't have bothered. She laughed.

"Not to worry, mine's broken too half the time. Want another?" she said, eyeing his empty glass.

"I'd better not." He leaned back on the stool and drummed the countertop a couple of times. "I've got to get back to the party, and it'd be better if I arrived sober seeing as I'll be required to continue talking to people."

She laughed again. The sound made him feel like he'd struck oil and used the slick black liquid to make art. A new medium, bright and exciting, a challenge. A weird assessment, but everyone has their dreams. She leaned forward and lowered her voice to a level only he could hear.

"Can you believe all these famous people are

here just to see some uppity artist? I mean, what kind of outrageous party is this when Madonna isn't even the highlight? The artist must be crazy-famous. In the art world, I mean."

He was fairly certain that there was a hidden insult in there, but he was too busy twisting around on the barstool to dwell on it. *Madonna was here? For him?* He'd never met Madonna before, and while he wouldn't call himself a mega-fan, he appreciated good art when he saw—or heard—it. "Papa Don't Preach" was an undeniably good song, one the woman in question wrote herself.

"Madonna's here?" he asked. *For him?* The idea was sobering even for a man who'd just inhaled two scotches.

"Yeah, she's here," the bartender said excitedly, reading his thoughts. "I only saw her for a second before her bodyguards whisked her off to a back room. I think she's set to perform later. Hopefully, I can hear her from here. But again, how is she not the highlight?"

"She might not have top billing, but she's absolutely the highlight. I would bet money everyone here is waiting to see her. The 'uppity artist' you mentioned is just a means to an end." Walter put the two words in air quotes, his private inside joke.

She picked up his empty glass and placed it in a sink on the opposite wall, then reached for a rag to wipe down the counter. "I don't know," she said. "I heard the guy sells his work for thousands of dollars apiece, maybe more than that. And it's calligraphy, not even paint. Who pays that much money for letters, anyway? I can write the alphabet on my own just fine, thank you very much. I don't need some other dude to do it for me."

It took everything in him to keep his laugh in check. Thousands of dollars, indeed. To date, Walter's most expensive creation sold for 2.2 million dollars and now hangs in a Roman museum. As for the "alphabet" comment, he barely felt the sting. She wasn't wrong; people wanted what they couldn't have and would pay nearly anything to get it. Case in point, his calligraphy. Nearly everyone at this exhibit knew how to write, but he guessed only one or two had the knowledge and skill to turn that work into a one-of-a-kind marketable product.

Still, even he could admit that two million dollars was obscene.

Not that he would ever turn it down. Walter wasn't an idiot.

"Want to walk over later and listen to Madonna sing with me?" he asked, nervously biting his lip when her eyes grew wide. "I'll wait at the back of the room and usher you in. No one will ask questions."

Everything froze in place, but her eyes; they danced around in search of the punch line. "Are you serious?" she finally asked. "You have the power to do that?"

"I indeed have the power, and I'm dead serious. If you want to come and can get out of work for half an hour, I'll bring you to the show. We might even push our way to the front row."

Her awestruck expression was nearly as endearing as the single dimple he just noticed on her right cheek. Just as quickly, her eyes narrowed suspiciously as the rest of her body thawed; she crossed her arms.

"What's the catch?"

The "womanizer" comment from earlier bounced in the air between them. "There is no catch. I'll get you into the show to watch Madonna, and then you can come back here to serve drinks for the rest of the night." Walter held up both hands in surrender. "I swear, despite how I came across earlier, I'm just trying to be nice."

She studied him for the truth until it appeared she'd found it. He smiled when her shoulders visibly relaxed. "My break is in a few minutes. I'll keep working until I hear her first song start to play, and then I'll walk over."

Walter grinned. "Perfect. I'll meet you at the back of the room when it starts."

"And...you're sure you won't get in trouble for letting me in? I don't have an invitation, and I'm hardly dressed for a party." She gestured to her casual outfit as though she wouldn't outshine everyone in attendance.

He shook his head. "I'm positive I won't get in trouble, and you look great. But what's your name? I'll need to give it to the doorman, and it'd be a good idea if everyone thinks we know each other."

The pink stain on her cheeks returned, arriving with a hint of irresistible shyness. "It's Sarah," she says. "Sarah Jones." Walter rolled it over in his mind. Sarah. Sweet. Beautiful. Kind. Princess. The name suited her perfectly.

"I'll see you in a bit, Sarah Jones," he said, taking a couple of steps away.

"What's your name?" she hollered after him. His grin intensified with the knowledge that this might be his favorite part of the night—of any night in recent memory, actually. Especially now.

"It's Walter." He sauntered back toward her and held out his hand. "Walter Lorry, resident 'uppity artist,' at your service. Nice to make your acquaintance."

Her mouth fell open in mortification right as he turned to leave, the sound of her, *"Madonna is here for you?"* causing him to throw his head back and laugh with delight. It was fun to shock people, especially someone as beautiful as her.

Favorite night, indeed.

"I CAN'T BELIEVE you didn't tell me you were an artist. *The* artist. And if we're being honest here, I can't believe you made all the things hanging in this room, either. Your work is amazing. I've never seen anything like it before."

Walter followed her gaze as it traveled from the wall in front of them to the ceiling, where elegant scrollwork told the story of early Hollywood, of Gable and Leigh, Bogart and Becall, and even Chaplin and Pickford. You had to squint to see it, study the center of each letter to find the makeup of traditional English letters before the swirls and loops distracted you from the heart of the story. But it was there for those who looked, available for those who valued real over pretty. He was one of those people.

Most people weren't. Hence the black and white photos that accompanied the words.

"So, you think my work is better than just "an alphabet" that any average Joe could do himself?"

Sarah looked at him sidelong. "I'm pretty sure I didn't say the 'average Joe' part. But yeah, I'll agree to the rest of it." She tilted her head back to see the words up high. "It's amazing, Walter. Really amazing."

"More amazing than Madonna?"

Her head snapped to him, and she scowled. "I wouldn't go that far. It's blasphemy, honestly. No one is better than Madonna, but you're a close-ish second."

Walter slapped a hand over his chest. "It's the 'ish' that really warms my heart."

"It's the 'ish' that makes you stand out among the other wannabe calligraphy artists, so..."

"Wow. High praise. Especially considering the calligraphy crowd is a hugely expansive one."

She turns as though looking for said crowd. There's literally no one standing nearby.

"Clearly. And you're welcome." Sarah smiled, and he found himself doing the same. A long second passed before it occurred to him that he likely looked like a lovesick schoolboy to random bystanders. He stayed that way until a guest interrupted.

"Walter, this evening was glorious. And how is our star of the night holding up? Not getting a swelled head due to all this praise, I hope." A woman dressed in gold silk paired with a triple strand of elegant pearls, a woman he recognized immediately as Gloria Vanderbilt, laughed so musically that Walter could almost feel heaven's angels studying her high notes. Madonna might be envious if she were still here to hear the sound.

"Glorious, indeed," he said, leaning with a

conspiratorial eye as though they were sharing an inside joke. They say flattery will get you everywhere, a half-truth that hadn't failed him yet. "Thank you so much for organizing it, Mrs. Vanderbilt. And for making this all possible. I wouldn't be here without supporters such as yourself." It was true. He wouldn't. It took money and clout to organize a showing of this magnitude, neither of which Walter had in excess—though some might claim otherwise—and there isn't a moment that went by that didn't find him gratefully aware.

"I hope you'll be back next year," Mrs. Vanderbilt said with a pat on his arm.

"If you extend the invitation, I wouldn't miss it."

"Rest assured, I will," she said.

They parted after a few more pleasantries, and then Walter turned to see Sarah standing back and staring dumbstruck, her two ice-blue orbs star crossed and unblinking. "Who was that woman?" she whispered.

"Um..." He looked over his shoulder to make sure the woman in question was far enough away to miss her name coming up in conversation, then turned back to Sarah. "That woman was Gloria Vanderbilt. She helped organize this gallery tonight."

She gasped. "Gloria Vanderbilt made my pants!" She twisted at the waist to show off what he assumed was the label on her pockets. Like the chivalrous gentleman he was, Walter took it as permission to eye her backside. And a nice backside it was, even with the Vanderbilt signature scrawled across one pocket square.

"I'm very impressed," Walter murmured, hoping she wouldn't catch his real meaning. He wasn't talking about the jeans. "Though I would venture to guess that she didn't personally make this pair with her own two hands. More likely used a factory full of minimum wage employees."

Sarah sighed. "That's a good point, I suppose. Still amazing to see her, though. Madonna too." She smiled at him. "Thank you for a lovely evening, maybe the best I can remember. But I suppose I should get back to work. The last thing I need is to find myself out of a job, even if seeing all these famous people might make it worth it."

He nodded. "My pleasure. I'm glad you were able to come. And thanks for the scotch. From now on, Glenlivet is the only brand I'll drink."

She beamed. "Don't forget to sip it."

"Wouldn't dream of making that mistake ever again. Goodnight, Sarah. It was lovely to meet you."

She hesitated, glanced at him as though she had more to say, then thought better of it with a shake of her head. Walter had never known such profound disappointment.

"Goodnight, Walter. I hope your art sells for more than you've ever dreamed."

He didn't tell her the money wasn't where he found his joy; the fame didn't matter. Instead, he smiled and said thank you, then watched her walk away, back to the bar, back to work. Even surrounded by all these people, those with large social circles and even larger bank accounts, suddenly Walter felt cold. Lonely. Alone.

Money can't buy happiness despite so many believing it might.

What it could buy, however, was another glass of scotch. Who knew? Maybe he would order club soda this time, keep his mind clear and his conversation skills sharp. One thing he noticed about Sarah: she'd never once pointed out his limp or commented on how tired he looked, yet another side effect of his condition. Whether she didn't notice or simply accepted both things as part of his human makeup, it made him want to be near her again.

Walter took a deep breath, walked away from his own party, and with a determined step that masked any trace of a limp, he headed back to the bar. He couldn't think of any better way to spend his time than continuing to talk to Sarah, not even the prospect of shoulder-rubbing or name-building or money-making. Not even if Sophia Loren personally asked him to dance—that *was* Sophia Loren that just walked past him, right? Walter rubbernecked in her direction for a quick second before remembering his mission.

Sarah and her affinity to pour a good drink, that's where he was headed. Sarah and her quick smile and wide-eyed innocence, taking in the evening like an adorable first timer might. Sarah, who'd walked into his party starstruck and walked out unaffected —both by the well-known personalities surrounding her and by the sacrifices each one had made to achieve it. Everyone envied the Hollywood elite, but Walter knew few people would if they knew the real stories of those who had 'made it.'

Going back to see Sarah turned out to be the best and worst decision Walter had ever made. Funny how—when hovering from a distance and with the benefit of hindsight—both things can be true at once.

7

PRESENT DAY

Piper

It's been two days—forty-five hours and seven minutes, to be exact—since I found the journals in Walter's back room and read the first two in their entirety, reluctantly stopping when I got a text from Bryant.

"Are you on your way?"

We were set to have dinner with his parents, and I was already late. Everything in me wanted to cancel, to stay under the surface of my deep dive into Mr. Lorry's former life, but I left the antique store anyway, quietly letting myself out the front door, leaving the old man sound asleep and none the wiser. Sure, I felt guilty for snooping, but only as guilty as one feels when reading an erotic paperback in the back pew of a Sunday church service. You probably shouldn't, but when the story is good, and the romantic tension is high, there's no way you're going to quit. At least not before you get to the resolution.

It goes without saying that I was distracted at dinner.

Sadly, it also goes without saying that no one noticed but me.

Those journals took up every inch of space inside my preoccupied mind. They still do, almost two full days later.

If you're being technical, it took me only a moment to realize Walter's journals were stacked in backward order, the most recent one being at the top. So, I flipped them upside down while Mr. Lorry slept and began again, making it to the end of the second notebook before the old man began making noises, the first of many in a restless slumber.

I still don't know what he's sorry about.

I still don't know why he believes he failed.

I still don't know about his "diagnosis" because it wasn't made clear in the writings.

And I still have no idea how I'm going to get back to reading them, to solve the mystery as to why Mr. Lorry is the way he is, why the town believes him a strange recluse who's lived some sort of fable-like existence with more rumors circulating around him than a supermarket tabloid that specializes in splashing about those sorts of attention-grabbing headlines.

I still don't know who Scotty is or why Mr. Lorry kept mumbling that name in his sleep. This is the worst of all the details that have plagued me this weekend. I'm a kid at Christmas with her gifts hidden in a cedar chest, one lift of the lid away from knowing every surprise held inside. I hate surprises. I read books back to front to see if the story is worth the time investment. I eat the inside of a Reese's peanut butter cup first because it's the best part. I like the bread before the entrée and the dessert before either one because the thought of being too full for cake fills me with sadness. Some might say it's because I've lost so much that I like to reap the reward before I've put forth the effort. I might agree with that assessment if I hadn't been this way for as long as I can remember.

Long before I ever lost a thing.

Long before my mother's diagnosis changed everything about my life.

All this to say that I don't like not knowing. And I still have twelve hours to go before I'm able to head back to the bookstore and attempt to reenter the world Mr. Lorry created, assuming I can find a reason to be alone with his journals once again. I'm aware he might not want me to read them. I'm aware it could be considered eavesdropping or nosy or my inane inability to mind my own business, but in the same way curiosity often kills the cat, not knowing things sometimes kills me. Or at least it makes me feel so off balance I'd rather be dead. Call it what you will; I need to read those journals.

"Which one is your favorite?" Bryant asks, shocking me out of my reverie and back into the moment. We've been in wedding-planning mode all weekend while his mother tagged along, and blessedly, we're almost finished. I'm standing in the middle of a bakery with a bite of some sweet concoction rolling inside my mouth—a cake testing, though I haven't actually tasted anything. I could be eating sawdust for as much as my senses are retaining. Chocolate, I think. With a hint of mint. The sensation comes rushing at me so fast I begin to cough.

"Not this one," I say. "Too strong. Too heavy on the cocoa. I hate dark chocolate." All these things are true but saying them all at once is just deflection. I can't have my fiancé know that our wedding cake is last on my list of priorities, coming in line behind cleaning toilets and scrubbing a ketchup stain out of my favorite white button-up. So far down the list that I'm uninterested in tasting it even while it's in my mouth. "Maybe the raspberry?" I can't fully remember if we've yet tried raspberry, but I faintly remember the flavor and just go with it.

"What about the lemon?" Bryant suggests instead, and I shrug. I've never liked the taste of lemon, something I thought my fiancé knew. Maybe he doesn't remember. I remind him.

"Cherry, then?" he says.

Julia makes a delighted squeal. "I adore cherry cake."

I shake my head to dismiss the idea. "I'm allergic to cherries."

Bryant emits an exasperated sigh while Julia waves a dismissive hand. "It's not like you'll be eating it anyway. You're the bride. We should go with the cherry."

This makes no sense, but Bryant starts nodding his head, eyes seeking his mother's approval. "It's true. Brides hardly ever eat at their own weddings."

He says this as though he's walked the aisle many times instead of this one, and I give him a look.

"Not cherry. I'm allergic." Repeating myself makes me think the words will stick.

They don't.

"I'll bring Benadryl, just in case." Leave it to Julia to come up with a solution.

"You'll bring Benadryl to save me from my wedding cake?" She can't be serious.

"Of course. We can't let you break out in a rash on your wedding day, can we?" Julia says as though it makes perfect sense.

"Great idea!" Bryant says while I just stare. Did neither one of them hear the irony in my statement? I look around for someone to provide backup, but everyone here is either busy rearranging petit fours or pretending to.

"Cherry it is," I say, giving up the battle. Fingers crossed I don't die, but whatever.

Julia smiles and crosses her legs while Bryant peruses the dinner options.

"Next up, we need to decide on the appetizers," says a woman I vaguely recall being introduced to when we walked in an hour ago. It's all I can do to keep my groan in check. We're using a one-stop catering company to meet all our needs, a prospect that sounded appealing at first despite the more expensive cost when we scheduled it last month. Now the whole thing sounds tedious and tiring. Walter's writings are all I can think about. I'm invested in a way that makes no sense, a passerby after a bike wreck, desperate to know if the victim will live. All I want to do is get back to reading those journal entries, to Mr. Lorry's story and history and all the mysteries that lie inside both, but I can't. Until our wedding reception details are firmed up, I'm stuck test-eating food samples for what could be the rest of the afternoon. Things could be worse, I suppose. I could be looking at paper samples or invitation designs or weighing the pros and cons of birdseed bags versus miniature bottles of bubbles or a hundred other uninteresting items on the list I've yet to face.

They say the quickest way to the other side of a problem is through it, so I straighten my shoulders and take a deep breath.

"Hand me a marinated olive," I say, waving my fingers toward Bryant. "Let's see if we can lock down the menu in the next half hour. If we're lucky, we'll have this wedding planned by tonight."

He gives me an *atta girl* grin while I slide the olive off a toothpick and chew.

"*I HAVE CANCER.*"

My mother spoke the worst three words known to the English language on an otherwise happy Thursday night over a plate of shared tacos on a rare dinner out to celebrate my first-ever straight A's. I was a senior in college, and I'll never know why she chose that moment to tell me. Maybe it was guilt, worry, or the simple fact that happiness can't last, but she told me right then like she'd been holding back the words for weeks. They burst out like a party popper, loud and sudden, confetti landing all over the table in the form of shared pain. I'll never forget how the spoken diagnosis felt like a sharp whack to my head, a baseball bat that cracked my skull and reverberated consistently over the next few weeks, never once letting up, not even when I slept. They never tell you that about grief; it infiltrates everything, occasionally letting up a half-second to make room for joy but quickly rushing back in to remind you how selfish you were to feel it.

Grief expects to be validated in tears. Nothing more and nothing less.

We'd been talking about my future, including first apartments, full-time jobs, and my impending dates with Bryant. You know, the kind of future filled with nothing but promise and possibilities, parties and potential. My mother met Bryant the first night we went out as an official couple, and she quickly grew to love him. That night over tacos, right before she blew up the world with her news, my mother voiced her hope that we would wind up together, make plans, and build a future that included marriage, kids, and years of contented happiness. That way, her burden would be lessened. The promise of my happiness was what drove her to the end, knowing my future would be secured by a boy who loved me and his well-established family who would one day take me in and offer me security for the rest of my life. When you're sick, apparently, it helps to hope in things that you won't be around to witness.

Of course, life isn't that simple. In the same way, a smile masks varying degrees of pain; sometimes you tell people what they want to hear to make their private torture wane a little bit.

"I want that future with Bryant too, Mom." The words weren't true when I said them. I dreamed of going away and starting over, meeting new people, and experiencing new things. But when my mother died, what drove me most of all was the desire to make her proud. A mother's dying wish is sacred, and I wasn't about to let her down. I would make my mother's dream my own if only to honor her memory.

The chemo only worked for a while; the cancer sprang back with a vengeance just when the doctor thought it was gone for good. It wasn't. This time, it attacked hard and fast.

It took only three years from start to finish. My mom died from advanced melanoma, an aggressive type of cancer that laughs at your pathetic attempts to fight it, especially when you discover it midway through the game.

After her death, nothing was the same, and like my personality, my sense of self died right along with my mother. I was a piece of target paper hanging by two clips in the wind, just waiting for life to fill her up with holes.

And fill me up, it did.

My neighbors and their sympathetic whispers.

My friends and their suddenly busy schedules.

My mind and its persistent niggling doubt.

My old dreams and their insistence that I listen.

My refusal to grant their wishes, no matter how loudly they screamed.

When Bryant proposed all these years later, of course, I said yes. It's what my mother dreamed of, what she counted on to bring her peace. What we talked of and planned together. What I still dream of late at night when new doubts creep in and a longing for what might have been plague my dreams. But I can't entertain such things because I won't be a liar. Bryant and me together; it's the last promise I made to her. And I'm grateful to fulfill it. So very, very grateful.

Mostly.

It's the *mostly* that still screams at night when no one else is around.

The *mostly* that increased in volume as I read those journals last Friday.

The *mostly* I try to ignore at all costs because the doubt could ruin everything.

"So, we're going with the chestnuts, then?"

I blink into focus only to find myself mid-bite

into a brand-new appetizer with no memory of the last one. What is wrong with me?

"What?" I say to Bryant, genuinely flustered and confused. That's when I taste bacon and barbecue. That's when I realize the olives are long gone and have been replaced by something much more delicious. The only problem is...I don't recall the moment it happened. It seems impossible to go from point A to point B without recalling the journey—in this case, going from tangy to savory in a lengthy series of appetizer eliminations. I've become a pro at blocking out whole pieces of my life, a side effect of trauma, I suppose. Unfortunately, that seems to include things I thoroughly enjoy.

I love bacon. I feel cheated.

"The chestnuts," Bryant says with a frown. "You're the one who asked to try them. And judging from the noises you're making, I'll take a wild guess and assume you like them."

I press my lips together and nod. "I like them." And I do. I just can't remember sampling anything since the olives. "I definitely want these at the reception."

Bryant sighs. "Then there's one thing chosen, at least. Only four more to go. Which will be difficult since we only have three more options to choose from, and you've eliminated all the others."

I have? I'm aware that thoughts of my mother

generally clear out all the extra space in my head and fill it with my memories of her, but I had assumed that unlike everything else in life, planning my wedding to Bryant would be the exception.

My college entrance exam? I had to take it twice.

My first job interview at a supermarket photo kiosk? I didn't get the job because I seized up on the first question. Odd, since "so you want to be a photographer?" is a standard issue softball question. But my mind had wandered, and my listening skills had taken off with it.

The lists are endless, but I didn't expect this.

"What's left to try?" I ask, hopeful that our remaining three options are the best ones.

Bryant rolls his eyes. "Pretzels dipped in cheddar, grape and white raisin skewers, and pickled okra."

A hard *no* to all three. Disgusting.

"Perfect," I hear myself say instead, ready to wrap this taste testing up so as not to embarrass myself further. Of course, it won't work, but five points for trying and bonus points for believing in the possibility.

"Really?" Bryant says, frowning like a man questioning his fiancée's judgment. That makes two of us.

The oxymoron involving grapes and raisins notwithstanding, I give a decisive nod and lean into the certainty of leaving this place. If the guests don't like the food, they can hit a drive-thru for something more substantial after the reception.

"Really. I think those selections are perfect."

Bryant presses both palms to his knees and stands, then offers a firm handshake to the wedding coordinator. "Pleasure doing business with you." The men shake hands, and Bryant turns to look at me. "According to my mother, next up, we need to choose napkins. I guess the real question is: do you prefer linen or cotton? Monogrammed or embroidered?"

Just when I thought the day couldn't get worse...

Gritting my teeth against the tedium ahead, I work to focus on my fiancé and the ever-present list of his mother's many requirements.

My mother loved him for me.

Like always, remembering that simple fact makes the task ahead easier to take.

8

iper

P I have one foot inside the door when Mr. Lorry addresses me with his unique way of speaking; sharp like a switchblade to my eardrums, muddy like waders sloshing through a strong current, low and gravelly like a good cough might clear it. He's angry; I can pinpoint that much.

"You read my journals."

I blink, stunned that it took no time for him to speak and also aware that his eyes appear tired, low lids shuttered halfway over his irises. They're perpetually that way. It surprises me that I didn't notice until now. I consider lying to save my neck; the man looks like he could slice through me and discover the truth tucked inside my cleanly picked conscience. The truth indeed hurts, but it's almost always worth the pain.

"I don't know what you're talking about."

I said, "almost." At this point, I'm committed to the lie. Besides, I only read one journal in full, so technically I'm telling the truth.

"I'm talking about how you opened my shoebox."

This lie might be a bit trickier. To give myself time to think, I walk into the store and let the door slam behind me, trying to come up with another partial truth. Eventually, I give up and fall into my original story, standing my ground like I'm not the one digging my grave. "I did no such thing. Now if you'll excuse me, I need to get to—"

"If you're going to lie about it, at least do a better job."

My head spins at his use of so many words at once. Wasn't it only three days ago that I believed the man was mute? I would be amazed if I wasn't busy taking issue with something he said. I pull my backpack higher on my shoulder and cross my arms.

"Excuse me. I'll have you know my lying skills are top-notch."

"According to the camera in the back room, you're awful at it."

Crap. Caught on camera, a dirty trick up the old man's sleeve I hadn't considered. If I hadn't walked into that back room like a trespasser, I would be offended at his gall to film me without consent. Stupid technicalities.

"Fine, I read one of your journals. They were just sitting out in the open like you wanted me to. Besides, they weren't even in the right order, just tossed inside that box like you didn't care about keeping them organized."

He takes a shuffled step toward me. "I don't care. They were sitting out in the open of a room you weren't invited to enter, and I didn't want you to read them. Those journals are none of your business."

His long statement is a lot to process, so I don't try for now. I'm too busy mentally working out my defense. "Maybe not, but now I'm invested. Who's Sarah, and why are you writing to her?" Weak as far as defenses go, but there it is.

I see him flinch before his gaze narrows. "That's none of your business."

I don't tell him it's all I thought about all week-end, making it my business whether I meant to or not. We're locked in a stare-down, a standoff, a clash of wills in a match that only one person has a right to attend, and that person isn't me. Still, I don't back down when someone tosses up a challenge. I need to read the next journal.

"They might not be any of my business, but—"

"Which one did you read?" he asks.

The sudden change in attitude accompanied by his slur of a question catches me off guard, surprising me in how it's delivered. Mr. Lorry works his bottom lip like a child at Christmas who wants to know what's inside the brightly wrapped packages without taking the cheater's route and opening them. Like a writer facing his first critique on a manuscript he tucked away years ago and just pushed out into the world. The papers were yellowed and worn, some written years ago. Maybe decades.

"First, I started reading one about—"

His hands come up to stop me, eyes wide with pleading.

"Never mind, I don't want to know. Read them if you want to. Just don't mention them to me again." He turns to go, then thinks better of it and pauses after a single step. "But you can only read the opened ones. The others…leave them alone until I decide what to do about them."

Do about them? I noticed a few journals with tape around them, but I assumed they were discarded drafts, middle-of-the-night thoughts he scratched out with no coherence, never to read again. Private thoughts, painful to share, safer to keep hidden away inside the semi-permanent confines of paper and glue. The idea that he may have plans for them piques my curiosity, though it isn't a thought I can consider entertaining. I nod to show agreement.

"I won't touch them; you have my word." It's the only thing I can say, the only choice I have. The man is trusting me, and something tells me that is a rare occurrence. For now, and for always, it'll have to be enough.

"That doesn't mean much from a woman who takes pride in lying," he says. He has a point, but that doesn't mean I like it.

"Hey, I'm helping around here like I said I would, aren't I?"

Mr. Lorry makes a grand show of taking in the room. "If you say so. The place still looks a mess to me."

"And whose fault is that?"

"Not mine, that's for sure."

My mouth nearly falls open at his ghost of a smile, but he walks off before I can say a word, shuffling toward the back of the store while I watch in fascination. It's his first attempt at teasing me, almost like we're at the beginning of a relationship not based on fear and intimidation. Maybe we'll grow to like each other at some point. Perhaps we'll even be friends? The word seems too much of a stretch, so I internally settle on *somewhat tolerant* and hope for the best. Still, I smile at his retreating form. Despite what everyone thinks, Mr. Lorry isn't scary as much as he is different. Awkward. I'm starting to wonder if maybe the best people are.

He disappears around a China cabinet while I slide my backpack to the floor and grab a mop. I spend the next hour cleaning, all the while alternating between wondering about the old man's history and wondering when I can get back to reading those journals.

The open ones.

But it's the closed ones that plague me all afternoon.

9

26 YEARS EARLIER, SUMMER 1996

W*alter*

They were three dates into what he hoped was a long-term relationship before he told her his secret. His prognosis. His life expectancy. His "handicap," as his father had so lovingly called it.

Myotonic Dystrophy. Not as severe as the muscular kind, but there would be—there already were—repercussions. Speech impediments, currently barely perceptible but a positively prominent part of his future. A left foot was already beginning to turn inward, not so noticeable yet and manageable with medication, but the mask wouldn't last forever. Someday, he might lose the ability to walk entirely. At the age of five and even before his diagnosis, his eyelids had begun to droop in a way that had his parents sending him to his bedroom for extra naps. His eyes looked perpetually tired even while wide awake, which was expected to worsen with time.

The one positive fact that flabbergasted even his doctors: his hands had been blessedly spared. As a child, he could play baseball with his friends and paint in his room after dark. As a young adult, his talent had grown stronger. As he grew older, his work had only been enhanced. Entirely unaffected by his disease.

No one had heard of Myotonic Dystrophy back then. But they all knew now. Boy, did they know.

And now, much to the dismay of his hoped-for future, so did Sarah.

Myotonic Dystrophy causes extremities to weaken over time, leading to slurred speech and obvious deformities. It wasn't an easy prognosis for him at ten years old, was even more difficult at forty, and had often been proven nearly impossible on his limited number of relationships. He was handsome at first meeting—he'd been told that plenty of times. It was the second and third meeting when his guard was down enough that his speech became more relaxed and, consequently, more noticeable, that was his undoing. Women didn't appreciate the slightly inebriated-sounding way he spoke. Their parents appreciated it even less. Worse still was the occasional fumble of his steps, one instance so bad that it sent him colliding head-on into a woman's chest. An accident, but she believed otherwise. After a slap that left a red mark on his cheek for two days, she marched away, and he never heard from her again. It stood to reason that he was mortified. It also stood to reason that he grew increasingly gun-shy as time passed. Even success didn't give him a confidence boost. He'd nearly sworn off dating entirely until the night of the Malibu reception. Until the moment Sarah poured him that drink.

With her, three dates were all it took to know he was already in love with her, and there was no going back. This breakup would crush him.

But Walter didn't know that Sarah had a secret of her own.

She could have told him she was eighty-five and looked young for her age, and it wouldn't have affected his heart. She could have said she'd been married four times already and owed alimony to every single man, and he still wouldn't have wavered. His mind was already made up; he loved her.

But even Walter had to admit it was a life-changing secret.

"I have a son."

For Walter, those four words changed everything in the second it took to hear them.

"You have a what?" He never heard her repeat

the words. His ears rang too loudly to hear past the noise inside his brain.

Sarah had a son. Walter didn't want kids. He had known that from his first memory of being a kid himself. Fatherhood wasn't on the trajectory of anything remotely related to his career aspirations or lifelong plan—he had one, of course. A chart, a graph, a list in alphabetical order in color-coded ink. And Walter's personal experience with fathers made fatherhood a non-sequitur. Very little about his childhood was pleasant. His father was domineering and angry, controlling and aloof, consistently critical while managing to be curiously absent. For his dad, fatherhood was a nuisance at best and a source of secondhand accomplishment at worst. *"That's my kid pitching the Little League game...My kid getting straight A's in grade school...My kid winning the wrestling match..."* Until Walter's diagnosis, that is. Up until then, Walter existed on this earth to be his father's link to bragging rights.

For a man like Tom Lorry, bragging about a kid who walked with a limp became hard. When calligraphy art became Walter's chosen profession, the silence turned to ridicule.

What man wants to tell his drinking buddies about his son, the professional calligraphy artist with a turned-in lower lip? Not Walter's father. He made that clear long ago. When Walter began studying calligraphy, his father considered it some-thing only a "sissy" would be interested in. When Walter sold his first greeting card concept, his father told him to pursue something more manly, like being a mechanic or a construction worker. When Walter was first invited to the White House, his father remarked that Nixon was a traitor to the country and *"Why would anyone want to be associated with the likes of that man?"* Nothing Walter did was good enough. Not ever.

Not until he sold his first million-dollar painting, that is.

That day, the phone started ringing. It had been ringing ever since. The only difference is, eventually, Walter learned how to ignore it. The man wanted money, not a father-son relationship like Walter had hoped...like he had wished for every single year of his life because that's all a kid wants; to be uncondi-tionally loved by dad.

So, above everything else Walter believed about life, he knew with complete certainty that father-hood wasn't on his radar. And he was okay with that.

Until Sarah flattened that belief with four simple words.

"You have a son? Like, a kid? One that belongs to you?" Walter had been considered overly bright and gifted his entire life. At that moment, he could barely string basic words together to form a semi-coherent sentence. Sarah just looked at him.

"I have a kid. And yes, I'm pretty sure he belongs to me. Has for four years, now."

Walter swallowed, a little flutter of nerves building in his chest. "He's four?"

She smiled. "He's four and every bit as precocious as you might imagine a four-year-old boy being. He's my whole life, and I thought you should know. Before this goes any further, I mean."

And just like that, despite a lifetime of absolute certainty, Walter's doubts fizzled in the light of instant clarity. What is doubt, anyway? Old-fashioned fear of the unknown, rejection, and discovery that you're not as equipped to accomplish something as you hoped. But what Walter felt now was pride. Sarah wanted him, maybe even wanted their relationship to go further. Hearing her give voice to the idea made him feel like he could conquer anything.

How hard could a four year old be?

Had a belief ever been more laughable?

Two nights later, he discovered four-year-old boys were a symphony of precocious and sweet, terror and hilarity. Case in point, their first meeting.

"Why does your mouth look like that?" little Scotty asked Walter point blank, while cautiously examining his face. They'd been locked in a stare down for a solid minute, Walter hunched over slightly at the waist for a better look, and Scotty pressed against his mother's backside, only partially visible as his little face peeked from around the hem of her blue pencil skirt. The question both surprised and delighted Walter. Most people didn't notice the way his bottom lip had begun to curl inward, or if they did notice, they tended to speculate in hushed whispers and sympathetic glances. Not Scotty. The little boy saw an outward flaw and wanted to know about it, plain and simple.

"Because I have a condition that makes my muscles get kinda weak. Sometimes it's hard to hold my lip up all the way. Today's one of those hard days. See?" he added, trying to smile and knowing it wouldn't quite work. "Probably not the best smile you've ever seen, but most days, it's better than this one. Tomorrow it might even work all the way."

The boy came around his mother's waist, his gaze drifting slowly from Walter's lip to his eyes and back, waging a clear internal battle on whether or not to believe the story. Finally, he held up his arm, pulling back the sleeve of his gray Carter's t-shirt.

"I got a bruise on my arm yesterday when I fell off the swing at daycare, but it don't hurt much. I can still throw rocks in the pond at the park. Can't I, Mom? We went there to feed the ducks last night."

Walter smiled, impressed, while Scotty regaled he and Sarah in all the ways falling off a swing set made him and Walter exactly alike. To a four-year-old boy, having a disease was on par with a flesh wound. Nothing to worry about, nothing to cry over. Just get up, dust yourself off, and go back to enjoying life.

Later that night, when Walter climbed into bed, he realized that it only took a single afternoon to know that he'd not only fallen in love with Sarah... but her little boy too.

THEY WERE married three months later. Some called it a whirlwind romance, but Walter was surer than he'd ever been about anything else in his life. A wedding was just the next step, like knowing the punchline to a brand-new joke by the time the teller speaks the second word. A given. The obvious choice. Inevitable.

After the ceremony, Walter whisked his new little family away to Puerto Rico for a week of sunshine and fun—all three of them—because he couldn't imagine a situation where he removed a little boy from his mother and forced him to stay behind, not even for a moment. Walter had grown up begging for attention and affection. Little Scott Jones wouldn't face the same fate on Walter's clock.

"Why does the ocean do that, go in and out all the time like the water can't make up its mind to stay or not?" Scotty asked during a quiet moment when the three of them stood by the shore. They stood at the water's edge, letting the waves lap against their toes and recede back into the sand, here one minute and gone the next. Scotty giggled at how his toes tended to sink into the sand a bit more with each in and out of the tide. Sarah ruffled his hair and laughed at the innocent question while Walter pondered Scotty's words and thought to himself, *"Why indeed?"*

"Because the ocean is a living thing, a bit like you and me."

"And my mom!" Scotty shouted. Walter and Sarah laughed.

"And your mom. And just like the way we can't make up our minds about what to eat or when to wake up or—"

"Or if we should have to learn to read books—"

"You don't have a choice about that," Sarah interrupted, eliciting a deep and dramatic sigh from her anti-book son. Walter looked on and marveled at how blessed he'd become.

"Anyway," he laughed. "Just like we can't always decide what we want in life, the ocean does that too. Just watch. The water wants to come to see you, but then it gets scared and runs away. Over and over because it can't make up its mind. It'll do this all day if you're willing to wait and watch."

"I am. But can we build a sandcastle while we wait so we won't be so bored?"

Walter suppressed a laugh. Nice to know he'd dropped five thousand dollars only to bore the life out of a little kid.

"We can build a castle."

Their little threesome relocated themselves a few yards away and dropped onto the sand, unloading buckets and shovels from a black mesh bag with the price tag still attached, a souvenir shop find that now served as quality entertainment. The upscale restaurant Walter had reserved for tonight likely wouldn't measure up. They built an elaborate castle mostly in silence, sending Scotty running after buckets of water when the sand was too dry to pack properly. It wasn't until Walter lifted the last bucket to reveal a surprisingly good shape of a fire-breathing dragon that Scotty delivered another question, dropped softly into the middle of their sand kingdom like a bomb on Hiroshima.

"You're not gonna do that, are you, Walter?"

Walter frowned, unsure of Scotty's meaning. "Do what, Scott?"

"Keep leaving like the ocean. Stay for a minute, and then run away scared? Mom said my dad did that, and I just wondered if you would do it someday, too."

Walter quickly glanced at Sarah; her eyes were already watery with unshed tears. What a question for such a small kid to ask. What a thing to think about at an age when your biggest worry should be choosing between having ice cream or a candy bar for dessert.

"I'm not going anywhere, Scott. I already made my choice."

"And you're staying forever?"

Walter watched as the child used his hand to pat down a piece of sandy roof that threatened to separate and slide away.

"I promise. I'm staying forever."

10

PRESENT DAY

Piper

Something about the beach scene
Walter described seems familiar. Hazy and
just out of reach. I'm mentally stretching my mind
toward the memory when the ding of the front door
rips me out of his writings—written more like individual journal entries, I've decided—and I growl.
Who's bugging me now, just as I opened another
journal? I've read through five notebooks so far
today instead of organizing the store like I'm
supposed to be doing, but still. Can't people see I'm
busy?

I've discovered something about Walter that
seems unique to me: Walter Lorry is not only a
super-talented calligraphy artist but also a fantastic
storyteller. Something tells me all those people who

spent thousands of dollars on his art might have fared well to demand the stories behind how he created them. As for the citizens of this town, they've gone and decided he doesn't add much value to anything. They've simply thrown him in a box labeled "weird" and left him there to collect dust. Just goes to show that you can't tell a thing about people when you size them up from afar. How often are we wrong while pretending our assessments are right?

Enough philosophizing for today.

It's three fifteen in the afternoon, and I am here to work, not to snoop through old notebooks in hopes of finding the missing pieces that make up one very haggard old man. Seeing as I'm the only person here, looks like it's up to me to help the customers. I've been in the back room of Mr. Lorry's store for well over an hour while he headed for his house next door. School just ended, so J.D. will be here any minute to help. If a customer hadn't interrupted me, I suppose someone else would have.

I lay the opened notebook on top of the cot and stand, my knees creaking like they belong to an arthritic elderly woman, not a soon-to-be bride, then walk out of the back room.

My step falters when I see the waiting customer is Ben Ratliff.

IT WAS their gestures that made me do it.

Instead of saying hello, I hid behind an old organ, ducking down to spy on the men. For two minutes now, Ben has talked rather animatedly to Mr. Lorry near the front door like both men just walked inside. No one noticed me at first, just as well since they seemed engrossed in a serious conversation. Now Ben's hands are up and moving rapidly while Walter's head is down. I can't hear them from here, but something about the posture of both men doesn't sit well with me. So, I come around the organ and clear my throat, hoping to end the discussion.

"Hi," I say. "What are you doing here?"

Ben's head snaps up, and his hands drop to his side. A surprised smile fills his face, one that somehow doesn't seem entirely genuine.

"Piper, my dear. I didn't realize you were here."

I nod and take a few steps closer, glancing at Mr. Lorry as I go. He doesn't make eye contact, just pats his own chest and scans the room as though looking for something to do with his hands.

"I've been here most of the day, same as always. Did you need something? Were you looking for me?"

Ben hesitates before nodding. "Yes, yes, I was. Julia is making dinner reservations for tonight and wanted me to find out where you might like to meet later. I mentioned Wildfire Grill would be a good choice if that works for you."

They have never, not once, asked for my opinion on dinner. Or anything else, for that matter. But I smile, ready to agree with whatever will make him leave the store and move away from Mr. Lorry. There's no basis for this, but I feel it like you feel an omen right before the car crash happens. The men don't like each other.

Or maybe Ben is like every other person in this town who sized up Walter from afar and decided they were right. Aren't I just as guilty?

"What time is dinner? I'll head straight there after I finish up here."

Ben frowns. "Seven o'clock, but you might want to change clothes first. Maybe..." he gestures in a long oval in front of me, "...clean up a little?"

My default has always been to change my clothes, my hair, my face, my image...to make myself more presentable, more palatable to be around. But I glance at Mr. Lorry with his raggedy appearance and curved lower lip, and for the first time since I showed up last week, I realize I'm starting to like the man. Maybe even admire him. There could be a lesson in the revelation.

"I'll probably just come straight from work." I tilt my head as though the thought hadn't occurred to me, then look down at my jeans with the hole in the knee and the vintage Blondie t-shirt I pulled over my head in a hurry this morning. "I think I look okay like this." Tonight, I'll just come as I am.

Ben doesn't try to hide his displeasure, but at least he doesn't protest. "If you're sure. Wildfire is an expensive restaurant." He mumbles under his breath.

I make myself smile. "Great! Then I'll see you at seven. I'll make sure to bring my appetite."

Ben nods and sees himself out with a backward glance to me and Mr. Lorry. I wait until he rounds the corner and turn to face my boss. Is he still technically my boss when I'm not getting paid? At this point, it's all semantics.

"What did he want?" I ask.

In true Lorry form, the only response I get is silence. Which I proceed to fill because talking is how I cope in uncomfortable situations.

"Was he looking for something in the store? An old frame for the wife? A vase with a crack down the side? An old pill box, perhaps?" For the life of me, I can't think of a single reason my future father-in-law would come here. Like olive oil and water, Ben doesn't mix well with dust and dirt.

"He wanted to tell you about dinner plans," Walter rasps with a nod that doesn't look convincing. "Just like he said."

Dinner plans. I would guess that Mr. Lorry is

lying in the way he won't look at me, but the man rarely makes eye contact, so my assessment might be invalid. Still, I can feel a lie hanging over us for the second time in as many minutes. So, I toss out an idea.

"Would you like to come with us?"

Walter's gaze shoots up in my direction, and I see it. Fear. Plain and simple.

"To dinner?" he asks, fuzzy on the letter d.

I nod. "Yes. Tonight, just like Ben said. You can be my guest." Bryant won't like it, and there's a zero percent possibility Mr. Lorry will agree, but that isn't the point. Mr. Lorry shuffles away, pretending to straighten things as he goes.

"No, thank you," he says. "There's too much to do here..." His slurred voice fades away as he moves toward the back of the store. My feet stay planted in place, eyes watching him as he goes.

He's afraid of Ben Ratliff; that much is obvious. What isn't so clear is why. Other than the unkind words my future father-in-law has said about him— the same sort of unkind words everyone else in this town has uttered—there's no reason for him to be afraid. Still, there's bad blood between the men, and I'm going to find out the cause.

That was the point.

11

25 YEARS EARLIER, SPRING 1997

W*alter*
There was a lot to having children that Walter had never considered. In part because his parents had never played an active role in his life. When you don't have children, you don't consider everything that comes with raising them. And when any of those things feed into the trauma of your own childhood, not thinking of them is just a way to survive.

Take school, for example. Walter hated school as a kid. By the time he reached third grade, all the kids were horribly mean to him. Why would he want to subject his stepson to such an awful reality?

Because the law said he had to, that's why.

"I still don't see why we can't homeschool him," he said to his wife on the first day of kindergarten registration. "School will eat him alive. Kids are awful, and so are the teachers. What if he's bullied, or worse, what if he's an outcast? What if they push him around or don't include him at recess? What if they—"

Sarah stopped walking to face him; her arms crossed in that no-nonsense way that let him know he was once again on the receiving end of one of her lectures. Walter pressed his mouth closed, suddenly feeling like one of those kindergarteners he was just criticizing. There's nothing like returning to school to make you feel like you never left. Even with a successful career that had afforded him more luxuries and opportunities than most people only dreamed of, right now, Walter might as well be standing against a wall on the playground, begging for someone—anyone—to let him join their game.

"First of all, you're projecting your own experiences onto Scott, who is right now very likely heading up his own game of ring-around-the-rosy at preschool." On this point, she was right. Scotty had plenty of friends, as could be attested at his five-year-old Chuck-E-Cheese-themed birthday party. Thank God Scott was nowhere near his unfounded tirade. "Second, the man travelling to New York next week, Glasgow the week after, and Denver at the end of this month wants me to homeschool? Are you serious? Your schedule is full from now to the end of the year, and it's probably already filling up for next year with things you just haven't mentioned to me yet."

She wasn't wrong. London and Edinburgh were already on the itinerary, but in his defense, he planned to make that second one a family vacation because it was set for next June. He couldn't help it if people continued to like his art and wanted to meet him.

"Touché," he said.

"I knew it!" She laughed, loud and obnoxious for all the parents around them to hear.

Walter narrowed his gaze and delivered his best glare. "What's your point?"

He tried to appear stern, but the thing he loved most about his wife was her inability to care what anyone thought. Which was why right there, on an elementary school campus with a few dozen anxious parents milling around them, she folded her arms around his neck and pulled his face toward her, giving him the kind of intimate kiss that made him want to abandon all thoughts of school registration and go pursue a different sort of educational endeavor.

Back at home.

More of a two-person game.

He liked one on one sports best, anyway.

But Sarah wouldn't be deterred. She pulled away

and looked up at him, all sorts of promises in her eyes, making Walter want to march inside that school and get this registration nonsense over with so they could leave. Leaving could be fun. Going home could be fun. Best idea he'd ever had.

"My point is," Sarah said, bringing him back to the moment at hand. "Thank you for loving me. For loving Scott so well. Even if you are a bit misguided while doing it."

"I've never been misguided a day in my life."

"Says the man who needs a road atlas to travel to the supermarket," she said with a wink. "Now, you want to go in there with me and get school registration over with?"

He grinned. "If you promise you'll go home and include me in one of your games when we're finished. I've never liked feeling left out, and I sure don't like it now."

"I'll include you in my games, Mr. Lorry." She winked. "If you follow me inside with a good attitude."

No one had ever been happier to register a kid for kindergarten than Walter was that day.

Except maybe Walter himself, later that night.

❧

THREE MONTHS LATER, happiness was more elusive than it had ever been in their marriage. Wouldn't life be so much easier if the good feelings stayed around...if darkness only crept in when you were prepared for it, or when boredom with life allowed it a brief stay just to shake up the monotony?

Not that his marriage to Sarah was monotonous; it wasn't. It just had a few more lows than most marriages seemed to endure, and all signs pointed to Walter as the reason.

It's common knowledge that when you're at your happiest point in life, that's when bad news gets delivered. And while things could be worse—aside from Walter's career—life with Walter was never smooth sailing. Choppy and wild, that was more like it, which made today like any other day. Except by all accounts to anyone looking on, it wasn't.

"There's nothing there," the doctor said. "By now, there should be growth of some sort, perhaps even a heartbeat. It's just as we thought, though I know that doesn't make things easier. I'll give you both a minute." The doctor exited the room, leaving Walter alone with his wife.

He held Sarah's hand as they stared silently at the blank sonogram screen, where there should have been a small bean, a heartbeat, a cell split, or anything that would point to signs of life. But the space was empty. A dark void of nothingness but organs and tissue that belonged to Sarah herself. Walter wasn't a doctor, but even he knew the road they began walking down six weeks earlier had crumbled into an abyss. Doctor Bailey had warned them that becoming parents together carried a minuscule chance at best, but a warning is merely a red flag waving the possibility of danger ahead.

It's entirely different to be hit with the white flag of surrender.

His wife lay silently crying while he sat next to her and wondered why he had let her say yes to him. Why God had let her love him when there were a million other men in the world she could have wound up with? Normal men. Healthy men. Men who didn't slur when they talked or limp when they walked; fairly subtle now on both counts, but one day it wouldn't be. None of it was fair to Sarah, but such was a life of living with him.

"I'm so sorry," he muttered over and over. It was all he could think to say. "So, so sorry. You wouldn't be in this position if you hadn't married me. I'm so incredibly..."

"Stop," she said, wiping her eyes with the back of her hand and looking at him with still-watery eyes. "Please stop apologizing. I knew exactly what I was doing when I married you, and I would do it all again in a second. Even now."

"But another man would—"

"Another man? I've known plenty of other men, Walter. There's not another man alive who would treat me as well as you do. No other man in existence who would treat Scotty like his own flesh and blood, no hesitation or questions asked. I don't want another man, not now or ever. I just wanted to be able to give you a child of your own and..."

Walter squeezed her hand, both to stop her and to communicate how fiercely he felt at that moment. "I *do* have a child of my own. Scotty is as much mine as any little boy could ever be. I fell in love with him the same day I fell in love with his mother, deeply and personally. Do I need to keep reminding you?"

Sarah sniffed through her tears. "It's just that most men want a biological child to carry their name. What if you change your mind someday? What if you—"

Walter laughed at her ridiculous questions. It seemed they both had insecurities that most marriages were different from theirs. Comparison was a cancerous pastime.

"I'm a forty-one-year-old man with a progressively worsening disease who was a lifelong bachelor until nine months ago, and you think I need a child just to claim a blood relation? For what, bragging rights? I wouldn't wish my blood on anyone, let alone a child. I just want you to be happy."

Sarah smiled. "I am happy. I have all I ever wanted." She was quiet for a long moment, thinking. "Except one thing," she finally said, untangling her hand from his and reaching to cup his face.

"What one thing?"

"I think it's time. After we leave here, I think it's time."

Walter's breath caught in his throat.

"Time for what?" He thought he knew, but imminent disappointment was a real possibility.

"For what you mentioned when we first got married. I wasn't ready then, but I am now. I think it's time to make this arrangement permanent. Then no one can claim you don't have a child of your own again. Including me."

Walter's throat squeezed, and his heart skipped a few beats inside his chest. He had ever truly wanted only a few things in life: his father's approval, a career he could be proud of, a woman to love him, and this. Was she saying what he hoped she was saying? Could it be possible? He couldn't trust his voice to work well enough to ask, but a few seconds later, he had his answer.

"I think it's time we make it official. I want you to adopt our son."

At that, the tears dripping on their conjoined hands no longer belonged only to Sarah.

∾

THREE MONTHS. That's how long it took for a judge to hear their case.

It's interesting that a woman can get pregnant, carry a baby to term, birth that baby, take him home alone, and raise him for the next four years as a fearless single mother completely without help and with no father involved. No one cares much about that. But when that same mother wants to add a permanent and supportive father to the mix, everyone in charge suddenly needs information.

Who is the baby's father? "He isn't involved. I left his name off the birth certificate."

What if he suddenly makes a reappearance? "Why would he do that when he has no idea his child exists?"

Why do you want Mr. Lorry to adopt him? "Because he's my husband."

What if he isn't fit to be a father? "I think I should be the one to decide that."

Are you aware of your husband's medical condition? "Yes, I am."

And you're not concerned this could be an issue in the future? "Yes, for Walter. But not for me or for my son."

What if his medical bills become too much for you to handle? "Are you offering to pay them for us?"

That last answer from Sarah nearly got Walter kicked out of the courtroom when he snorted with laughter; the judge was none too pleased. One thing to remember about a single mother: You shouldn't mess with them. They've seen it all and heard it all and done it all, and men with self-appointed superiority complexes would do well to remember it.

Eventually, Walter was granted temporary custody of Scotty. Followed by legal guardianship, which meant permanent adoption was officially on the horizon. All they had to do was make it through the six-month waiting period. For now, they had reason to celebrate.

They celebrated later that night when they asked Scotty what he wanted to do and proceeded with a plan five-year-olds everywhere would also choose. They went to Chuck-E-Cheese. Again.

"You're cheating!" Walter mock-yelled at Scotty, eliciting a giggle from the boy.

"I am not! It's not my fault you're not good at this game." To prove his point—and Walter's—Scotty climbed onto the Skee-Ball game, walked his ball to the ten-thousand-point hole at the end of the lane, and dropped it in. This, folks, is cheating at its finest. Unless you're five years old and don't know the literal definition of the word.

Walter giggled himself as Sarah snapped photos in the background. Her camcorder sat on the gray carpet at her feet, for once getting a well-deserved break in the action. She hadn't played a single game, claiming a need to document the occasion so she could play it back one day at Scotty's high school graduation. Mothers were always thinking in advance, Walter was quick to discover.

"Just play one game," Walter coaxed her, not for the first time that night.

"Yeah, Mom. Play one game with me," Scotty echoed.

She dropped her camera with a sigh of defeat, outnumbered once again. But Walter saw her smile clear as day through her fake annoyance.

"Fine. One game. But Scotty, you better not cheat. And Walter, you better take pictures."

"I wouldn't dream of letting a single moment pass that I don't document."

She shot him a pointed look at the same time Scotty yelled—

"I'm not cheating!" The boy wailed the way only a little boy can, loud and screeching. Sarah laughed and handed Walter the camera. Taking it from her hand, he lined up the first shot and began to click.

A photo of Sarah picking up a ball.

Another of Scotty's arms wrapped around her legs, trying to keep her from playing.

A photo of Walter's brown loafers because he lowered the camera and accidentally clicked.

A photo of the Skee-Ball machine exploding in lights when Sarah landed the ball in the center hole three times in a row *without cheating,* as she so graciously pointed out to another round of outraged giggles from Scotty.

A final photo of the three of them in the parking lot, taken by a kind elderly grandfather heading for the entrance with his granddaughter in tow. In the photo, Sarah is holding a giant stuffed teddy bear, and Scotty has a red balloon affixed to his wrist. Both were positioned perfectly in the frame, save for the top of Walter's head. It was cut off right above his eyebrows. Still, there's no mistaking how happy he was. His smile filled his face, despite the absence of his forehead. Had a man ever been happier, more in love with his nearly permanent family? None more so than Walter that day.

They didn't know they had five more months to enjoy life.

Five blissful months before everything began to crumble.

12

PRESENT DAY

iper

P I drop the notebook when my phone buzzes from inside my bag. I'm ripped from the story like a teenager awakened from a good dream, grumpy and angry, forced back into real life when all they want to do is slip back to sleep. All I want to do is delve back into Walter's old life. Dinner plans suck today, like school sucked back then.

One glance at my iPhone screen tells me I'm already late by five minutes. Reluctant or not, I stand and slip into my fur-lined slides.

No one dines more formally or often in this town than the Ratliff family. In the beginning of our relationship, I adored the cloth napkin way of living; five-piece place settings, crystal goblets, candlelight, and proper conversation. Only high-class people lived like that, and I'd never been considered part of that category. Nowadays, I'd give anything for a microwave pot pie, a can of Dr. Pepper, and a couple of episodes of reality television from the comfort of my sofa.

I'll never hear of the end of the tongue clicks when I show up late. Or the teeth-sucking judgment when they take one look at my outfit—the ripped jeans and Blondie t-shirt I promised to wear and am now second-guessing with the force of a woman who committed to skydiving and just watched the airplane hatch open.

So much for formal. Impetuousness has never been my friend.

Mr. Lorry still hasn't returned. He walked out after J.D. went home; I assume he left to take a long stroll or run an errand. That was an hour ago, when I had planned to leave but got sidetracked by the sight of the journals peeking out from under Walter's cot. I might be concerned about Walter's lengthy absence if the man had ever informed me of his whereabouts. He never does; he just disappears like a thick mist you can't hold onto. Mr. Lorry is nothing if not a loner, though you wouldn't know it from reading his journals.

Once upon a time, he loved people deeply. That much is clear.

Why it all stopped...that's still the murky part.

Maybe if I just—

I see something then, a loop of fabric poking from the bottom of the box, one I didn't notice before. Curious, I carefully lift the entire stack of journals so as not to get them out of order and to place them on the bed. Then I flip the box over and scan the underneath, heart pounding at what I might find like I'm a detective and just discovered a clue. Tugging at the loop, I open a flap to reveal a hidden compartment, a false bottom of sorts. And there, right in front of me, I see them and gasp.

Walter's pictures.

A small stack, the one on top revealing a blurry photo of a pair of now outdated brown shoes.

The pictures he took during the celebration at the arcade.

I flip through the first three quickly. Sarah is holding a ball in the second photo—more stunning than even my overimaginative mind could have conjured up—so beautiful my throat swells. A Skee-Ball machine, just like Walter's writing described it, lit up in faded colors that had likely once held bold proof of her winning hand that day. Another of—

My phone vibrates on my lap, and I glance at the screen. It's Bryant, sending a third text in as many minutes, none of which I've answered. *Where are you?* this one reads, his growing irritation coming through the line. Rudeness is not a character trait I want to call mine. So, in a split-second decision, I scoop up the remaining photos and stuff them in the bottom of my bag, planning to study them thoroughly tonight and return them to the box tomorrow before anyone notices their absence. I place the journals back inside the box and slide it deep under the bed. Out of sight, possibly out of Walter's mind.

Moving quickly, I race to the front door, hoping to make it to dinner before anyone gets too angry with me.

WHEN I SET foot on the front porch, I find him, my eyes taking a moment to focus through the already prominent moonlight. The sun sets before dinnertime in Silver Bell in early November, though it's still too early for bed for most people.

But there's Walter, sound asleep on his cot, a single dried tear streak leaving a temporary mark on his left cheek. Crying oneself to sleep is to him what counting sheep is to everyone else, a knowledge that makes my heart stutter. If I had time to study his profile, I would. I might imagine whatever keeps him there night after night, a thin military cot making a poor substitute for the soft bed in his home only twenty paces away. Curiosity got the better of me a few days ago, and I looked inside the windows of his house before I came inside to work. I knew all too well that I could ask him any number of questions about why he sleeps here, why his house stays locked up tight most days, why he keeps the house at all if he rarely plans to use it... and that he wouldn't answer me. Mr. Lorry only speaks when necessary and never talks about himself. It's a fact I learned rather quickly. While most of us spend our time filling the shortest silences with unnecessary chatter to stave off our uncomfortable thoughts, to Walter, words are a chore. They should only be spoken to convey a particularly meaningful message. As for me, I only wish I could master the art of translating what he's trying to say.

I'm counting on the journals to enlighten me, though their meaning is still a mystery. As mysterious to me now as the reasoning behind the man's odd affinity for sleeping under the stars. I watch him for another long moment, trying to imagine varying possibilities, until I hear voices.

Whispers. Sharp like an argument, soft like a breeze, floating over from the tree line across the street.

Curious and momentarily forgetting all about dinner, I follow the sounds until I hear the familiar voice of J.D. talking with his friends.

"I'm not sure he really has them. I looked, but his back seems pretty normal to me. Almost like he's—"

"What are you boys doing back here?" I quietly demand, coming up behind their little group of four without being noticed. "Honestly, J.D. You're still spying on Mr. Lorry even though you see him at work every day?"

Three sets of pupils look from me to J.D. in wide-eyed wonder. "You see him every day? Like, inside his store? Up close?" one of the boys asks, awe filling his words.

J.D. shrugs like it's no big deal. "Yeah, she makes me help her clean the floors like I'm a maid or something." He gestures to me like his preposterous statement is true, and I scoff.

"I don't make you help, J.D. I *pay* you to help. You volunteered to last week when I caught you spying on us through the window." I turn to face the kids. "He's around me and Mr. Lorry every afternoon, and neither of us has killed him yet. Emphasis on the *yet*." I say, inserting an ominous tone into my voice just to scare the kids a bit. "As to Walter Lorry's wings, I'm not much of an expert on those." I sigh and begin to examine my fingernails, casual as you please. "But I did see them once."

A pause. A collective breath. I sense four sets of eyes trained on me, unblinking and wide as quarters.

Looking up, I nearly laugh at the fear suspended on their faces.

"You saw his wings?" croaks a towheaded blond in the back, the smallest kid in the group.

"Sure did. You haven't?" It isn't a sin to lie to kids when they're lying to you first. I think I read that somewhere.

"No, we haven't," goes a chorus of awestruck voices.

"Well, you'd better get out of here," I say, turning at the waist to study Mr. Lorry, still unmoving on his cot. "You never know when he'll put those wings to use, especially considering it's a full moon tonight." I look up at the sky and make a face. "Seems like prime flying weather to me, especially for a man who might actually be Santa Claus. I wouldn't want him to catch me watching him, not if I were you..."

At that, three kids scatter. All but J.D., who stays in place, blinking up at me.

"You didn't really see them, did you?"

I wink. "Nope."

"Then why did you tell the kids that you did? It's not nice to lie."

"It's also not nice to spy on people when they're trying to sleep. Plus, I think Mr. Lorry likes having you around. I wouldn't go getting on his bad side, kid. Not if you want to keep helping out around the store."

To my surprise, J.D. smiles. "You think he likes me?"

"Don't push it. Besides, I'm not even sure he likes *me* yet. But I don't want to risk upsetting him too much. Honestly, I'm kind of starting to like him myself."

J.D. grins. "Me too. I won't tell my friends our secret that Mr. Lorry doesn't have wings."

I tilt my head and frown. "Oh, I didn't say he doesn't have them. Just that I've never *seen* them. There's a difference."

Again, J.D.'s eyes go round like walnuts, doubt creeping back in. Nighttime is a landmine for over imagination. I bite my cheek to keep from smiling when the kid takes a few steps back.

"I gotta go home," he says, and I nod.

"I'll see you tomorrow?"

He nods silently at me and takes off down the street.

I watch him go until he disappears into the darkness, then turn to head for my car. I'm well past late for dinner now. If I'm lucky, I'll make it to the restaurant before dessert is served. Ben Ratliff is many things, but primarily he is a man who never skips dessert, particularly at Wildfire Grill. They have excellent bread pudding with whiskey sauce.

Just as I open the driver's side door to climb inside the car, I'm startled by the sound of a voice.

"It's about time you left. I can't very well fly with an audience, can I?"

I'm so rattled that I nearly miss the car seat, catching myself on the floorboard with an ungraceful thud. Mr. Lorry is making…a joke?

"You heard that?" I ask, brushing myself off as I stand, my heartbeat returning to normal rhythm.

"I always hear it," he says.

I try to smile at him, but the words register before my mouth tilts upward. He always hears them, the whispers. The rumors. The unkind words that spread through this town on a feeding frenzy looking for public takedowns. What must it be like to be the object of ridicule and know about it every second of your life?

"And you don't mind what people say?" I ask.

There's a long pause, and then… "Even if I did, what can I do about it?"

I take a deep breath, ruminating on his words. "Nothing, I suppose." And that's the truth of it. You can't stop gossip. People will talk, and people will whisper. People will say whatever they want just to feel better about themselves. And what will any of us do about it when faced with the option?

Nothing.

It's like trying to kill the world's mosquito population one swat at a time. Keep stepping outside in summer, and you'll keep getting bit, golden summer skin slapped with angry red welts. Keep hanging with the same people, and you'll find yourself turning into them.

Which means the only way to avoid it is to be yourself and live life the best way you know how. For someone like Walter Lorry, it might lead to a lonely existence. But as I'm beginning to discover, living alone might be better than being surrounded by people who judge you. Misery might love company, but the wrong company only serves to make you more miserable. A vicious cycle that spins and spins. Clearly, I have lessons to learn.

"Goodnight, Mr. Lorry," I say, climbing inside the car.

I don't get an answer. He simply rolls onto his side and falls back to sleep.

THE ICY RECEPTION I received when I finally showed up to dinner—during the end of dessert, mind you —has thawed slightly, thanks in part to the new bottle of wine Julia ordered because the first one was already empty. Normally, I'm not much of a drinker. Now, I'm contemplating paying for a third bottle just to get the focus off my tardiness. And my outfit. Surprise, surprise, no one liked it. Bryant even offered me his jacket to cover myself up like the unsubtle gentleman he is.

The cabernet is half gone already. One more glass apiece should loosen everyone up nicely. I pick up the bottle and offer to pour the round. Three glasses are pushed toward me. A silent victory.

Yet, like all victories, the moment is short-lived.

A woman in a severely hair sprayed-blonde bob does a double take as she passes our table and stops to say hello.

"Ben! Julia!" she says, stopping to air kiss them like we're in an episode of Real Housewives and not sitting at a restaurant in small-town Arkansas. I glance at Bryant for help, but he only shrugs. He's as much in the dark as I am. "It's been ages. How are you both?"

For the next few minutes, small talk abounds. It isn't until a lull develops in the conversation that the woman focuses on me.

"You must be Bryant's fiancée. Pippin, is it?"

Irritation scratches across my skin like the misstep is intentional, but I offer a smile. "It's Piper," I say, extending my hand for a shake. "Nice to meet you."

"Oh yes, Piper." She smiles. It appears to freeze and hold. "I must say, there was once a day when I thought my Jessica would marry your fiancé. She and Bryant sure liked each other way back. Dated each other for a while, if I recall."

I glance at Bryant to see him shift positions. His face reddens as he leans slightly away from me. So much for being in the dark. I smile up at the woman, doing my best to appear unaffected.

"That must have been when they were children, seeing as I've known Bryant nearly thirteen years now and he's never once mentioned her." I place my hand on Bryant's thigh in subtle ownership.

"That's because we went out when we were fifteen," he mutters.

But the woman simply laughs over him. "I heard you two have been dating for a long time. My my, that sure took a lot of time to finally make up your minds. Fish or cut bait, that's what I've always believed. I'm glad Bryant finally fished."

"Or maybe I'm the one who fished," I say, but we all know I didn't. "And your daughter? I assume she's happily married now. Any grandchildren to speak of?" My face is the picture of innocence. My eyes burn with murder.

The woman's smile flattens. "No grandchildren or spouse yet, but I'm certain she'll meet the right person one of these days."

"Let's hope so. If you take too long in the kid department, you'll eventually run out of time. Bryant and I want four," I say, taking a casual sip of wine.

I'm not completely sure we even want two children, but I despise this woman and will say just about anything to get rid of her.

She narrows her gaze at me.

"Did I hear correctly that you've been helping out in Walter Lorry's antique store?" she asks, her change in subject like a swift swipe to the leg.

I blink, for the first time feeling caught off guard, a weird irony. Undermine my love life, and I'll come out swinging. But ask me about Mr. Lorry and my barricades go up. For some reason, protecting him seems essential.

"Yes, I have been for about a week now," I say. "It's been an interesting experience." I didn't mean it to be funny, but all around me, people start to laugh. Including Bryant, who stops when I send him a pointed look. "Why do you ask?"

"No reason. Just...watch your back around that man. He's been known to go off the handle." She turns to Julia and Ben. "Don't you remember years ago when that trial happened, and the judge found him—"

"Well, Amelia," Ben says, standing abruptly to kiss the woman's hand. "Please tell John I said hello. We should probably finish up dinner and head home..." He leaves the sentence hanging, much like the words she didn't finish. A judge found him, *what?*

"I suppose I should go," she says, leaning down to air-kiss Julia again and to pat Bryant on the arm. "I told John I was running to the powder room, and he's probably wondering where I disappeared to." *He's probably relieved you're gone*, I think, then give myself an internal chastising. Wasn't I just lamenting all the ways people mistreat one another? Mistreating her mentally doesn't give me a pass.

When she walks off, Ben sits and shares a look with Julia, one she interprets immediately with a sigh.

"That woman is a lot," she says.

"That woman is impossible," he echoes. "And you dated her daughter for what, a week?" he says to Bryant.

He responds with, "Two, maybe three." Bryant rolls his eyes at his father, but he doesn't look at me. He does, however, press a kiss to my temple and reach for my hand. A silent apology for leaving that minor detail out, not that I can blame him. How much does anyone know us, really? How often do we let them?

My mind swings back around to Walter Lorry.

I'm both angry on his behalf and worried for myself.

He was found guilty of what?

I'm suddenly desperate to discover the truth.

13

_____

P_iper_

"For the third time, let's go!"

It's two days later, and Bryant keeps calling for me from the kitchen. I feel bad—I do, especially since I initially told him I needed a quick second to brush my teeth. That was ten minutes ago. Now, I can't make myself move from the desk chair in my bedroom. He's gotten weary of my many "just one more second" replies, but this is important. Yes, registering for wedding gifts is important too, but when you're weighing the value of a new KitchenAid against the sad fate of an ostracized old man, the scale tips heavily in Mr. Lorry's favor. Especially when I just discovered Mr. Lorry moved here to Arkansas with his wife and child back in 1998 and bought the house next door to the antique store. There was a picture of the three of them standing in front of a "Sold" Coleman Realty sign, Walter and Sarah smiling at the camera while little Scotty tried to break free from his mother's grasp, arms outstretched, fingertips barely touching in that way children everywhere do seconds before they escape.

I smile at the photo, mentally attempting to insert myself into the scene.

Happy family.

New adventure.

Whining child who simply wants to check out his new bedroom.

Realtor so proud to have sold the large home to such a famous—

The door flies open. "Piper! My mother is already at the store. You can finish up whatever it is you're doing later."

I jump up and push the chair underneath the desk, feeling more than a little guilty. I'm supposed to be *excited* to plan for the wedding, not stalling for time.

"I'm doing research."

"You said you were brushing your teeth."

"I did that already." Sometime this morning, I forget when, but I keep that tidbit to myself.

"Researching what?"

Whether or not my boss is a murderer, I think, but I

can't exactly say that. So, I settle on, "Work stuff," and hope for the best.

"It's Sunday."

Bryant's right. It's a day of rest. A holy holiday. A day that frowns on snooping for the criminal history of an elderly recluse on the internet, if I remember the Bible right.

"I couldn't think of anything better to do."

I immediately know it's the wrong thing to say.

"Um, you could hang out with your fiancé? Plan the wedding we're supposed to have in five months?"

"You played pickleball at the club all morning and were an hour late to pick me up. By then, I was heavily involved in what I was reading. Plus, it didn't seem like hanging out was a huge priority."

He lands on the bottom step and glances over his shoulder at me.

"All the more reason I thought you would be ready."

"I was ready, but then I got bored and opened my laptop..."

"What 'work stuff' are you researching, anyway?" I'm not sure I like the way he air-quotes those two words.

"Just...antiques." It's only a half-lie. Yes, antiques, but only indirectly. Ever since that horrible woman made those comments about Mr. Lorry at dinner last night, I haven't been able to shake her words from my mind. A court case. A guilty verdict. But for what? I lay awake all night tossing and turning, mulling over her words, trying to convince myself that her claims were none of my business. I got out of bed at sunrise, washed and folded two loads of laundry, cleaned my bathroom and color-coordinated my dresser drawers, took a shower and made a grocery list, got dressed, and then ran out of ways to occupy my time.

That's when I headed for my laptop. If Bryant hadn't spent the morning playing games, I would have been saved from falling down the rabbit hole I've spent the last hour trying to dig myself out of. Essentially, our lateness is his fault.

"I think it's weird that you've developed such an affinity for old things." He climbs behind the wheel and slams the door. I slide into the passenger seat and reach for my seatbelt.

"What's weird about it? Antiques are a link to the past, a bit like a history lesson."

Bryant shrugs. "If you say so. I'd rather have new things, myself."

"Hence the reason we're leaving so quickly now."

He glances at me sidelong.

"We're leaving quickly because we're late. My mother has already called twice. The good news is she's already picked out our towels and comforter set."

I study the road. "Isn't that something we should do? You and me? Seeing as we're the ones who will be using them."

He rolls through a stop sign and turns right. "It doesn't matter to me what we use. Plus, it makes her happy."

"That's fine, but what if I don't like what she chose?"

Bryant exhales slowly. "Just let her have this. It's only bedding and not worth the hassle."

Except this is his answer for everything. It's only this. It's only that. Which means his mother controls most of what we do and has planned the majority of what we'll have in the future. Becoming a Ratliff has never been a two-person experience. When you marry one person, you align yourself with the whole family. And their interests. And as long as their interests align with Julia's, it works. It's a fun little maze that's nearly impossible to navigate. I, for one, keep getting lost inside it.

"You say that every time," I say.

"And you argue with me every time."

"I guess I just thought being your wife meant I would only be married to you."

He laughs as though my words are a joke but stops when he realizes they aren't. "We've talked about this so many times, Piper. You *will* only be married to me. But there's also my parents to consider; I am their only child. And there's the business I will be taking over someday; I'm going to be the president of the company eventually, and that will take up a lot of our time. Not to mention the non-profits that we're all set to head up and the dreams my father has for me politically."

"I know, it's just that—"

"I'm starting to think it isn't me that you want to marry, but some version of me you have in your mind." He laughs again, this time more to himself.

But I stay quiet and stare out the windshield, his words rolling over inside my mind.

That's the crux of things, isn't it? We both have differing versions of the other in mind. Ideals that have never necessarily matched, at least not at the same time. Bryant wants a wife who will be a business partner in every sense of the word, quick to stand by his side in a well-tailored suit with an ever-present smile, quick with a handshake and a "thanks for coming, isn't my husband wonderful?" Happy to head up fundraisers and attend dinner parties, maybe even join his bid for Congress someday— stand front row center at rallies and make introductory speeches on his behalf. As for me, I want a husband who'll hang with me on the sofa, curl beside me with a book, and be as proud of me when I'm wearing a dress as he is when I spend all day in ratty pj's.

I want what my mother wanted, what she dreamed of for me back when everything was innocent and new. Thirteen years is a long time to try and live up to a dream that never existed.

"Piper, you do want to marry me, right?" Bryant asks in an undertone that implies, *of course, you do,* hidden inside a smile. Everyone either wants to marry Bryant Ratliff or wants their daughters to. To be a bigwig in a small town is the highest goal most people dare to aim for. It's a dream I've spent a third of my life aiming for. But in my quest to belong to something—to keep the past alive—have I been focused on the wrong thing? Should I have been looking outside this town toward a world much brighter and vast? There are forty-nine other states filled with places I've never discovered and people I've never met. Partly out of fear of the unknown but mostly out of an unwillingness to travel too far from my memories. But how long can you hold onto the past before you find yourself still living in it? How long can you live someone else's life instead of formulating your own?

Should I be looking outside myself, trying to find the answers?

Or should I simply look inward, and be honest about my own desires apart from anyone else's opinions or expectations? When it comes down to it, isn't self-awareness the scariest thing to uncover? To be raw and real in a world built on a façade is the hardest thing of all.

I still don't know if I can do it. Maybe I'll never be able to.

"Of course, I do," I say, my eyes following a tree line on my right until it slowly disappears to nothing but dirt. "Of course."

We don't speak the rest of the drive.

All I can think is...did I tell him the truth?

14

25 YEARS EARLIER, FALL 1997

W*alter*

"Sarah, she's your mother, and she needs you. Some of us should be so lucky."

He'd struck a nerve; one he hadn't intended to come so close to touching. But unlike him, Sarah had parents who adored her and would move mountains to see her happy, even though most of the mountain moving had come in the form of letters and phone calls over the past few years. Her parents were in their late seventies, and travel was getting difficult. Nearly impossible now with her mother's newly fractured hip that had happened only the week prior. The outlook was on the iffy side, at best. Walter was only trying to make her see reason.

His wife's head whipped around, her eyes

narrowing into laser beam slits as she took him in with his calligraphy pen poised in his hand. He was making a piece for a client, a special order for one Whoopi Goldberg. In it, she was dressed in a nun's habit, some movie role reference Walter had never seen. The words "Wake up and pay attention" were in the process of stretching across both shoulders. What the phrase referenced was anyone's guess except for his wife's. Sarah had seen the movie twice and squealed in delight when he told her about the project.

At this moment, however, she wasn't impressed. Annoyed was more like it. Walter knew reason often had a bruise that wouldn't stand to be poked. There was danger on the horizon. He softened his tone because he could sense that danger approaching.

"I'm just saying you should consider going. Maybe just for a month or two, long enough to assess the situation and make things more comfortable for her. Then we can get back to normal."

The slits rounded out a little, and her shoulders dropped a couple of inches. He began to breathe a little easier, but he knew his wife wasn't truly angry when she sighed long and deep. Sarah was bothered. Maybe even worried.

"Walter, when I left Arkansas, I promised myself I wouldn't go back. Not ever, not even for my parents.

It's the reason they've come here twice since I moved away. And now you're asking me to—"

"I'm not asking. I'm just pointing out that based on your mother's condition, it might be a nice gesture to help your parents out for a few weeks. We don't have to stay there long, just long enough to get your mom released from ICU and settled into long-term care and to fill up your father's pantry with food so he has very little to do except worry about your mother. After that, we can come back here, get Scotty enrolled in first grade, and continue life as though we'd never left. It would just be for a few weeks, and summer starts tomorrow. It isn't as if we'll be missing much. I can take my work with me anywhere, and you've mentioned wanting to quit your job."

"I like my job," she protested.

Walter raised an eyebrow. He knew she liked it... sort of. He also knew she kept her job as insurance, her own private backup plan in case he ever left. Walter wasn't going anywhere, but convincing a woman who spent four years as an ostracized single mother is about as easy as persuading a wounded bear cub that the cage you need to put them in is for their own good. Try it once and said animal will bite. Try it twice, and you're likely to be missing a limb. At minimum, a finger.

Walter softened his delivery. "You said just the

other night—and I quote—'if I never have to pour another whiskey for a cheater meeting his mistress for drinks, it won't be soon enough.' Well, babe, it's only Wednesday. Can't get much sooner than that."

She plunked a hand on her hip just as the front door opened and closed. "I hate it when you throw my words back at me."

"I'm not so much throwing them as handing them to you on a gold-plated serving platter. And you love it because it's proof I'm paying attention." He winked. "It's okay to put your job on pause for a bit. If you still want it, it'll be here when we get back."

He watched his wife as she worried her lower lip, knowing her mind was weighing the pros and cons of trusting him fully. Finally, she let out a slow breath and looked him in the eye. If he had blinked, he might've missed her ghost of a smile, gone as quickly as it appeared.

He grinned. "So, are we flying to Arkansas?" Walter had been to forty-two states so far, but Arkansas was not one of them. He was excited about the prospect of checking another state off the list.

She closed her eyes for a long second, then relented. "I guess we're going."

"Going where?" Scotty asked, dropping his backpack on the floor, kicking off one sneaker followed by the other, each arching through the air and landing ten feet apart from one another in the living room, one upside down, one cocked sideways. The boy hated shoes, hated clothing even more. Some days, he left a trail of clothing so perfectly symmetrical one might think the rapture had happened and left behind Scotty's human-shaped outfit like he'd simply lain on the carpet and been zapped into heaven.

Walter sent an apologetic look over Scotty's head to Sarah. He hadn't meant for the boy to overhear their conversation, but he'd also forgotten to keep his voice down. To his relief, Sarah came to his rescue.

"To Arkansas, buddy. Where Mommy grew up. What would you think of us heading there for a few weeks this summer? That way, you can meet your grandma and—"

"I'll go pack!" Scotty raced for the stairs and clomped his way up them, no coaxing needed. Everything's an adventure when you're six.

They watched him go, then locked eyes with dual shrugs. At that, Sarah gave a soft laugh.

"I guess I'll go pack, too."

Walter reached out both hands and pulled her to him, leaning down to cover her lips with his own. God, he loved this woman. Loved her and Scotty with his entire soul, and for a forty-one-year-old man who never planned to have a family of his own, it was a heady realization. He pulled back to study her. It never got old.

"I guess you should."

Four days later, they were on their way.

HE SHOULD HAVE LISTENED to his wife.

Sometimes life turns with the flip of a coin; quick, clean, heads up, seven up. The odds are in your favor so high that it would be a great time to buy a lottery ticket. Other times the quarter wobbles a bit, makes to land on the upside, pauses on the rim, and then takes a last-second turn and comes to rest on the downside. So close to winning, but you taste the bitter bite of loss in the end.

Such was the case only seven days later, and no one was prepared.

It happened so quickly, the accident. One minute Sarah's father was behind the wheel, on his way to visit his wife and Sarah, who were waiting at the hospital while Walter entertained Scotty at the new Star Wars movie. The next minute, her father's Corolla was smashed into a mangled mass of metal and rubber with the top shaved off and one wheel missing.

A semi blew through a red light on Main Street at one o'clock in the afternoon. Its driver was on hour twenty-seven of sleepless driving, against the law in every state. Lack of sleep can inebriate a person just as much as alcohol if combined with monotonous inactivity. There's nothing more monotonous than sitting behind the wheel of an eighteen-wheeler headed north, especially when the radio's out, and there's nothing to listen to but the dull cries of your overly exhausted mind.

Sarah's father was halfway through the intersection when his vehicle was struck at full speed, smack into the driver's side door. The car folded in half like a tortilla in a hot oven, soft and pliable, burnt on the outside edges; the engine went up in flames to prove it. Started at the engine and traveled to the underside right beneath, where the man sat blessedly dead. The car exploded in minutes, drowning out the sound of sirens as rescue vehicles approached.

Doctors said her father never saw it coming, a fact the family desperately clung to in the days that followed. It's difficult enough to think of your loved one being here one second and gone the next. Add pain to the mix, and 'difficult' can crack the mind in half. Walter and Sarah hastily planned and carried out a funeral two days later—on what would have been her parent's forty-first anniversary. What was supposed to have been a celebration dinner planned in the hospital room complete with white tablecloth covered bed trays and candles—as romantic as one can get considering the circumstances—was traded for hors d'oeuvres sent to an after-funeral reception at Sarah's childhood home.

The next week, the last of the mourners left town. Walter was self-employed, and Sarah was out of a job. Her mother's care naturally fell to them. It was clear they wouldn't be returning to California, not now, maybe not ever, though Sarah fought against Arkansas for days, weeks even. For reasons known only to her, she hated the state. She especially hated the town.

For all its oddities and quirks, Walter found Silver Bell charming. The perfect place to set up shop and continue his work; Hollywood still called, and there remained a waiting list for Walter's work that extended seven months. Money wasn't an object, making taking care of Sarah's mother the immediate next step. Paying her medical bills and moving her into a long-term health facility the only correct thing to do. Not to mention, Scotty loved it. There were very few trees to climb in Beverly Hills; as for fishing ponds, the idea alone would draw nothing but blank stares. After all, fish were sold at the market, a civilized way to buy them. Both were abundant in Silver Bell, and the boy couldn't get enough. Between climbing trees, fishing, and midnight star gazing, it was heaven in a small town for a little boy from California.

Their Beverly Hills home sold in less than forty-eight hours. They bought a house in Silver Bell for a tenth of the profit and banked the rest. Well, nearly the rest. There was the matter of Sarah's lifelong dream to attend to. Walter was determined to line her broken heart with a ribbon of silver.

So, they bought the tiny one-story house next door to their new one in Silver Bell, made plans to turn it into an antique store, and opened for business by the end of the summer.

"I can't believe we're doing this," she said just before they turned the "Closed" sign around to "Open" on the very first day. "I've dreamed of owning a business for as long as I can remember."

"In that way, we're alike. And if I get to do something I love every day, why shouldn't you? I'm proud of you, wife," he said, pulling her into his chest and bending his head to nuzzle her neck. "What do you say? Shall we open the door and usher in your newest fans?"

Sarah laughed. "I don't have any fans. You're the one with those."

"Not after today, my brilliant, sexy wife," Walter whispered in her ear. "Not after today."

They stayed in each other's arms for another long minute, enjoying the hum of excitement that stirred in Sarah's soul and the contentment that snaked through Walter's veins, both emotions long dormant since her father's death. Finally, Sarah sighed. She couldn't remember smiling in weeks, but she felt the corners of her mouth inch up just a bit.

"Let's open the door," she said.

And they did. And that's how things stayed; their little antique store opened for business, rarely closing, inventory brought in on a rotating basis even as customers carried purchases out by the armloads. Sarah found her products at market, at resales, from customers wanting to make a little money by unloading some of their own personal items to her. As for Walter, he brought in items from overseas trips and cross-country art shows to add to her collection, then set up an art studio in the back room and worked side by side with his wife on his off days, wanting only to help fulfill her dream because he wanted to see her happy.

And she was.

Oh, how happy she was.

Until her mother died four months later.

And any remaining chance at happiness was taken from her, too.

15

PRESENT DAY

Piper
    I drop the journal and slap both hands over my eyes, then slide them to the sides of my head and try not to cry. Both her parents, dead? In the very same year?

My own grief suddenly pales by comparison, a difficult fact to comprehend, considering I've spent well over a decade drenched in sadness. Two parents are too much loss for one person to endure. The scales seem off-balance, considering some people sail through life unscathed.

How did Sarah make it?

There's only one way to know for sure, and there's only one more unsealed notebook. No matter how many times I scramble through the box's contents, count them out, and check the tape, the result is the same: ten opened journals and three sealed ones. My heart is both relieved and panicked, a nervous juxtaposition of wanting to know how younger Walter transformed into the current one and feeling frightened of the truth. Both are so vastly different that something truly horrible must have happened to him. So horrible that it changed everything. When it comes down to it, maybe we're all just one wrong choice away from completely side-tracking our lives.

But there's a good chance the final unsealed journal won't reveal much of anything.

And if it doesn't, I might walk away from Walter's story without ever knowing the ending.

"I won't open the sealed notebooks. You have my word."

I hate myself for having a moral compass that always comes to rest on the high side. Opening the sealed notebooks now couldn't be explained away as an innocent little white lie. It would be a bold-faced one, black and blue and ugly, directly violating one of God's commandments—though I can't remember which one.

When there's a top ten list, I guess that makes them all important.

∾

"I THINK I'm going to head home early today," I say, walking into the main room to find Walter ringing up a customer. I come around the counter to help, pulling a stack of large white paper across the counter, wrapping each China plate in a sheet, and transferring them to a brown paper bag. The woman has chosen a porcelain tea set I've never noticed before, scalloped around the edges, a blue flower pattern that seems to bleed into the white, the whole thing trimmed in expensive-looking gold leaf. There are eight pieces in total, each carrying the same trademark stamp on the bottom. My mother would have loved them. All at once, my throat clogs with emotion.

Silently, another tear falls.

"What is this pattern called?" I say to them both, turning over a teacup in my hand before wrapping it in paper. Walter says nothing. I didn't expect him to.

"Flow Blue," the woman says curtly, giving Mr. Lorry an exasperated glance. "I've been asking him to find this particular pattern for months now, and he finally got around to it last week. You'd think customer service would be a little better around here..."

Walter counts out change from the four-hundred-dollar total and wordlessly hands it back to the woman. I watch as she slips a ten and two one's back into her wallet, the hairs on the back of my neck giving an irritated tug upward.

"Or I suppose customer service could be considered pretty darn good if Mr. Lorry is the one who found them for you. Considering Google exists and there is such a thing as ordering things yourself nowadays." I smile to soften the effect of my delivery. It doesn't work.

"If I wanted to order them myself, I would have," she says.

"So, it seems." Another smile because I won't be swayed.

Finally, the items are wrapped and in the bag. I hand it to the woman and clock her dramatic exit, complete with loud stomps and an attempt at a firm door slam, but the door was newly affixed with a spring, so the door only snaps quietly. I roll my eyes with a sigh.

"I don't know how you put up with customers like her," I say. "This whole town is full of rude people more entitled than a library full of books."

"That's the wrong use of the word 'entitled,' but I agree."

My eyes go wide. It's the quickest response I've gotten from Walter to date, and a tiny zing of victory zaps my spine. One thing I'm beginning to realize— Walter's slur becomes less noticeable over time. Or maybe it's simply that I hope so much to earn a response from him that I've learned to like the sound of his voice when it happens.

"Maybe so, but you get my point. Why do you put up with them?"

"I don't." He says it simply, like he believes the words.

"Yes, you do. Every day, people come in here to buy things, and they treat you badly. If I were you, I wouldn't let them in."

"I have a store to run, and they buy what I'm selling. You think I shouldn't let them? How would that make sense?"

I'm nearly reeling from this unexpected conversation but keep my face neutral. "Because they should learn how to treat you with respect. If someone talked to me like that, I'd punch them in the face."

He lowers his chin to give me a disapproving look. "Or you could simply learn not to respond."

I blink. "Not respond?"

He nods. "Yes, not respond. People are going to hurt you for the rest of your life. Everyone thinks the best way to react is to hurt them back. But you know what drives people crazier than anything else?"

I shake my pounding head. Or maybe that's my heart making all the racket. Currently, both organs are crossing wires and collectively freaking out. I'm about to learn a lesson from a man who rarely talks.

The profoundness behind the moment isn't lost on me.

"What?"

Mr. Lorry pats the top of my hand. "Ignoring them completely. Mean people hate to be ignored." He slides the stack of paper to the edge of the counter, returning it to its proper place.

Is that why he never speaks to customers? Not because he's ashamed or embarrassed by the sound of his voice but because he wants nothing from anyone besides their money. Meanwhile, the insults flow from townspeople who desire a reaction and are eternally frustrated by never getting one. I'm a reactor. I lash out. I can't imagine not reacting to someone who deserves it.

"So, you just...say nothing?"

He glances back at me, almost like I've already become an afterthought.

"I say nothing." He busies himself with straightening a rack of postcards that no one ever buys, turning the display a quarter clockwise every few seconds until he's satisfied with the result. Finally, he stops to study me. In that moment, I do indeed discover an important lesson about life. When someone who rarely speaks finds it in themselves to use their voice, you can bet the words they choose are going to make an impact. Maybe even change your life.

I brace myself for what's to come.

"It's okay to walk away from something that no longer serves you, Piper." It's the first time he's said my name. An unexpected tear slides down my cheek. "Remember that. It's okay to walk away from anything you've outgrown or no longer require. At the very least, you can choose not to expend any of your precious energy on it anymore. Some things just aren't worth crying over, not if you've cried about them for too long already."

He looks me straight in the eye for a long moment, and then Walter Lorry walks away. He's said his peace, and he's finished for today, leaving me to reflect on his words while he disappears around a display of antique doors. *It's okay to walk away. Okay to ignore what isn't meant for you. Time to stop crying.*

I know he's talking about his own life and how he's chosen to respond to circumstances he can't control. But a small part of me believes he knows my struggles of late and is speaking directly to my soul. *It's okay to walk away. Okay to decide you want something different.*

Walter's last unsealed journal nearly burns my skin from my back pocket, where I tucked it away earlier in my quest to leave. I couldn't wait until tomorrow to know the ending of his story. I'm taking the journal home to pour over tonight because I need to know what happened back then and what happens next. I'll return the journal to the box tomorrow, almost like it never left.

A plan for Walter's life, even if mine is still undecided.

It's okay to walk away from something that no longer serves you. It makes sense and brings with it a sense of relief. But with that relief comes a whole new question that desperately needs an answer.

Sure, I can walk away.

But what am I walking toward?

It's midnight before I'm back in my apartment and sliding between the discounted white satin sheets I found at a bath store clearance sale last month. The evening had been filled with wedding plans—which band would play at our reception, what napkin color to use at the rehearsal dinner, whether we should have guests toss birdseed or blow bubbles at us in the receiving line. So many details, none of which I found entirely interesting. Apparently, you could tell by the look on my face.

"What's the matter with you?" Bryant asked for the third time when the discussion turned to gold flecked or solid white China plates, neither of which I wanted, but Julia made clear they were the only acceptable color options considering the brides-maids were wearing lavender. Her argument was a poor one, though she presented her side with such conviction that Bryant wound up nodding along as usual. All I could think about was that I wanted practical pottery plates in the same way I wanted my bridesmaids to wear black and how that opinion got vetoed two months ago.

"Black? At a wedding? Do you want people to think you're distraught at the idea of having to marry my son?" Julia had asked back then with a frown. So out went the black dresses and in came the lavender, the color Julia herself had chosen for her wedding to Ben.

Of course, Bryant agreed that lavender was the absolute best out of all the options on God's color wheel. For the bridesmaid's dresses, that is.

For the China, they collectively decided on gold flecked while I sat by and said nothing, testing out Walter's theory and fuming in the process. Clearly, the old man's method was a flawed one. If you never speak up, don't you just get walked over?

I decided then to test the theory.

The moment the stemware choices were presented to us, I stood up.

"I'm going to head home," I said, two shocked faces looking up at me amidst color wheels and fabric swatches.

"What do you mean? You're leaving?" Julia said. "We still have so many choices to make, and we need to finalize them tonight."

I pull the strap of my purse up to rest on my shoulder. "I'll leave you and Bryant to it, then. I'm tired and just want to go to sleep."

"But you're the bride," she cried at the same time Bryant said, "Piper, don't be ridiculous." I hadn't been ridiculous up until that point, but I figured it was high time I started.

"That's the thing: I'm not being ridiculous. I'm being me and giving you my opinion, but you don't want to hear it. You're both going to have the wedding you want no matter what I say, so starting now, just plan it and tell me when and where to show up." I moved to leave.

"Piper, please stop," Bryant said.

But I didn't.

"I guess we could go with the pottery." I heard Julia mutter. And I smiled to myself at the irony. Maybe Walter is onto something after all. It's quite possible that the quietest among us have the loudest sense of humanity. Maybe we would all do better to listen to what they say when they finally muster the will to speak.

My smile fell when I walked out the door and into the parking lot.

The problem was, even after hearing Julia's

words and deciding Walter was right, I wasn't sure I cared anymore.

Sometimes when people push you far enough, you might not feel like coming back.

I TAKE a sip of steaming peppermint tea and open the last journal. I'll deal with the fallout of walking away from Bryant and Julia tomorrow, once and for all, and without looking back. I have a future to figure out and a clean slate to start filling.

But tonight, I want to spend one last evening living in the past.

Taking a deep breath, I open the final unsealed notebook and begin to read.

16

---

24 YEARS EARLIER, SPRING 1998
WALTER

"What do you mean, cease to operate?" Walter said, turning the envelope over in his hands. Elrod and Hart was stamped on the address; he'd seen the sign on Main Street downtown and recognized the law firm, though he had never dealt personally with them before. Walter's lawyers were based in Los Angeles, and he would be calling them today. "Did it give a reason?"

Sarah chewed a fingernail. "Something about the house. Like, someone else owns it or something."

Walter ripped into the letter. "But we bought the house. How can someone else own it when we paid the asking price and have a deed of sale?" They'd gotten a good deal, too; almost too good, come to think of it. The price was bottom basement; they already owned the home next door. Letting the opportunity go to waste seemed the worst choice, and Sarah had always wanted to run her own business. Walter had vowed to give her the world, and for the past three months, he lived up to it. This woman was his life, and despite all her recent heartbreak, she was thriving. The idea that someone might try to take her dream away had him tearing through pages of legalese, looking for the loophole.

"Can you make sense of it?" Sarah asked, moving from destroying her fingernails to pacing up and down the tiny store hallway.

"This says someone paid the taxes on the house years ago when the property was in foreclosure. Now they're claiming ownership and want the house back."

"Who?"

"The name was left off the document."

"Well, can they do that? Just stake a claim and take the house? This is our business, Walter. You can't just come along and take someone's business away from them, can you?" The crease between her eyebrows was deeper than Walter had ever seen, and he wanted to smooth it away with a fingertip. If only life were that simple. It wasn't. Someone could and would if the claim was real and the opportunity was viable. Besides, the real issue was deeper. This belonged to Sarah, not him. Walter already had a thriving career that would carry them financially through retirement years and beyond. She wanted that same security for herself; it wasn't enough for her to rely solely on him, something he understood. Loving her required it from him. She had more to lose than he did, and they both knew it.

But Walter would be damned if she lost anything at all.

"I'll take care of it," he promised, hoping to God that he could.

THE STORE WAS SHUT down less than two weeks later.

As hard as he fought, Walter's lawyer couldn't find a clear point to remove all doubt about the Lorry's claim to the property—an outsider had paid the taxes on the building a decade prior, a distant relative of a resident of Silver Bell. Names were to remain anonymous until the case was heard before a judge. Until then, a cease in operations was in effect.

Sarah lost her store, at least temporarily. Even the prospect of a brief pause in business didn't assuage her broken heart. When you've lost a father and a mother in a few months' time, one more loss only adds to the pile-on. A soul can only take so much before it becomes crushed under the weight of grief. The day they turned the lock for the final time was both the worst—and best—day they could have asked for. The worst because the finality felt real, even if it might not be in the end.

The best for an unexpected reason.

The old woman came inside the store ten minutes before closing, her red-headed grand-daughter in tow.

Everyone in town knew her name and had seen her emerge from her hiding place one step at a time over the past five years. She was a legend in these parts, though not necessarily the good kind. She'd been a punching bag if you will. A reason to finger point, whisper behind opened palms, to snicker at and spit, turn away from and judge. As bad as it sounded now, Walter was told it used to be much, much worse.

"Can I help you?" he asked, hearing his wife inhale sharply, the kind of deep breath that appears from a sudden shock. He glanced Sarah's way only to see her wide-eyed stare, then breathed a little easier when she began to smile at the small child holding the woman's hand. Sarah was kind to her deepest core, but sometimes it took a moment for her to warm up to new situations. You can't fault anyone for first reactions; it's the second reaction that matters the most. That's the one that reveals true character.

"I'll help her, Walter," Sarah said, finally

speaking up. "What can I do for you, ma'am? The store is closing in a few minutes. It might be a while before we reopen again, but I'll help you however I can right now."

Walter smiled. That was his girl and her sweet spirit. He busied himself with counting receipts and balancing the cash drawer. Sales-wise, this had been their best day yet. Poetic justice at its finest, a bitter-sweet victory.

"I don't need nothing," the woman said roughly, her chin jutting out as she scowled at Sarah. "Though my granddaughter might could use one of your lemon drops there," she added with a nod toward the small jar Sarah kept on the counter, especially for small children and adults who needed a sugar fix. Sarah quickly fished a lemon drop out and handed it to the child. In went the drop. Out came a gap-toothed smile that reminded Sarah of Scotty only last year. The space in her son's mouth had already filled with adult teeth, a sentimental reminder that life moves at a lightning pace, even as you wish it would slow down. Scotty was nearly seven and losing more teeth by the day. Any second now, he would be a teenager.

Sarah straightened and looked the old woman in the eye. Walter watched the pair sidelong to make sure all was well. He needn't have worried.

"Grandma, can we go home and make cookies

now?" the small child asked hopefully, tugging on the old woman's skirt. She smiled down at the child, and the old woman's face transformed entirely. It was a wonder to behold; the way being with the right person at the right time can light up a soul from the inside out.

"Oh, what kind of cookies?" Sarah asked, putting a dash of over-excitement in her voice. The child jumped up and down, clapping her hands together.

"Oatmeal raisin, my favorite!" she said, and Walter suppressed a laugh. Scotty hated raisins. Only last week, their son hid under the kitchen table when he found one in his cereal that Sarah had missed when she picked them out one by one. Scotty's favorite cereal was Raisin Bran minus the raisins, and don't even think about tricking him with that Wheaties crap—kids know what they know and will make you miserable for attempting to make your own life a little easier.

"That sounds delicious," Sarah said, a lie. She hated raisins too. Like son, like mother, because that's how the world spins. "Well, if you're sure you don't need anything else..." Sarah said, returning the lid to the lemon drop jar.

"Don't let them push you around," the old woman said, voice low and level, startling them both. Walter stopped counting. Sarah clanged the lid as it dropped and blinked at the old woman's forcefulness.

"What do you mean? Don't let who push us around?" she asked.

The old woman gave a single nod at his wife. "You. Just you. Don't let them push you around. This town will try, but don't let them do it. You got to push back. You know how to fight?"

A slither traveled down Walter's spine, though he was lost for a reason. The woman seemed to speak from experience, and he began to wonder at the history of this town. Not for the first time, either.

Sarah blanched, going pale like a paperwhite. And then she nodded.

"I know how to fight." They stared at one another for a moment as the old woman sized up Sarah's sincerity. Finally, her mouth twitched like she'd found a kindred spirit.

"Good. I'll hold you to it, then."

And with that, the old woman left, her scowl replaced with a bright smile down at her granddaughter as they walked out the door. You could hear their voices blend into one as they ambled down the front steps.

"Hurry up, grandma. I'm hungry."

"Sally Anne Hardwick, you just ate a lemon drop..."

They disappeared into the afternoon, leaving

Walter with a whole bunch of questions and not a single plausible answer to any of them.

THEY BOTH FOUGHT—THEY did. But how many times can you get back up when the circumstances hand you one blow after another, up and down and up and down until you find yourself spinning in a dizzying wind tunnel?

A whole lot, that's for sure.

But not enough.

The process to adopt little Scotty didn't carry over state lines, so the process had to begin again. And with so much free time on their hands, now seemed as good a time as any. For Walter's part, he was busier than ever, with orders coming in from Florida to France, from Paris, Texas, to Prince Edward Island, Canada. Travel had picked up as of late, so Sarah filed the paperwork with a lawyer she found in the yellow pages, a woman attorney named Georgia Ford. The adoption papers were filed the day before a court date was set for the antique store, exactly one month to the day after the door was locked for the last time.

Sarah wanted nothing more than to get both her business and her little family back in working order, so she did what any woman living on pins and needles might do in her situation: she filled her time with housework. She swept the garage. Dusted the ceiling fan blades. Moved the couch to a different wall and then decided all the furniture in the house needed to be rearranged. She potted new plants and painted the kitchen a lovely shade of deep red, as was the fashion of the time.

And then she began the task of cleaning out the attic.

She was dragging a box down the ladder when the neighbor came to call. He wasn't there long, only five minutes or so. Walter pulled into the driveway just as the man stormed out of their garage, red-faced and angry as he marched across the lawn and climbed into his car, a silver DeLorean like the one in that time-travel movie. The lowering of the driver's door was something to see, even if Walter was confused by its presence in front of their home.

Walter retraced the man's steps back toward his garage, where he found his wife crying at the bottom of the pull-down attic ladder, a box in her lap, two dirty tear streaks running down her chin.

"Who was that? And where's Scotty?" he asked, his voice beginning to shake. His words were slurred worse than normal, as they tended to get when he was overly agitated. Sarah hadn't noticed him until then. She looked up with wide eyes, fear ringing her irises, gaze darting from side to side.

"He's inside watching television. When did you get here?" she asked, her voice quaking on every word. His wife was afraid of something that was plain to see. He couldn't think of a single reason she should be.

"I just pulled up. Who was that man that left just now?"

Sarah stood then and wiped her eyes with both palms, walking across the garage with purpose, though it looked more like a woman trapped inside a cage...albeit one inside her own mind. If Walter gave her anything, freedom was at the top of the list. She sniffed and looked at Walter, shaking her head. The tears were gone, but the combination of mascara and dirt left a smudge.

"No one important. Just a neighbor who didn't like all the noise I was making. I was using a...leaf blower, and he was trying to work."

To Walter's knowledge, his wife didn't know how to use the leaf blower. That and the fact that it was still sitting on the shelf with the cord wrapped tight at the base, just as Walter had left it last week. Sarah was lying to him, something she had never done. Not to his knowledge, at least.

"So, he drove over here to tell you to stop using it?" He carefully measured each word, letting his skepticism take center stage.

She waved him off. "He was probably leaving his

house. That's my best guess. What does it matter? He is gone now."

More pacing, more sniffing, more of that trapped feeling radiating off her countenance so strongly it made him dizzy.

"Sarah." One word that ushered in a thousand questions, with a couple of accusations thrown in because they existed. He didn't like being lied to, not by the one person he trusted always to deliver the truth. She was cornered.

"What, Walter? I already told you who he was, and now he's gone. Can't you just let me get back to work in peace? I have too much to do and don't have time for this conversation."

Something was wrong with his wife, something she didn't want him to know.

"Okay, then I'll go find his car and ask him myself. Seeing as he lives just down the street, and that car is pretty easy to spot."

"Walter, stop." She had never sounded so angry. Or so afraid. Nothing would make him stop, not when it came to protecting his wife.

"If you're not going to tell me, then I'll go ask him. I'm guessing he came from..." he swept a purposeful gaze down the street, "...that way. I'll be back in a bit."

"Walter, don't leave," Sarah said. "I'll tell you."

So, she did. The truth should have calmed him

down. It should have answered so many questions that had reared to life the last three years since their first meeting at that hotel bar. It both did and didn't. Walter listened like a man trained in information gathering, rapt at attention and careful not to get distracted.

But he *was* distracted. Sidelined by his rage at her explanation. Both at her and on her behalf.

In the end, he wound up leaving, claiming a need for space, a minute to clear his head. Walter became the self-appointed victim in a situation that somehow had very little and everything to do with him. And just like a false victim in very real circumstances, in that moment Walter managed to make Sarah's situation about him.

So, he left to nurse his wounds, seeking solace at a bar on the other side of town. Nothing nurses a wound like three whiskeys and a side of fries.

He came home three hours later, calmed down, filled with regret, ready to talk, and drunk. He should have arrived sooner; he shouldn't have left home in the first place. A less selfish man wouldn't have.

Instead, by the time he showed up, Sarah—his beloved wife of nearly three years—was already splayed out on the garage floor, fading in and out of consciousness, blood pooling from her head from a wound he couldn't see.

Walter tried to ask what happened. Tried to call for help. Tried to stop scrambling to feel her head, her shoulders, her mid-section, her legs. Tried to stop cursing himself for drinking so much. Tried to rewind time with the strength of his own pleas to God. He tried it all.

But she just kept saying the same thing.

"Watch over Scotty. Watch over Scotty. Please watch over Scotty."

He promised to watch over them both for as long as he lived on earth. He promised. He promised over and over.

Long past the moment his wife took her final breath.

It was an eternity before he knew Sarah was lost to him. Gone. All the promises in the world wouldn't bring her back.

Exactly one week later, Walter's son was gone too.

17

Piper

It's Monday morning, and my brain is a one-track railway pointed two decades back. Sarah died? I mean, of course she's dead—I knew that. But from falling off a ladder? Alone? With no one around to help? My mind can't compute. And what did Walter mean by "gone?" Did Scotty die like his mother? Was he taken? Or he simply...left? This whole time reading the journals, I took it for granted that a happy ending was coming, even if that meant Walter now lived alone like so many his age do. I assumed he and Sarah had a long life together, that she died of natural causes, perhaps even in the past year or so. Death is the inevitable end for all of us, after all. And as my grandfather used to say about people like himself, Walter is no "spring chicken." But to die from an accidental fall so many years ago, back when they were so happy together? What the heck happened to Scotty?

The chime over the door tells me Walter is finally here. I hear him cough in the front room and stand up to ask him. No, to demand answers. It isn't fair he let me read these journals, knowing I would be left suspended in a state of discovering nothing but awfulness. Who lives this kind of life? Who even writes things like this in the first place? I march into the main store and look around, but I don't see Walter anywhere.

Bryant stands with his hands in his pockets, staring right at me.

There comes a time in a person's life when you face a T in the road: you can turn right into the future you've built for yourself onto a freshly paved road with very few twists and turns, free of bumps and potholes. Smooth travels ahead, the scenery in front of you flat and predictable, just like the world you've already come from. Or you can turn left and see what happens. Perhaps you've never turned left before. Maybe the road looks sketchy, dotted with gravel, with no median to buffer bad navigation. Bumpy and rough, caution up ahead, so please fasten your seatbelt. Chances are you'll make it. But for safety's sake, watch out for falling rocks and narrow pathways.

But the thing about T's in the road is there's no going straight ahead. You've got a choice to make, and neither one is easy. But then your fiancé looks at you, and your heart cracks a bit, and you remember why you love him, why you said yes to his proposal in the first place. And then he says this:

"I can't believe you just walked out on my mother like that. You'll need to apologize and make it up to her if this is going to work for us…"

And he keeps talking, but you don't hear the words because everything becomes perfectly clear.

It doesn't matter if you love him. It doesn't matter if it hurts. What matters is the way you can already feel 'love' turning into 'loved,' because you've already swung a left and driven miles down the road.

Leaving your old life, your old dreams, and even your mother's long-held wishes for your life behind you.

Of course, it hurts. Burns like dry ice to a middle fingertip.

But you just keep driving because you have no other choice. Heartbreak aside, the new path is yours.

～

I CRIED myself to sleep but woke up at midnight. I've been Googling for six hours since then. When my eyes opened, my cheek was stuck to the pillow, adhered to the satin case from my tears drying into the fabric. Just because you decide to end things with your fiancé doesn't mean it's an easy breakup. The heart wants what it wants, even if it's merely attached to a familiar routine and balking from the shakeup.

I reached for my phone a dozen times to call Bryant last night, even fisting my car keys and racing for the door in three different attempts to leave the apartment. Finally exasperated with my weak self, I went to bed, cried for an hour, slept for twenty minutes, then dragged myself out of bed to pour a glass of wine and research. A private eye, I'm not. But just like outrageous imaginations, distractions come in odd forms in the middle of the night. Convincing myself I could be best friends with Enola Holmes was embarrassingly easy at two a.m.

Walter's journal said that Scotty was gone.

Not that Scotty was dead.

Just...he was gone.

There are many interpretations of the word "gone." After scouring articles on obituaries, abductions, custody battles, adoptions, and cases of juvenile delinquents for two and a half hours, I finally found a possible correct one.

Scotty was relocated. Possibly to a relative, maybe to another family entirely. He could have been fostered, adopted, or simply raised to blend in with people he already knew. Sarah was an only child, as was Walter, but that didn't mean neither had other family members to speak of. Distant relatives exist for everyone. All I knew was Scott Lorry was a real person; maybe he still lived nearby. A long shot to be sure, but not out of the realm of possibility.

Now all I had to do was find the right Scotty. You don't change the first name of an eight-year-old boy, right?

I hoped to God no one had.

Typing in Scotty Lorry, son of Sarah, stepson of Walter, took me on a virtual manhunt that led to Scott Hampton of Mesa, Arizona—the wrong Scott, which led to Scott Jewel of Huntsville, Alabama— also the wrong Scott, which led to five other Scotts with varying last names—all the wrong Scotts. The internet is a tangled web of false information that led me to all the wrong things.

Until I located a man named Scott Crawford of Little Rock, Arkansas.

Chocolate hair.

Brown eyes.

Thirty years old.

An age that matched the timeline.

Children's occupational therapist.

A profession that tugged at my heartstrings.

But when I read "adopted at age eight from Silver Bell, Arkansas by Mr. and Mrs. Amelia Crawford..." that cinched things quickly, even though I spent until sunup making sure all the bullet points lined up. You can't just knock on someone's door to demand things nowadays without the right information, even though that's exactly what led me to Mr. Lorry's door in the first place. It's what I hoped to do again this time, preferably with similar results.

I reached for my car keys and grabbed my bag, then locked up the apartment and headed for the car.

Assuming this Scott Crawford is Walter's Scotty, his office opens in two hours. It's a little over an hour's drive to Little Rock from Silver Bell, and I want to make the round trip before the afternoon. Before Walter wonders where I've gone. Before I lose the nerve.

If I leave now, I think I can make it happen.

Pulling out of my parking space, I shift the gear in Drive and pull onto the road. When you don't know what to do with your life, it's time to do the next thing, the only thing that makes sense. For me, nothing makes sense except finding out what happened in the end. With thoughts of those journals sitting unopened in the bottom of Walter's memory box, I point the car west. My only hesitation is wondering how Scott Crawford will react to what I plan to say.

No matter how it turns out, it's time to find him.

PART III

18

Scott

"I know it hurts, Sierra, but we just have one more minute to go. Can you push through the pain one last time? And then, I promise, we'll go to the swings." The "swings" are two rope buckets tied to the ceiling in the middle of the room, a design meant to accommodate the widest variety of patients; the entirely self-sufficient and the barely mobile who need full assistance in and out of them, occasionally with body gear in tow. Sierra is in the former group and loves holding onto the ropes.

Her face brightens like a lightbulb turned on from behind her eyes, and I grin. This little girl is something special.

"Swings! Swings! I want swings!" she says.

Now I'm full-on laughing. "Let's finish your exercises first." Thank God she was my first patient today. Her good mood usually sets the tone for the not-so-pleasant ones.

Friday mornings are, by design, the best and worst workday of the week. Best for all the obvious reasons—the impending weekend, the chance to sleep in, bacon frying and pairing it with an omelet, a Saturday morning ballgame or two on television, shots of whiskey at a bar with friends, and time to nurse the inevitable hangover the next morning.

Worst because everyone either calls in for a last-minute appointment, desperate to see you before the weekend, and is upset when your schedule won't allow for it. Or they call to cancel because they forgot about their weekend plans. The only upside to that second one is a wide-open hour and room to fill it with a patient who makes work feel more like play. Don't get me wrong; I love working with children. I just love working with exceptionally well-behaved ones most.

Four-year-old Sierra attempts to press her palm to mine with all her might, an adorable little divot appearing between her eyebrows. At the same time, she concentrates, still making only the slightest progress but working her hardest for the tiniest millimeter of a second. She was born with mild cerebral palsy that presented primarily in her palms, causing the last three fingers on both hands to turn inward. We'd been working to strengthen the muscles in them for five weeks now with little progress. But not zero. By my best estimation, she'll have better use of those fingers by next July if her treatment stays consistent.

"I did it!" she says excitedly when the timer goes off, signaling we have five minutes of our session to go. It's playtime. She didn't do it, exactly, but twenty-five minutes of work and five minutes of play is the schedule I live by, one that makes the hard work worth it. She'll catch on eventually; children always do. They aren't as rigid as adults. The world hasn't pissed them off yet.

"You sure did do it," I say. "Now let's swing, little monkey." I tap my shoulder, she climbs on for a piggyback ride like always, and we head to the swings. Behind us, I hear the front door open to signal my nine o'clock appointment. Little Billy Brewer, right on time. He is one of the more challenging kids because he has a temper he can't always help. Still, he's a cute kid, so the next half-hour shouldn't seem too long, despite the screams that'll have my nerves begging for a sedative.

Since the waiting room is freshly stocked with coffee and snacks, I focus on Sierra and let Billy's mom make herself comfortable. Knowing the receptionist will help make sure the kid isn't too wild while they wait, I strap Sierra into the swing and give it a push. As always, she squeals with delight while I sit on the ground and pretend to snatch her feet when she comes toward me, making her squeal even louder. Funny how two kids can scream, but the happiness level makes all the difference.

After a few short moments, our time is up. Like always, Sierra climbs out of the swing and hugs my neck tight, her fingernails scraping my skin in a way she can't help because of her curled hands, but I don't mind. The fact that she has nearly full use of her limbs gives me a glimpse into her bright future, a prospect not all children who walk through my doors share. Squeezing her tighter, I stand to walk her to her mother where she waits on the sidelines each week. After a few rounds of questions and instructions for follow-up therapy at home, they leave the office. I turn to greet Billy and his mom, preparing myself for the battle it takes to coax him into therapy each week, reaching for the piece of bubble gum in my pocket that usually does the trick.

Billy isn't here. I look around, but the only person in the room is a young woman I don't recognize.

Figuring she's a salesperson or someone here to inquire about a job—both happen a lot—I bypass her for the receptionist's desk.

"Billy still coming this morning?" I ask Barbara, the receptionist who's worked for me since I opened the doors four years back. As a mother of four with a granddaughter on the way, Barbara is a parental figure of sorts, even more so considering she's my mom's best friend. They met when Barbara's son Daniel and I were fifth-grade classmates in middle school. My mother was PTA president, and Barbara was secretary, and they've been nearly inseparable since. When I told my mom that I was opening my office in downtown Little Rock, she called Barbara to tell her the news. The next afternoon, Barbara called about a job, I hired her on the spot, and our little team of two was ready for business. We've been veritable partners since, though part of me suspects Barbara is secretly here to spy on me at my mother's request; more precisely, to be on the lookout for any single women that might wander in and out of the office. She wants a grandchild and I'm not getting any younger, both of which she reminds me weekly at Sunday lunch. I've threatened to stop showing up if she doesn't quit nagging me, but we both know I'm lying. My mom's apple pie is my favorite.

"Billy's mother called because she's waiting on a grocery delivery. She says they'll be here, but it might be late."

One glance at the wall clock reveals they're five minutes late already.

"How late?"

At Barbara's grimace, I know it's inconvenient news. "She said forty-five minutes?"

Great. Now my entire morning will be off, which is bound to anger at least one parent or two. I would be more annoyed if I didn't need another coffee, one that didn't come from an occupational therapist's waiting room, no offense to Barbara. Her coffee is occasionally decent; more often, it tastes like day-old flavored water. I take a step backward toward the exit.

"Then I guess I'll make the best of it. I'm running to Pour Joe's for coffee, but I'll be back in fifteen." Halfway out the door, I remember my manners and duck my head back inside. "Want anything?"

Barbara glances to the side, then back to me. "I don't need anything, but this young lady has been waiting to speak with you if you have a second before you go..."

I pause, really look at the chick as she stands up to face me, and feel my throat go dry. She's about my age, much hotter than first impressions allowed—especially when you're holding a toddler whose talon-like claws are jammed into your neck—and she has red hair. Not apple red—brick red. Cinnamon red. Utah-desert mountain red. The kind of red you want to play with, tunnel through, climb up, dive inside, and never escape.

I have a thing for red hair, have since I saw Julia

Roberts in Pretty Woman right as my unfortunate case of delayed puberty began to kick in. It didn't matter that I was thirteen, shorter than everyone in school, and didn't have a lick of hair anywhere on my body, not even under my arms. I took one look at that woman on the screen and, well, let's just say you never forget the first woman who made you...feel things. Ask any man out there, and they'll tell you the same thing. Red hair is my weakness. My kryptonite. My go-to when I think of the perfect woman.

With a single shake of my head, I swallow and tell myself to calm the heck down. The woman is openly nervous and doesn't need me to make her more so. She clasps and unclasps her hands like she doesn't know what to do with them. A nervous tick. Suddenly I get it and feel like an ass; while I'm standing here practically objectifying her, the poor lady just wants a job.

"Sorry," I say, walking back through the door and letting it close behind me. "We're not hiring right now, but if you come back in a few months, we might be looking for—"

"Oh, I'm not here looking for work," she says, progressing to rubbing her hands together and worrying her bottom lip, the telltale sign of a mother in distress. What is wrong with me? It's like I don't even remember the reason I work here.

"If you need to make an appointment for your

child, you can check with Barbara, and she'll fill you in on our openings." I glance at my receptionist to see her grinning between me and this new chick like she could read all my hot-and-bothered thoughts. Great, my mom will be calling me tonight. *'What's this about a pretty woman showing up at work today?'* I pull in a breath and focus on the redhead. "You have a referral?"

"No, it isn't that. It's just…" Her hand comes up to twist her hair, then falls as though she doesn't know what to do with herself. She clears her throat and swallows, and I frown. Back goes the hand to the ends of her hair, and now I'm at a loss. Intrigued, but still lost. I've been told that in a room full of people, I'm hands-down the least intimidating person there, probably because I work with children. But this woman is nervous to be around me. This is new.

"Just?" I prompt, but nothing. I look to Barbara for help, but she's still grinning and useless. The clock is ticking, and I really need coffee.

"My name is Piper Moore," she finally says.

That stops me.

Piper. A nice name, kinda cool. I've never heard of her or seen her before. She doesn't elaborate further. This whole conversation isn't starting off well, so I work to make it less awkward, and come up with an idea I might regret sometime in the next two minutes. But an idea's an idea, and it's all I've got.

Billy's mom could walk in any minute now, and I've got to get to the coffee shop. Only nine a.m. and I already have a raging headache.

"First thing's first, Piper." I say. "Do you like coffee?"

A spark lights up her bluebell irises, a good sign. As far as me so distinctly noticing the color of her eyes...I decide to ignore that part.

"I love coffee," she says with a relieved smile, her voice slightly musical. I steal a quick glance at her left hand; there's no ring on her finger. I can almost hear my mother pumping her fist and cheering at home. I roll my eyes at the thought, but there's undeniably something about this woman that constricts my chest muscles. Trying my darndest to ignore it, I open the door and casually gesture for her to walk through it. Thankfully, she does. Her backside is as nice as her eyes.

"Then let's get coffee."

Maybe I'll pour some on my face just to get a grip.

19

Piper

He's just so nice.

In the two minutes I've spent with Scott Crawford, not to mention the ten minutes I observed him with that little girl at his office—a sight that nearly made my ovaries fall out of my body, by the way—that's the one big standout so far. He's nice. Patient. Quick with a smile and a joke. He is already familiar somehow, most likely because of the journals I've read, but also just because he...is. His eyes, his smile—both bright and mischievous in the way Walter described. But gone are the lanky limbs and childlike features that Walter might remember, all impressively replaced with muscular arms and a chiseled jawline that would make runway fashion models envious. They absolutely have me internally gawking. The boy has absolutely turned into a man. Dark hair swoops over his brow, one wavy lock stubbornly insisting to fall over his left eye like a defiant child fidgeting in church. Scott pushes the strand back often, but there it falls again in a way that has me wanting to push it back myself. Bedroom hair, some might call it. The thought alone has me mentally scolding myself.

I shouldn't be thinking of bedroom *anything* where Scott is concerned. Or any other man, for that matter.

Still, it's almost like I've known him for years and not just a handful of minutes. Like we might have been friends in high school. Someone I could be easily comfortable with, even though we've exchanged so few words yet, because I'm a nervous wreck and have no idea how to begin. How do you tell a stranger that you know all about their history? No matter how many times I play the scenario out in my head, there's no way it can go well.

I'm almost certain this is Walter's Scotty.

I'm definitely certain I don't want to tell him.

I'm dreadfully aware I don't have a choice.

But he's headed toward our table with two drinks in his hands, so the countdown inside my head winds up and releases. He sets one mug down in front of me, a frothy caramel concoction with a heart-shaped design inside the foam that starts my

mouth watering immediately. Art in a porcelain cup.
I pick it up with both hands and take a slow sip to
buy time. Delicious, but it hits my nervous stomach
with a jolt and a flop, not the soothing liquid I was
hoping for.

"Good?" he asks, with a hopeful raise of an
eyebrow.

I swallow, hot milk burning the back of my
throat. I nod with a cough and take a deep breath.
"Very good, but I should probably let it sit for a
minute. It's hot." And it's making me nauseous, but I
skip verbalizing that part.

His wince turns into a smile, something that
comes easily to him, I've noticed. "Yeah, this place is
great, but they are known to be a little temperature
happy. Gotta start slow and ease into it. I should
have remembered to tell you."

"That's all right. I can handle the heat." A bit of a
metaphor, considering my current situation. Feeling
a dot of foam resting on my upper lip, I lick it off
without thinking, immediately cursing myself for
not using a napkin. When I glance at Scott, it's clear
he watched me do it. He swallows forcefully, and my
neck grows hot. I push the mug away an inch and
settle in my seat. "But you're right; I'll wait."

Scott takes another sip before setting down
his mug.

"So, Piper, what did you want to talk about this

morning? I'm assuming you're *not* a mother with a special needs child?"

"What gave it away?" I'm stalling. Wishing to go back to him being just a hot barista who serves me coffee, but that isn't possible.

"Um...your lack of child was the first clue," he says.

I try to smile, but the countdown stops. Time's up. I take a deep breath.

"No, I'm not a mother. I'm just a friend of an elderly man I met last month. An employee of his, technically."

"Technically?"

"He doesn't pay me."

Scott laughs. "That sounds like a job I would "technically" quit." He puts the word in quotes, and I nervously laugh.

"I would quit, but it's more like we're exchanging services."

When his eyebrows go up, my eyes go wide, and my face heats in a flash. I rush to explain. "Not *those* kinds of services. He's nearly seventy."

Scott holds up both hands, leaning back in his chair. "Hey, I'm not one to judge...much." He gives me a look filled with mock judgment, but I see the smile he's hiding. "Everyone has their thing."

I'm mortified at the idea. "That is absolutely *not* my thing."

"He probably wishes it were," he says, pointedly giving me the once-over.

"Oh my gosh, stop it."

I cover my face with both hands and giggle nearly uncontrollably at his quick wit and my knack for always saying the wrong thing. If poor Mr. Lorry knew the way we were speaking about him right now...

That sobers me, and my laughter fades. For a second, I nearly forgot the reason I was here. Interesting how Scott so easily puts me at ease. I sit up straight and nervously fiddle with the corner of a paper napkin.

"The man I work for is an artist."

This puzzles Scott, and his head tilts a bit.

"What sort of art, and how can I help with it?" He stretches an arm over the back of the chair next to him and looks at me, a question in his eyes. "That is, I assume you need some help. Unless you came in for a different reason, in which case I am completely lost."

I smile, a pebble turning over low in my stomach. "I do need your help; I just don't know how to...what to..."

He waits while I gather my thoughts, and I try to steady my racing pulse.

"He's a calligraphy artist. A pretty famous one, at that. Used to be, anyway."

I study his face, but his expression doesn't change. There's nothing. No recognition at all. Maybe this won't be as difficult as I thought. Maybe Scott doesn't remember a thing. Maybe I somehow have the wrong Scotty. It's the worst possible outcome imaginable, even worse than being on the receiving end of his hurt or anger. I forge ahead, rip off the proverbial bandage, hoping that something I say will trigger his memory.

"The man I work for...his name is Walter, and he owns an antique shop in Silver Bell, the town where I'm currently living. His last name is—"

There. I see it the moment it happens, the exact second my words visibly register. His eyes flicker, his jaw hardens, and the muscles in his neck constrict. I have no choice but to finish what I came here to start.

"His last name is Lorry."

His arm slides down the back of the chair and into his lap. Limp. That's how I would best describe him. Lifeless even. This is what shock looks like when watching it land in real-time. He remembers.

I have the right Scott.

FOR THE LONGEST TIME, we don't speak. I don't dare to take a sip of coffee, breathe, or even blink to risk scaring him away. Maybe he has a temper. Maybe he'll turn it on me and yell right here in the café. He could ask me to leave or calmly walk out. He could accuse me of setting him up or manipulating him—which I technically did, even if it wasn't intentional. So many awful things that could happen, none that I'm ready for. I hold my breath and wait.

"Walter Lorry," he finally says with a single humorless laugh. "I haven't heard that name in years."

Not the response I expected, but he doesn't seem angry. I tentatively approach.

"But you *have* heard of him." It's more a statement than a question, but I don't know what else to say. Scott looks at me. I can't read his expression.

"Of course, I've heard of him. He was my stepfather until he wasn't. He just disappeared. Left without a word, and I haven't seen him since, thank God. No father worth anything would do that, so in the end, I was better off." There's bravado in his voice. Some might call it indifference. But I hear the hurt, the ticked-offedness, even if he doesn't mean for me to.

"I'm not sure that's exactly how it happened."

His eyes shoot to me. "Were you there? Because I'm pretty sure you weren't." It's a challenge, the first time a touch of anger has escaped through his countenance. Of course, I wasn't there. This isn't my battle to fight. But I can't shake the feeling I'm on the right side of it, nonetheless.

"No, I wasn't there. But I read the journals."

He blinks. "What journals?"

I'm not sure I was supposed to share this part, but I'm already halfway into it. "He wrote stories about your life together in notebooks, I think to process what happened back then. I read most of them, and I'm not sure he just left in the way you might think..."

Scott stands up then and pushes in his chair. He's mad but can't abandon his manners. Someone did something right by raising him.

"Look, I've got to get to work. It was nice to meet you, but I think we're done here. Now if you'll excuse me, I'm already late for an appointment. Tell Walter I said hello." He stops. "No, you know what? Scratch that. Don't tell him anything. I'll show him the same courtesy he showed me. None at all."

Scott barely glances my way as he turns and walks toward the door, shoving it open with force. It bounces against the wall outside before catching and slowly closing behind him. I stare at the empty space he leaves behind, feeling dejected and sad and so catastrophically worthless. This isn't how I expected things to go, though I couldn't pinpoint clear expectations. I just know this wasn't it. At the very least, I wanted to talk to him more. You can't just let someone live an entire life believing they were abandoned, not when it happened at such a young age. I know the feeling of being left behind. At the very least, I thought I could let him know I understood.

Dreading the drive back to Silver Bell, I stand to gather my bag and discard the latte in the bin against the counter. I couldn't drink more of it anyway, not without making myself sick. With a longsuffering sigh, I heave myself out the door, slip my sunglasses over my eyes, and then look toward the parking lot across the street where I left my car, taking inventory of my life. I have no fiancé. No family. No photoshoots lined up for a week. No reason to stay at the antique shop since there's no need for invitations. No idea what's inside those three unopened journals. No reason to find out now that Scott has shot me down. And evidently, no purpose for anything.

What a waste. What a stupid, stupid waste.

I fist my keys and click the unlock button, then walk toward the sound of my car.

That's when I see him standing outside his office, leaning against the side of the building, looking straight at me. I make a misstep and trip a bit before righting myself, surprised to see him waiting for me.

"What journals?" he calls sharply, unable to notice how my pulse skyrockets. This is how hope feels when it pulls you from a pit. It strikes me then that it's been a long time coming, that in me at least, hope has lain dormant for years.

I stop in front of him. "He wrote you journals. I've read ten so far. There are three more sealed that I promised not to open. From what I can tell, he's been writing them for years. They're long. Detailed. A couple made me cry. And for the record, he has no idea I'm here."

Scott crosses his arms. "Why didn't he come find me himself?"

I shake my head. I have no answers except my very best guess. "I don't think he knows where you are. And I'm not sure he would want you to see him even if he did." My gut tells me that, even if my instincts are sometimes off.

Scott frowns. Behind him, a bell dings as a mother and son walk into his office. He doesn't turn around. "Why wouldn't he want me to see him? What's wrong with him?"

I could be tired. That might be why my eyes begin to sting. "He has a disease. Some kind of muscular dystrophy, I think. He can't walk or talk very well, and the people in town make things worse with how they treat him..."

His chin comes up. "How they treat him?"

"Just...they aren't nice."

Scott sniffs and looks down the sidewalk. "How

do I know you don't just have a bleeding heart for some weird old man in town? The Walter I remember dumped me like last week's trash after my mom died."

My heart sinks at the mental image. Little Scotty was only eight. "I guess you can't know that for sure. Maybe I can't, either. But I don't think it's as simple as him dumping you. From the journals I read, he seemed distraught about whatever happened back then, and I think he's been punishing himself for it ever since."

"Punishing himself, how?"

I look over his shoulder, staring off, coming up with a mental list.

"For one thing, he rarely talks. He has a speech impediment, but I think it's more than that. He's stooped and aloof, almost like he doesn't want anyone to get too close. For another, I think he stopped painting. Or drawing. Whatever it is you call calligraphy art, he stopped doing it abruptly. He has a whole storage room filled with art that he could have sold but didn't." I look up at the sky, clear and blue, not a cloud anywhere. "Then there's the way he sleeps on his front porch every night like he—"

"What did you say?" The question is so sudden that I blink.

"His porch. He sleeps out there on a cot every single night. I have no idea why, but everyone wonders about it. It's so odd considering he has a house next door. But I never see him go inside it, which is also strange because..."

At the look on Scott's face, I stop talking. His face has gone pale, his eyes red-rimmed and glassy as he stares down the street. Memories live behind them, stories I haven't read in Walter's journals. I want to ask what he's thinking, beg him to tell me, plead with him to give Mr. Lorry a chance. But I don't, unwilling to interrupt whatever state his mind is living in. Finally, he clears his throat.

"Think you can hang out here for an hour? I have an appointment right now, but I'll have my receptionist clear my schedule for the afternoon if you can stay."

I find myself nodding, agreeing to an unknown agenda, unclear where we're headed but desperate for Walter's sake—and my own—to find out.

"Sure, I can wait. I'll go back to the coffee shop and stay there until you're finished."

"Okay. Here." He pulls out his wallet and hands me a twenty-dollar bill, a confusing and unnecessary gesture. "Order yourself a drink you'll like this time."

I start to protest, but he holds up a hand. "Consider it an exchange of services, like I'm paying for your time. Might not be as exciting as what you're used to from other, much older men, but..."

I raise an eyebrow, secretly thrilled that he's in

the kind of mood to tease me. That's a good sign, right?

"For your information, that would cost you a lot more than twenty bucks." I pluck the money out of his hand, deciding to buy myself breakfast too.

He laughs, walking backward toward his office. "I'll see you in an hour."

I feel lighter on my feet somehow. Like we might be making headway. Like Walter could have a happy ending after all. Maybe. Just maybe he will.

At the same time, I can't shake the feeling that Scott seems familiar.

Like I've known him forever, even though we just met this morning.

20

Scott

    "Do you see it, Scott? If you relax your eyes a bit and look a little to the left, you'll be able to make out the way the stars make a box of four in each corner, then dip and narrow off to the left like they're forming a handle for pouring. Do you see it, Scotty? Do you see it?"

    "I see it! I think I see it!"

    He didn't see it, but he really, really wanted to.

    "That's my boy. Now when I'm out of town, you can come out here at night and look up at the sky, and you'll know we're looking up at the same spot at the same time. It'll be like I'm right here with you. Like I never left..."

    I'm so entranced in the memory that the gel pen I'm holding drops from my fingertips and lands with a thud on my desk. I catch it as my eyes snap into focus and take in the mural hanging on my wall in front of me, the one I bought in college from a Beale Street thrift store in Memphis during finals week junior year. I walked into the store on a whim while the group of girls I drove with were getting pedicures. I hadn't expected to find much, maybe a vintage jacket or an old guitar, but it was the mural that caught my eye. It hung on the wall behind the register; an eight by ten tapestry of a farmhouse, a full moon, a night filled with stars, and a sky streaked with purple, orange, and gold. It reminded me of my childhood, of the parts I could remember. Before life went to hell and I was forced to trade one existence for another faster than most people decide where to go for dinner.

Luckily, the trade worked out okay. Most kids are fortunate enough to have one set of parents who love them. I had two, and you'll never hear me complain. But before the happiness came the loss, an impact so profound that it remains so today, my life divided into two distinct parts. Little Scotty lived next to an antique store and slept under the stars every Friday night with his parents—a mother named Sarah and a father named Walter. And older Scott, who played soccer and baseball and took piano lessons every Tuesday after school, who was officially adopted at age eight by Kathleen and James Crawford, and who took a longer time than most children to adapt but did catch on eventually. Both parts make the whole me, but I've seen life in before and afters since I was a little boy that came home to a dead mother and a grief-stricken stepfather who left after a week of listening to me cry and never returned.

Some habits are impossible to break.

I just thank God none of them ever broke me.

"I hate you, I hate you, I hate you!"

My palm still occasionally throbs from the old tear in my nerve endings when I slammed my hand against that brick wall at the police station and failed to see the nail poking from it. It bled for a week. It still hurts today. I shake my head to clear the memory and grab my jacket. It's been thirty minutes since I sent Billy and his mother away and ninety minutes since Piper left for the coffee shop. I'll think about my sad early childhood later.

Right now, I have a girl to meet.

PIPER LIKES PUMPKIN SPICE. I file that mental note away for later but don't allow myself to dwell on the reason. Who says there's going to be a later? My obviously broken mind, that's who.

She sips from a takeaway cup when I walk in, then forks a bite of an orange-looking muffin as she stares out the window. The scent of pumpkin engulfs the table, not unpleasant, but a bit overwhelming. She's a big fan of autumn, that much is clear.

She startles a bit when I pull out the chair across from her and sit, her eyes large round saucers that morph into delighted curiosity at the sight of me. When she smiles, I'm stuck commanding my mind not to entertain thoughts of Christmas and New Years and Valentine's Day or any day after the one we're currently living through. Holidays are better when they don't require buying gifts for significant others, anyway. That's what I tell myself.

Problem is, 'myself' isn't listening. On to other topics.

"Tell me about Walter."

She wipes her mouth with a paper napkin, wads it into a ball, and drops it on her plate.

"Want to walk and talk, or would you rather stay here?" she asks.

That's an easy one for me. I'll always choose fresh air when given the choice.

"Let's walk."

I gather her trash and toss it in the bin, then open the door and wait for her to walk through it. My mom raised a gentleman. I'm just not sure which mother launched that character trait of mine. In a single morning, my memories have blurred together, and I'm not sure how I feel about it.

Piper steps off the sidewalk onto the patchy grass of the neighborhood park, one where children play on the swing sets after school, and little league ball games can be heard just before sundown. For now, it's blessedly quiet. There are a handful of moms with toddlers playing on a slide about fifty yards away, but otherwise, it's just the two of us. There's no one around but Piper to witness my reaction to what she has to say.

"I've only known Walter a couple of weeks, but I'll tell you anything you want to know."

"Tell me how you met him."

She hugs herself and looks at her feet while she walks. "I wanted him to design something for me with his calligraphy, so I went to his shop to ask him. He said he would do it, but I had to help him straighten up his antique store in return, which was a mess. That's the exchange of services I was talking about," she says with a grin, "though so far, I'm the only one sticking to my end of the deal. The store is still a mess, and he hasn't made a thing. Not that I need him to anymore..."

I stopped hearing her a few sentences back.

The store. I vividly recall the sound of breaking glass and the distinct scent of weathered, musty paper. Other details are fuzzy, like trying to glimpse a sunrise through a thick layer of fog. I recall breaking a cobalt blue tumbler by running head-first into a bookshelf after my mother said to settle down. A set of twelve matching tumblers wobbled while I watched helplessly and tried not to cry. Blessedly, the others stayed upright, so my tears quickly abated. Besides, Walter explained that they were only items and could be replaced. I, however, could not.

"What did you want him to make for you?"

She sighs. "My wedding invitations."

My insides deflate like a balloon stabbed with a machete. "You're engaged?" I pretend to say it like the news is something to be happy about, all while thinking how immensely unfortunate it is for me. The good women are always taken, and I'm starting to wonder if she might be one of the better ones out there. I'm not a fan of Walter Lorry and haven't been for years, but a woman who cares for the elderly is a woman I want to know. Considering she drove all this way without knowing how I would react, I'd say Piper cares pretty deeply.

She's oddly silent for a long beat. "I was engaged. Up until last night, actually."

My pulse runs a victory lap at the promise of a breakup; stupid since I barely know the woman and shouldn't be invested in her marital status.

I look at her sidelong. "What happened?"

She shakes her head. "We're too different. Plus,

there's the fact that he likes his mother better than me."

I don't mean to laugh, but it shoots out like a rocket aimed heavenward.

"That can't be true."

"It's absolutely true." She looks at me. "Do you know what kind of wedding cake the two of them picked out?"

I wait for her to continue. She doesn't disappoint.

"Cherry. We taste tested fifteen different cakes, and they chose cherry."

There's a story here, one that I'm missing. "I'm guessing you don't like cherries?"

She looks up at a bird flying overhead. "I'm allergic to cherries. And when I pointed out that little fact, they both agreed that since I'm the bride, I probably shouldn't be eating cake anyway. You know, because it's important not to get fat while wearing my dress, even at the reception. But not to worry, because my impending mother-in-law kindly offered to bring a bottle of Benadryl as a backup plan. That way, I probably wouldn't die if I accidentally took a bite."

"She did not offer that."

"Oh, but she did. And my fiancé thanked her for it. Former fiancé that is."

It's both hysterical and incredibly sad. Unless there's something wrong with this chick that I haven't learned yet, she seems kinda great. If I were lucky enough to have her, you can bet I wouldn't be foolish enough to let her go. I absolutely wouldn't offer her food that might kill her or make her break out in an itchy rash. The things we do for love.

"And you dumped him, I assume?"

"Not as quickly as I should have, unfortunately. But yes. And then I took his car on a joyride through downtown Silver Bell. A little poetic, don't you think?"

"So that BMW I saw you standing next to earlier is his?"

"No. I felt too bad to leave town with his car, so I switched his out for mine."

"We all have our limits."

"Apparently, mine extend to the county line and no further."

I smile. I'm having a nice time despite the subject we're still dancing around. I let the feeling linger for a long moment until I can't anymore. There's a reason we're talking, and that reason is a ghost in our otherwise pleasant two-person stroll.

"So, back to what we were talking about before..." I dutifully say, sad to see things get serious again. She takes a few steps, seeming to mull the subject over. "Anything else you can tell me about Walter?" We walk to the edge of the park. A pond sits in the back, sunlight glistening off the surface of the water while ducks and a lone goose glide across the middle like they haven't a care in the world. Oh, to be them. I've had about a thousand cares in life and just passed my thirtieth birthday. "Anything that would help me understand what happened?"

She picks up a piece of discarded old bread and tears a piece off, then tosses it into the water. Two ducks swim quickly toward it, the smaller of the two gobbling it up. Piper aims another piece for the bigger duck. Fair is fair.

"I think there might be an answer in the sealed journals. So, I'm not sure. But I did read enough to know that he loved your mother. And you. As for the rest of it, maybe you should ask him. Walter doesn't talk much, but I have a feeling he would talk to you."

"Not sure I'm ready for that. What if you just bring them here and let me read them first?"

She shakes her head. "I promised him I wouldn't open them."

"You wouldn't be the one to open them. You would give them to me, and I would do it."

She looks at me then, her eyes roaming over my face. "Somehow, that still seems like a breach of trust."

My temper spikes at her gall; I don't like my hand being forced, but she's doing it. She's the one who came here to open Pandora's Box, to unload information about something I've pushed into the recesses of my mind for years quite successfully; thank you very much. Who does that? Who gives someone false hope and then leaves them to flail around all alone in the aftermath? I'm pissed and livid. Blood pounds against my neck so forcefully it's all I can do not to punch something.

Even though she kind of has a point. Keeping a promise matters. In my experience, most people don't. This Piper lady must be trustworthy, even if her loyalty lies to a man I've spent my life resenting.

"So, you're not interested in helping me out?" Trustworthy or not, I'm still mad.

She sighs. "Of course, I am. It's why I'm here. If there is a chance for you to fix things with Walter... Let's just say if I had that same chance with my mother, you can bet I would take it."

There's a flicker of pain behind her eyes, but she doesn't elaborate. Maybe someday I'll convince her to. I rub the back of my neck to ease the tension caused by the morning's developments, but it doesn't help. Some days are weird as hell.

"Can I think about it and let you know?"

She nods. "Sure. I need to get back to Silver Bell anyway. I'm already late as it is."

"You're heading to the store?"

"Yes. There might not be a wedding, and I may not need invitations anymore, but Walter still needs help, and I still have a few days left to give him. That store is a total mess."

At this, I take a clear breath. Trustworthy and honest, a fulfiller of commitments. Check, check, and check all boxes that matter. Piper gets more interesting by the minute. I shouldn't ask the next question. I know I shouldn't, but I can't just let her leave without putting it out there.

"Can I have your number? You know, in case I decide to show up one day next week. That way, I can warn you beforehand, so you're prepared." I'm dancing around the real reason in a series of little white lies. I want her number so I can call her, plain and simple. Whether or not it involves Walter is yet to be decided.

"Give me your phone," she says, holding out her hand. I place my phone in her palm, then watch as she sends herself a text from me. "There," she says, handing my phone back. I laugh when I read the message. *"Thanks for being the best person I've ever met. Can't wait to talk again soon."*

"Wow, someone's humble," I say.

She shrugs. "It's been a bad week, so I decided you would be the one to cheer me up."

"Did it work?"

When she winks, my pulse trips. "Let's just say you're a really good texter."

I hold out my hands. "Glad to be of service."

We walk to her car, and I open her door as she climbs behind the wheel. Just before she closes the door, she blinks up at me. I've changed my mind about the bluebell; now the blue looks exactly like the fifth color of the rainbow, full of promise and maybe a little good luck.

When did I become such a sap?

"I hope you call," she says.

"I hope I do too." And I mean it, in more ways than one. I step back as she pulls away, standing in place as she drives out of the lot and onto the road. When she disappears behind a row of downtown buildings, I head back into the office.

This rest of the day is a crapshoot, at best, despite canceling everything.

A clear schedule isn't fun when your mind is filled with thoughts of an antique store five towns away.

More specifically, of the woman who works there.

21

Piper

It's been four days without a word from Scott, and I'm rapidly nearing the end of my time at the store. I have a photoshoot scheduled two days from now, many more on the books the following week, and there's no credible reason to stick around. There's no wedding, no invitations to make, no viable "exchange of services," if you will. Besides, Mr. Lorry hasn't asked me to stay.

Something tells me he won't.

Bryant has stopped by twice—once to beg my forgiveness and another to tell me I'm being unreasonable and ungrateful and to remind me that anyone else would jump at the opportunity to join his family. The first time he showed up, my resolve began to crack. The second, I remembered all the reasons why I hated myself for staying as long as I did. It's a third of my life that I can't get back.

My mother loved Bryant. But I remember enough about her to know she never settled for anything—not a man, not a job, not an easy way out disguised as an opportunity. The only thing she eventually settled for was her fate. And yes, I've spent my life wanting to honor her plans for me. But now that I'm older, some might argue even a little bit wiser, I figure my life would be better spent honoring her memory.

"What time is it?" J.D. asks from his spot on the floor, where I sent him to alphabetize books when he arrived after school. While I dust off and rearrange a stack of dishes poorly displayed inside an old curio cabinet, J.D. is chest high in old volumes of fiction and non-fiction, two of which I set aside for myself because it isn't every day you find a second-edition Stephen King and a first edition Johnny Cash shoved underneath a pile of ancient Time magazines priced for ninety-nine cents. When I asked Walter how much he wanted for the books, he mumbled, "Five dollars" while I stared at him in disbelief. I argued their value, but he didn't respond, not even when I announced that I'd be paying him ten dollars each, hoping to get a reaction. Ten dollars, it is. I'm a common thief compared to what they're worth.

"I think it's after five o'clock," I say to J.D., knowing he needs to get home for dinner. Sure enough, the kid scrambles to his feet, another comic book tucked under his arm. He takes one every time he comes in but always brings it back. I never mention it to Walter; it keeps the kid happy, and I doubt Walter would care. "Which one did you find this time?"

"Captain America!" he hollers, holding the thin book up for my inspection.

I laugh at his enthusiasm. "All right, just bring it back tomorrow."

"I will!" he says, racing to the door. He flings it open and nearly collides with Walter. When I came back from visiting Scott last week, I noticed the old man exiting the house next door, something I hadn't seen him do once since I first showed up here. He seems to avoid the place, at least when I'm around. In three weeks, he's never strayed from sleeping on that front porch at night, the large house next door seemingly just a piece of real estate he holds on to for sentimental reasons. But the past few days have been different. Suddenly, he makes a visit each afternoon. Never for long, but still he goes. I'd ask him what's changed, but I'm certain he won't tell me.

Walter stumbles backward and clutches his chest, huffing a big sigh when the boy runs by without breaking stride.

"Good riddance," Walter mutters, but the way he watches after the boy tells me he doesn't really mean it. For the first time, I wonder if J.D. reminds him of Scott.

"He's in a hurry," I quip, watching Walter carefully while reaching for another plate.

"Kids these days always are," he mutters, more to himself than anyone. He finally looks my way and closes the front door, an unmistakable touch of regret in his expression. His mouth tilts briefly in something akin to a smile, but just like that, it's gone.

Walter still rarely speaks, but he has warmed slightly to me. I barely noticed the slurred words anymore. They've faded into the sound of his accent just like someone else might speak with a southern twang or an Irish lilt. His voice is just...Walter. Same as his slightly stumbling gate. People are quick to judge the smallest things and rarely like differences in the same way a gossip loves an audience but doesn't care much about the truth. As for me, I've decided that truth matters above all. Flaws and differences are what make people interesting. How boring it is to surround oneself with copies and pastes of the same personalities. That sort of life is no longer for me. Maybe it never was in the first place. I set the plate down and pick up a teacup.

"Where'd you go?" I ask, not for the first time. He doesn't answer, also not a first. "I thought I saw you going into the house next door..." My words trail off, an invitation to elaborate. He doesn't, but I don't miss how his gaze flicks to me, irritation clear in his expression.

"It's my house, you know..." He speaks, after all, and I smile to myself.

"Yes, it is. And a nice house it is. Maybe I could come over sometime and—"

"No. You're already reading my journals. Isn't that enough?"

I set the cup down a little too firmly, chagrined by his tone. Door closed; invitation not extended. What is in that house that Walter doesn't want anyone to see? And what does his house have to do with the journals? I suppose everything, considering the house is part of the story. Maybe my curiosity should roll over and surrender, but instead, it's piqued. If only I had more time to nurse it.

"I'm done reading them, actually," I say, closing the cabinet door and locking it with an antique key. "And as for time, it turns out I have to leave in a couple of days. I wish I could stay longer, but I need to get back to work."

"What about the invitations?" he asks. We haven't spoken of them since that first day, so part of me is surprised he remembers. The other part of me knows Walter Lorry spends more time observing life than busying himself with activity, so I suppose I should have realized he wouldn't forget.

"I won't be needing them after all," I say, leaning against the cabinet and folding my arms. "Bryant and I are no longer getting married. I called off the wedding last week."

"Good. I don't like his family."

I breathe a laugh and look up at the ceiling. "That's obvious, although I have no idea why."

He says nothing, leaving my imagination to wander. Ben Ratliff is the type to throw his weight around, to manipulate people and situations to work to his advantage. I still don't know why he was in this store that day last week, wearing an angry expression directed straight at Mr. Lorry. Despite reading the journals, there's still so much I don't know.

Then again, I've kept a few things hidden as well.

"I need to tell you something..." I say, pulse ratcheting up just as the bell dings over the front door. "...about why I was late to work a few days ago. I know I told you I went to visit a friend, but the truth is—"

Movement over Walter's shoulder catches my eye, and we both look over as Scott closes the door behind him.

The moment of truth, whether I'm ready for it or not.

I look at Scott, his expression fidgety with nerves.

I look at Walter's profile; his skin already faded to a pasty white. Fading more, even as I watch him stare at the figure coming closer. At Scott's dark brown hair with the cowlick at the part. At his green eyes ringed with brown that pull you forward like a lighted tree at Christmastime. At the chiseled jawline that pops and locks when he swallows. At the prominent cleft in the middle of Scott's chin that I'm just now noticing for the first time.

He knows.

All at once, I can tell Walter knows.

"Hi," Scott says to both of us while making eye contact with no one.

"Hi," I say, smiling tentatively, first at Scott, then at Walter. My smile fades when I look at Mr. Lorry's face. Annoyed one second ago, it's now washed in pain.

He looks at me.

Says, "What have you done?"

And the next second, he faints.

Clutches his chest and falls straight to the floor.

He doesn't wake up.

"Walter, can you hear me?" There must be a limit to the number of times it's healthy to slap the elderly lightly on the face, but I've been doing it for what feels like minutes to no avail. I keep at it while Scott talks on the phone. "Wake up, Walter, please wake up." He doesn't. His collar is dotted with water from what I now realize are my falling tears. Despite the old man being an emotionally closed door, I've managed to wiggle my way inside and desperately want to stay there. "Is the ambulance coming? I feel like they should have been here by now."

Scott hangs up the phone just as the low sound of sirens rings in the distance. "They're almost here. Sorry, I had trouble finding the address." He joins me on the floor and takes Walter's hand. "Walter, wake up. I need you to wake up." The old man remains motionless between us, even as paramedics file in with a gurney, load him into the ambulance, and drive away. We hop in my car and follow, knowing we're the only ones who will. A lifetime spent in the same small town, and the only people who show up have known you three weeks and twenty years prior, consecutively.

Two hours later, we're told Walter had a stroke.

It's unclear whether he'll speak from this point on. Until he wakes up, there's no way of knowing anything.

Funny how a feeble voice turns strong when the alternative is no voice at all.

22

S cott
    "*Mama, you want to lay here and look at the stars with us?*"

"*On that cot? There's barely room enough for the two of you as it is. Where would I fit?*" *The porch creaked under her foot as his mother moved around them, a blanket draped over her shoulders to warm her against the cool night air. Lying flat on his back, Walter reached to hook her around the knee. With a giggle, she fell in a heap on top of him while Scotty moved quickly out of the way to avoid getting crushed by his parents. His mother and soon-to-be father, anyway. Walter was gonna adopt him as soon as Arkansas finished with his paperwork.* "*Blasted state,*" *he heard his stepfather say more than once since they'd moved here.* "*If we'd stayed in California, we'd be legal already.*" *Scott didn't know much about*

Arkansas except that the new store made his mother happy, and the old law made Walter mad. He decided he fit best down the middle, happy to live here but never too loyal to leave.

"You could fit next to Walter. I'll lay down here on the blanket." Scotty tugged the blanket from his mama's hands and spread it on the wooden planks next to his parents, then tucked his body under the cot on his mama's side, where she lay above him next to Walter. "Want me to tell you everything I know about the Big Dipper?" he asked her.

When his mama said "yes," Scotty began a basic explanation, using his arm to point out the stars in the sky. Some facts were real, and some were based in seven-year-old imagination, but wasn't that the truth about all the best bedtimes stories?

THE PORCH IS what I remember most, the thing that has me climbing inside my mind even now, wanting desperately to recreate the brief but joyful childhood I spent here before the moment disappeared like the ambulance that carried Walter away.

When I arrived in town this morning, memories assaulted me from every side, like I was an actor in a movie about asteroids, doing the worst possible job of dodging falling debris while struggling to keep a brave façade and calm demeanor. Trying to push the memories away but being hit with another one each time I turned a new street corner. I was seven years old when I left, but the two years I spent here thoroughly made its mark. They say you can't go home again when you grow up and make your own way in the world, but right now, all thirty-year-old me can hear is a phantom seven-year-old me shouting in my ear to look around and pay attention. Redos don't come to us often, but my chance for one just showed up.

Walter was a great stepfather. I have no doubt he would have made an even better father in the legal sense. He treated me like flesh and blood, treated my mother like a lone gemstone found glistening on a public beach—he knew she was rare, knew they were in the wrong place at the right time, knew the chance to love and be loved by her wasn't something to toss away. Together, the three of us made up a family in every sense of the word, possibly made easier because Walter had never married before and had no kids of his own. I was it for him, he was it for me, and my mother was it for both of us.

Until she died, and everything stopped.

Until a man came inside the house and packed my bags, grabbing everything I owned but a favorite stuffed eagle my parents' won for me at a town carnival the summer before.

Until I was removed kicking and screaming from Walter's home while he sat on the front porch with his head in his hands and didn't say a word.

Until a man I'd never seen before asked if Walter had hurt me or mistreated me and wouldn't listen when I repeatedly said no, no, no, the same answer I would give even today.

Until another couple showed up, and I was moved into their house where they gave me a new stuffed eagle that I immediately threw in the trash.

Until we showed up in court, and I was adopted by that couple that wasn't from the family I belonged to.

Until we moved to a town an hour away, far enough away but not too far for the people 'in charge' to visit, as my parents used to say.

Until my cries for my mother and Walter and my old home stopped, and I grew accustomed to my new life because—say what you want—my new parents did love me a lot.

Until I sat in the therapist's chair to discover all the reasons my life seemed to be shadowed by a permanent sense of loss that I couldn't explain like every stitch of good was waiting to be unraveled by the bad.

Until Piper showed up at my job four days ago.

Until Walter was taken away just now.

Until we sat at the hospital, learned he had a

stroke, and we came back here to get his few meager belongings, so he would have something familiar when he wakes up.

Until now, here on this porch, all of it flooding back like the memories were held back by masking tape, and an unknown force just ripped it away.

Until I followed Piper inside the store to Walter's back room, where he keeps a change of clothes.

Until I saw that old stuffed eagle lying on a cot in the corner like it was just waiting for me to come back and pick it up.

Until I do. Until I'm filled with despair and relief and a rapidly growing sense of nameless injustice.

Why was I taken from Walter all those years ago? Who was the man that packed my things? Why did it all just happen to me without any explanation?

And above all, why am I just now questioning it?

"ARE YOU OKAY?" Piper asks when she looks back to see me sitting on the cot, that eagle pressed to my chest like a toddler holding a security blanket. She pushes a sweater of Walter's into a duffle bag and reaches for an old Stephen King paperback. "Or are you just a big fan of stuffed animals, too?"

"Too?" I ask, my voice flat, dull.

"Like Walter. That eagle is always in here." She

smiles sadly. "I even caught him napping with it once a couple weeks back."

I finger a feather poking out of the toy's face, pull it out, and turn it over in my hands. "It's mine. The only thing that man didn't pack when they made me move away."

Her forehead creases in confusion. "That man?"

I shrug. "I have no idea who he was. I just remember him coming in, packing my things, and telling me I was leaving. Right after that, I did."

Piper lowers herself next to me, her leg innocently brushing against mine. "Did anyone tell you anything about him?"

"No. They all told me Walter wasn't a good man, and they found somewhere else for me to live. It all happened fast. I was young, so I never thought to question anything. But I was angry. That much I remember."

"As you should have been." We sit silently for a long moment. "The 'not a good man' part doesn't make sense. The Walter I know is a very good man. A bit awkward, maybe, but I suppose we all are in some way. In his case, after everything he's been through…"

"What do you mean?" I ask.

I feel her eyes turn to me, so I look at her. This probably isn't the time to notice how they've darkened from a light bluebell shade into a brewing storm cloud or how beautiful the change is to witness, but I notice.

God, do I notice.

"The way he lost your mother that day. The way he lost you right after." I blink. It never occurred to me, not once, that she might have answers to my questions. "Scott, you do know this, right? What happened back then?" From the sound of her voice, she's only now realizing I don't.

"I don't know anything because no one ever told me."

"Scott..." She reaches for my hand and drags it to her lap, interlacing her fingers with mine. Empathy or sympathy, or maybe they're one and the same in this moment. Either way, I let her hang on because it's the only thing that holds me together. "You never knew about your mom? About how she died?"

I shake my head. "The better question is, why does it seem like I'm the only one who doesn't know?"

"I can't believe no one told you. Maybe everyone assumed you were too young to—"

"I wasn't too young to be affected by it, even if I couldn't name the reason. But I remember her, Piper." She's hazy around the edges like you might remember an old babysitter, but I do remember some things.

Just not as much as I want to. "Show me the journals," I say. This time, I'm not asking.

Her head shakes slightly, probably from the shock of my request more than anything.

"I can't...I promised him I wouldn't..."

"You promised him you wouldn't open them yourself, and I'm not asking you to." I keep my voice steady, calm. Piper is my only ally here, the direct link to over two decades of my life's unsolved riddles. "Please let me have the journals. Let me read them all. When Walter wakes up, I'll take the blame."

"And if he doesn't wake up?" Her eyes widen at her own reckless question, but we both know she isn't the only one thinking it. What if he doesn't?

"Then that's even more of a reason for you to let me read the journals now," I say. "Walter's been forced to stay quiet long enough. It's about damn time someone gave him a voice."

I READ through the open journals on the way back to the hospital while Piper drives us there, the first two on the drive and the last eight while sitting inside the parked car in the lot. Piper went inside to check on Walter, then came back to the car when the nurse told her there had been no change. Walter was still asleep; we were still helpless and waiting.

So, she waited with me while I read, reaching for my hand when I got to the last notebook which explained the whole sordid event.

My mother died from a fall from a ladder while Walter got sauced at a bar across town, and I watched television inside the house. But the journal implied the fall wasn't an accident. And if it wasn't...

Someone may have killed my mother.

Or at least watched her fall and left while the life drained from her.

I lower the notebook to my lap and run a hand across my mouth.

"It's been more than two decades. What am I supposed to do about this now?" I ask Piper, having no answer but desperately wanting a clear one. Next to me, she silently mulls over my question. There's no right answer here because the wrongs can't be corrected. No matter what, my birth mother remains dead, and Walter still sleeps in a hospital bed with no signs of waking. Anyone who could tell the real story of what happened back then...can't.

Piper sighs. She hasn't let go of my hand, and I'm glad. "I suppose that depends on what you want to do. Pursue the truth, mend your relationship with Walter, neither of those, or both."

I lean my head back on the seat. "Thank you for making that clear as mud. You literally just listed every option."

"That's because you have all of them in front of you." She looks away from me out the window. "What you could do, before you decide, is read the last three journals. Maybe they'll give you direction. At the very least, it might give you closure. Maybe you'll find your answer in Walter's voice."

I like the sound of that. Walter's voice.

My mother's, as well. The two of them may have a lot to say.

As for me, it's time to listen.

I break the seal on the top journal and begin to read.

23

24 YEARS EARLIER, THE FIRST UNOPENED JOURNAL, NOW OPENED

W *alter*

It unfolded like a dream, the way he met Sarah and then—subsequently —Scotty. The expression "walking around in a fog" had never applied to anyone more, not even Borda, the hideous mythical witch who lived her life as one with the fog itself. Walter learned of Borda as a child when his father regaled him with stories of her as punishment when Walter wouldn't sleep at night. What sort of bedtime story doesn't involve Italian witches who blindfold and kill people just for walking around in the dark? His father's clear message was, *"Don't get out of bed and wake me up again if you know what's good for you."* The unclear message was his father's lasting disappointment in his only son and his affinity for taking it out on the kid at every opportunity. Walter was a teenager before he knew most dads didn't treat their kids this way.

He was an adult when he vowed never to have children. By the time he was forty, he actually meant it and folded his cards on the parenthood game.

And then Walter went to an event being held in his honor at a bar in downtown Malibu, and before he knew it, the cards picked themselves up and dealt a royal flush. Just like that. Jackpot. Game over. Walter won the ultimate prize.

Sarah.

And Scotty.

And you know what was the luckiest thing of all? They both seemed to love the same weird things he loved, always seemed interested in hearing his aimless ramblings, even when his words slurred or his thoughts all crashed together in a stumbling effort to make line-item sense of them, not an easy thing for Walter Lorry.

When you live with an illness such as Myotonic Dystrophy, success comes when things are approached one item at a time. Try to introduce two, and you'll wind up with a mind too jumbled to untangle.

The first night the little family slept under the stars was perhaps the best night of Walter's life, aside from the wedding, of course.

"But what about bugs?" Scotty had asked. "What if mosquitoes bite me or a lion comes up on the porch and eats us while we're sleeping?" Such a vivid imagination for such a young child, so many fears a kid his age shouldn't yet have.

"There's quite a big difference between the two," Walter said, laughing at the discrepancy of the mental image that filled his mind. "And I'm fairly certain I've never seen a lion roaming these streets, but I won't let either one of them eat you if they show up."

"Promise?"

Walter smiled. "I promise."

Sarah chose that moment to join them on the porch, walking out of the antique shop with three mugs of hot chocolate and a plate of sliced banana bread balanced on a tray in both hands. There was butter on the tray, along with a jar of peanut butter that didn't make sense to Walter. While peanut butter is a food group staple, he couldn't imagine what would possess someone to put it on a perfectly good slice of banana bread.

"What are we promising out here?" she said, handing a mug off to first Scotty and then Walter. She sat on one edge of Walter's cot, a bed for one that he was bound and determined to share. No space was too small for Sarah to fill, not his home, not his heart, and definitely not his bed. Not even a cot built for one.

"I'm promising Scott that I will not allow a lion— or an elephant or a giraffe or the Loch Ness monster if that is on the list of possibilities—to eat him. Not tonight or any night thereafter, cross my cold and hardened heart."

Sarah slid a questioning look between the boys. "First things first, let the record show that your heart is possibly the softest ever made. But second, I grew up in this area, and I can assure you that no lions are roaming the streets. Unless you bought us a home with a ready-made zoo and failed to tell me about it?"

Walter held up both hands. "Busted."

"That's what I was afraid of. But not to worry, Scotty. If Walter can't fight off ferocious animals, you can bet I will."

Scotty smiled then, his shoulders sagging in relief. He took a sip of his cocoa, then set the mug on the porch and slid onto his back to stargaze, both arms tucked behind his head. Within a few short moments, both his parents followed his lead. There was something about lying under the stars and letting them speak to you that soothed a troubled soul. Walter knew it, Sarah was learning, and one day Scotty would join the ranks of individuals who believed nature was the best remedy for what ailed you.

Nothing ailed Walter that night.

It would be a full six months before everything did.

But that night...

"This is nice," Sarah said, her soft voice reverent as she settled in next to her husband.

"Yes, it is." Walter nuzzled her neck, nearly forgetting they were supposed to be studying the heavens. Or maybe that's exactly what he was doing as he worshipped his wife.

"Promise me we'll do this every night forever and ever?" Scotty said, oblivious to the way his parents weren't even watching.

"Sleep under the stars?" Sarah asked.

"Yes, promise me!"

Sarah balked, but Walter smiled. "We might not sleep out here every night, but we'll plan to do this for at least a few minutes every night before bed. Deal?"

"Deal! But in the summer, when there's not any school, we can sleep out here," Scotty added as a caveat, always finding the loophole in any negotiation.

"Perfect. As long as we're physically able, we'll sleep out here under the stars. That way, no matter what happens every day, every evening will be a new adventure."

Scotty liked the sound of that.

A few minutes later, he was fast asleep.

"Do you believe in Santa Claus?" Scotty asked him a few hours later, now wide awake due to an owl hooting in the distance, the moon still high in the sky, stars twinkling overhead like they had forever to shine, like the sun wouldn't soon creep up to steal their spotlight.

"What?" When you're nearly forty-two, it's a special kind of torture to be ripped from a dream, especially when the source of that ripping is a six-year-old kid with a high-pitched voice.

"Santa Claus. Is he real? And do you believe in him?"

Walter rubbed his eyes and looked around for his wife, only to find her long gone into the inviting warmth of their pillow-top bed inside the house. Smart woman, that one. Now, how to answer this doozy of a question.

By deflecting, that's how. "Do *you* believe in Santa?"

"Walter." Scotty wasn't having it. "That's not what I asked. I want to know if he's real or not. So, is he?"

Walter cleared his throat. "Well, see..." Stalling usually worked wonders, but for some reason, right then, it wasn't. Finally, he went with the safest choice, the one he knew wouldn't get him in trouble with his wife. "Personally, I think he's real. And if he isn't, I darn well think he should be." Walter was proud of himself for covering his bases so thoroughly.

"Me too," Scotty said with a gap tooth grin. "I think Santa Claus is about the coolest man who ever lived."

Walter decided not to be too jealous of Scotty's declaration. After all, he was only human, and who could compete with a man who flies around the world delivering toys every Christmas Eve?

"I think he's the coolest, too," Walter said. "Plus, he has access to all the best gifts."

"Yeah," Scotty said, somehow bouncing in place while lying prone on the wooden porch. "That would be the coolest job ever. When I get big, I want to be Santa Claus. Then I can sneak into everyone's homes and fly!"

Walter smiled to himself at the combination, every kid's dream. "Then I suppose when I get big, I want to be Santa Claus too."

Scotty giggled. "You're already big." He dropped his voice to a whisper. "You could grow your beard out and everything. You already have the gray hair started. And your belly could get even rounder until..."

"What do you mean, *even* rounder?" Walter sat up in mock outrage and tossed his pillow at Scotty. "Is my son calling me fat?"

The boy giggled, threw the pillow back, and tucked his hands behind his head.

"You're not fat yet..." Emphasis on *yet*.

They both laughed up at the night sky, at least one of them imagining himself flying as he drifted back to sleep.

24

*S*cott

Next to Walter's head, a machine counts out his heartbeats, keeping time with the raindrops currently slapping against the hospital roof. There's a clip-on Walter's finger to measure his oxygen level, a full tumbler of water with an unused straw sticking out sitting on a tray next to his bed, and an overnight bag stuffed with a change of clothes and a paperback that Piper and I packed so that Walter would have something familiar with him when he woke up.

We've been here since yesterday. Walter is still asleep.

Whether temporarily or permanently remains undecided. With nothing else to do to pass the time, I've been reading the journals. First, the ones Piper had already read, in the order she read them. Then I opened that first sealed journal and read it out loud, nervous about sharing something so personal with someone I only just met but knowing without a doubt that she was an ally. When it comes down to it —strangers or not—we're on the same team.

There's something about Piper that I trust.

Plus, I like her. Already a lot more than I should. So much that I want her to know everything.

"DO YOU REMEMBER ANY OF THIS?" Piper asks me about the first unsealed journal. I don't answer right away. The lump in my throat makes speaking impossible.

I remember that night on the porch as clearly as if it had happened last week. It was the first time Walter had referred to me as "son" without being asked.

"Am I your son?" I used to pester over and over in that annoying way kids do when they're searching for a response different than the one you've already given. *"Of course, you're my son,"* Walter would reply. My insecurities began to ratchet each time Walter introduced us as "My wife, Sarah, and her son, Scott," to anyone meeting us for the first time. I knew Walter was just being polite; I even knew that

he thought of me as a son. I just wanted to know I was his son in the way my mom knew she was his wife. It's hard to be a kid when you're not sure who you belong to.

That night on the porch, I brought up Santa Claus for that very reason, figuring that since Walter had fully claimed me as a son, I could tease him like a dad. The "even rounder" thing became a running joke. *"I'd better not eat any birthday cake, or my stomach might get* even rounder," Walter would exclaim. *"Does this sweater make my belly look* even rounder?" *"I got invited to Paris for an art exhibit. I sure hope my* even rounder *stomach fits on the plane."* Walter was trim from riding his bicycle every night, the best form of exercise for his "condition" as his mom called it. I never knew what the condition was, but besides a limp he sometimes walked with, there wasn't anything wrong with my stepfather.

Nothing wrong I could see, at least. Later, people would claim all sorts of things. Now I'm wondering how many of those things were true.

More accurately, how many were lies?

"I remember all of it," I say to Piper.

"You remember the porch?"

I nod. "I remember the nights we slept out there and the ones where we just stayed out until the moon came all the way up. I remember a couple times when it started raining on our heads, the wind blowing so forcefully it scooted the cot sideways."

Next to me, Piper remains still for a long moment. "You think that's the reason he sleeps outside now? Because he's keeping the promise he made to you?" Her voice cracks on the last word, like emotion got the best of her. It's one thing to keep a promise; it's another to alter a whole life around it.

But I wondered the same thing while I was reading. "I think that might be a big part of the reason, but I think there might be more to it."

Piper shifts in place, sliding her leg up on the hospital sofa until her calf is pressed to my thigh and she's facing me head-on. "What do you mean?"

I lean back and lay my head on the sofa. "I'm not sure yet what I mean. I just think we don't know the whole story yet."

Piper leans her head back. "Then I guess you should open the next notebook."

I guess I should.

25

23 YEARS EARLIER, THE SECOND
UNOPENED JOURNAL, NOW OPENED

W *alter*

There are a few moments in life when you can plainly see the turning point, the exact moment life pivots from before to after, from how things are to how things used to be. The only problem is that you almost always see the change after the pivot, when it's too late to stop it, and it's impossible to change anything.

Walter knew he shouldn't have gone to the bar that night; he knew it but did it anyway because his wife told him her story for the first time, and he was angry. Not angry at her, per se, but at life dealing its blows one shot at a time, all of which felt aimed straight for Walter's head. Maybe this inner mentality made him a victim, but Walter had spent his childhood dodging mental blows from people like his dad, his teachers, his classmates. Then in his adulthood, he worked hard to convince himself hadn't deserved the ridicule. It takes years to undo something when you've been trained to think the opposite. Even with all his success, Sarah's story seemed to drag him right back to that place. The place that said, *"Life never stays happy, not for people like you."*

It was the "like you" part that replayed in his mind all afternoon. The "like you" that propelled him to the bar in the first place. The "like you" that took him back home in time to see that silver DeLorean pulling out of his driveway once again right as Walter turned onto his street. Later, he might wonder if he'd imagined the whole thing. Later, he might think himself paranoid. Later, he might wish he had chased the car down and demanded answers. But Walter was drunk and later didn't come. At least, not right away.

First, he had to get through the moment three days earlier when he walked into the garage to find his wife.

His wife. Barely conscious. Splayed out on the garage floor. Her leg bent at a weird angle. Blood pooling around her head. He called an ambulance. Crouched low next to the woman he loved. Grabbed at her everywhere, trying to find the source of... everything. What had happened, where it hurt, how to fix it, how to rewind the afternoon. It took Walter a full ten seconds to speak. But once he started, he couldn't stop, his inner monologue struggling to keep up with his rapid-fire questions.

"What happened?"

"Are you hurt?"

"Can you stand?"

"Can you tell me what happened?"

Sarah never answered, just kept mumbling the same thing over and over.

"Take care of Scott."

"Don't leave Scott."

"Take care of Scott."

"Don't leave Scott."

He promised that he would, and he wouldn't, over and over and over until he heard sirens, soft like an alarm clock when you're deep in the throes of sleep, loud like a bullhorn in your ear when you finally wake up. He didn't want an ambulance. He didn't need an ambulance. He didn't want to be in a place where he needed an ambulance.

But two minutes later, when his wife stopped breathing, and he walked back inside the house to find his son still watching an old episode of Andy Griffith like the day hadn't just flipped on its axis and shaken them into another galaxy entirely, all he could think was...

The DeLorean. I'm going to find the owner of that car and kill him.

Driving to the funeral home two days later, he saw the DeLorean parked outside the bank and pulled into a parking spot next to it. A few minutes later, the same man Walter saw exiting his garage three days prior walked out of the bank, then stopped in his tracks when he saw Walter waiting for him. It didn't help that Walter had just picked out his wife's casket. It didn't help that he was gutted and sleep deprived. It didn't help that he was simultaneously hungry and too nauseous to think of eating. It didn't help that he blamed himself for everything—for moving here, for opening an antique store, for walking out on his wife in a fit of self-pity and selfishness—or that he blamed the man for everything else. It didn't help that he was grieving and broken and senseless.

It wasn't smart that he got out of the car. Or that the next two minutes would set in motion the very event that fully ruined his life.

Walter approached the DeLorean.

"You, there!" he shouted, those two words coming out slurred and slick like he'd spilled them quickly without bothering to enunciate. It's how he spoke when he was agitated, nervous, angry, or sad, even worse when all four emotions intertwined. Usually, he hid himself safely at home and didn't emerge until he had full control of himself. Walter had lost control three days ago and didn't care to ever control himself again.

He should have. Oh, he should have.

"Are you talking to me?" the man said, looking over one shoulder and then the other like surely there was someone else behind him.

"Yeah, I'm talking to you." Walter kept walking and shoved him; the anger already at ninety from a starting point of zero, like it had been shot out of a cannon. He shoved him again before the guy knew what had happened, and the man fell backward.

"What the hell, man?" the man said from his spot on the ground, working to stand up. But Walter side-swiped his leg, keeping him effectively down. "Who do you think you are? Do you know who you're messing with?"

"I have no idea who I'm messing with, and I don't care. You assaulted my wife years ago, you piece of trash. And I saw you leaving my house earlier this week. Why were you there? Why were you there?" Walter's voice rose to hysterics with each question, and he kicked him, feeling a weird satisfaction when the heel of his shoe connected with the man's shin. Walter had never struck another person in his life. "Did you kill her? Did you kill her?"

"I don't know what you're talking about but keep your voice down." The man managed to rise and stumble a few paces back, out of Walter's reach. "Now, what is this about your wife?" He swallowed and looked around, his skin three shades of pasty white. "You're not making any sense."

Walter breathed heavily, heaving from the shoulders down.

"Sarah told me what happened back when she worked for you. Before she moved to California. Before she—"

Any fake concern disappeared before it had a chance to morph into sincerity.

"Ah, Sarah. Yes, she was a terrible worker. Had to fire her for always showing up late, napping on the job, crying at the drop of a hat. A mess of a woman, that one."

"But not so much of a mess to force yourself on her."

The man's mouth came unhinged on an incredulous laugh. "I did nothing of the sort. Is that what she's trying to claim?"

"She's not trying to claim anything. She's dead."

Behind them, a door opened, and the man sneered and stepped closer.

"Keep your voice down. One more word of this, and I'll ruin you. You hear me? I'll ruin your whole life. By the time I'm finished, no one around here will have anything to do with you. Not your friends, not your customers, not your family. Nobody."

Walter got right in the man's face. "Go ahead and try it. No one will listen to you when they find out you're the kind of man who assaults women and runs them out of town. The kind who fathers children with employees who aren't his wife." As soon as Walter said it, he wanted to stuff the words back in and swallow them deep into his gut.

"I'll bury you," the man threatened, low and menacing. Heat prickled the back of Walter's neck, but he was too far in to back down.

"Then you'd better find a shovel."

Footsteps came closer, heels that clacked on the pavement behind them.

"I'll ruin your life by the end of the week." Walter had never seen so much hate reflected in another human before. He felt dizzy with fear.

"Mr. Ratliff!" A woman called. "Are you all right? I was looking out the window and saw you fall! The most important man in town, falling out here on the sidewalk. I'll talk to the board about filling in the potholes, so it doesn't happen again! Mr. Ratliff? Ben? Are you okay?"

Ben Ratliff. The man had a name.

The woman kept talking until Mr. Ratliff fully assured her he was fine. He had the audacity to wink. She had the boldness to blush. Walter was going to be sick. *The most important man in town.* Walter's mind went to Scotty. What had he done, and how could he undo it?

"I'm fine, Mrs. Neely. Just a little clumsy this morning, but this kind man helped me up." He offered an arm to the woman, and she took it, clutching it a little too tight as the two of them walked back toward the bank.

"Oh, that was kind of him. For a minute, it looked like maybe he had pushed you..."

Mr. Ratliff turned back to Walter and laughed. "Of course not, Mrs. Neely. If anyone is going to do any pushing around here, it's me."

She laughed right back while Walter went cold.

Less than a week later, Ben Ratliff had indeed pushed.

Pushed for a court order.

Pushed Scotty out of his home.

Pushed another family to the forefront, a childless couple, former employees who desperately wanted a child.

Pushed the town into believing Walter was dangerous, crazy, and a threat to even himself. Not hard to do, considering his limp, and his increasingly raspy voice.

Pushed the judge—a close personal friend—to side with him.

Pushed Walter straight over the edge.

By the time he finished pushing, Walter had lost it all.

His wife.

His livelihood.

His will to live.

His son.

The only thing he had left was the store. In the end, no one cared to claim it. Not even the person who'd stepped forward all those months ago to challenge the Lorry's ownership. It was almost as if, once Walter had lost everything, the man had let Walter have the store just to watch him try to save it.

Not that Walter cared.

There comes a point in every battle when you lose the will to fight.

26

Piper

PScott doesn't move as I snatch the journal from his hand, my heartbeat ricocheting in my ears as I flip through the pages looking for the punchline. It can't be right. Scott must have mispronounced the name, translated it wrong, reversed a couple of letters, or something. My eyes scan Mr. Lorry's intricate penmanship—the same handwriting I've spent the last two weeks reading—and stop. Ben Ratliff. It's right there in perfect script, clear as day in inky black confusion. I drop the paper to my lap, feeling my blood grow cold in my veins and hot between my ears, a heady concoction that feels the opposite of good.

I'm going to faint.

From the look on Scott's face, so is he.

"When he referenced 'assault'..."

Oh god, oh god, what fresh hell is this? Ben Ratliff? Ben? I drop my head between my knees and command myself not to black out. The man is egotistical and entitled and generally awful, but this? I leave the chair to stretch onto my stomach and press my cheek into the cool hospital tile, closing my eyes against an onslaught of emotions, almost all of them making me sick.

It's only a second before I feel Scott's hand between my shoulder blades.

Scott. More wrapped up in this mess than I am.

"Piper, are you okay?" His words are caring, but his voice is lifeless. "Can I get you something? Some water? A plastic bag? Not sure why I said a plastic bag..."

For some unexpected reason, laughter bubbles up my throat, and I slowly sit up. When I look at Scott, the laughter fades. Nothing about this is funny. His childhood was difficult enough without adding this to the mix. Ignorance is bliss, but luck is short-lived. It's only a matter of time until it fully clicks inside his brain. I'm surprised it hasn't yet.

"I'm okay," I say, a palm to my forehead, trying to steady my racing brain. "Are you?" His hand stays on my shoulder, beginning to knead in a slow circle that would feel amazing under different circumstances. Right now, it only makes me sad. He's comforting me. It won't be long until he wants nothing to do with me.

He doesn't answer, only asks a question of his own.

"Who's Ben Ratliff?" Scott finally asks. "Do you know him?"

I wish to God I didn't, but yes, I know him. I've known him for years, except I'm only now finding out that maybe I never really did. Maybe none of us did. How well can we know someone, anyway? We all bury our secrets and hide our darkest thoughts out of fear of being judged or being different from everyone else. And that's okay. It's when we hide our worst actions that lead us into trouble, especially when those actions are sinister and ugly.

Possibly even criminal.

"I know him," I say, closing my eyes against what comes next.

"Who is he? The journal said he was well-known around here..."

I nod. "He owns Ratliff Masonry—the biggest manufacturing plant in Arkansas, next to Wal-Mart. He's a millionaire with more connections than your average LinkedIn profile. He's powerful. Extremely so."

"And he assaulted my mother?"

My insides drop to my shoes.

"It sounds that way."

Scott's eyebrows push together. "And he ran her out of town because she was..."

Pregnant.

"You're not gonna do that, are you, Walter?"

Walter frowned, unsure of Scotty's meaning. "Do what, Scott?"

"Keep leaving like the ocean. Stay for a minute, and then run away scared? Mom said my dad did that, and I just wondered if you would do it someday, too."

At the look on Scott's face, the words of Walter's journal rush back to me.

Because right there, that's when it happens. The moment Scott realizes what the journal was referencing, what it means for *him*. Scott's father never left. They fled from him, from the worst kind of person.

Scott's face goes slack, even more pale than it already is. Much the same as mine, I suppose. My heart splits down the middle at his shell-shocked expression.

No one wants to discover they're a child of assault.

Almost like no one wants to discover that the man they were engaged to has a brother he never knew about. A *younger* brother, which means Ben was married to Julia and had already fathered one-year-old Bryant when this happened. Or that Bryant's very brother is sitting right here in front of me, watching his life fall apart like Walter's did all those years ago. I look over at Walter, unmoving on the bed, machines keeping steady track of his vital signs while mine and Scott's go haywire here on the floor.

"Piper, how do you know Ben Ratliff?" His words are slow and measured like he already knows the answer. My brain is screaming, "approach with caution."

I look Scott in the eye. He deserves that much.

"Ben Ratliff is Bryant's father. He was nearly my father-in-law until I broke off my engagement last week. According to that journal, Ben Ratliff is your biological father. And according to Walter, Ben's the one who—"

"Assaulted my mother. Ran her out of town. Killed her when she dared to come back. Took me away from Walter out of spite," Scott fills in the blanks for me, the implication now a reality that makes me so sick the room starts to spin again. "When Walter found out what he did, Ben Ratliff made him pay."

I breathe slowly and look at Scott, working to gather my bearings. He looks hard back at me, questioning, fists opening and closing, whole body on alert, ready to seek his revenge. I can't let him do it. Can't let him act in anger. I look to Walter for help, but he remains unmoving, unconscious. I'm alone in this, back in that place that feels as familiar as breathing.

"What are you going to do?" I ask with a shake in my voice, one that weirdly matches the permanent shake in Walter's.

Scott stands up, and paces back and forth to the door and back again and again. Finally, he grabs his jacket and shoves both arms through the sleeves, and my chest crumbles as I watch what I suspect is the moment history begins to repeat itself. Violence isn't the answer, even if the target deserves it. I know it even if Scott doesn't.

"I'm going to find him," Scott says. I don't bother to argue. I haven't known him long enough to earn the right.

"And when you do?" I lean forward, my head in my hands, peeking reluctantly at him through splayed fingers.

"I'll figure that out when it happens," he says.

"Scott, please don't—"

"I'm leaving," he says, throwing open the hospital door. It bounces back in protest, angry at being tossed about.

"You're not going anywhere, son."

Scott stops walking, and I spin around.

Walter. He's awake, staring between both of us, his voice quiet but clearer than I've ever heard it. Scott stumbles back into the room, hand on his chest, the fight suddenly gone and replaced with tired relief.

"You're awake." He says it like a prayer, one I'm currently praying too.

"I'm awake. More awake than I've been in years. Now sit back down before you make the biggest mistake of your life."

Walter closes his eyes as he points to the sofa. Message clear. Scott isn't going anywhere.

I watch Scott do as he's told.

When he sits, I sit next to him and reach for his hand.

We stay that way for another hour, watching Walter, already back to sleep.

I LEFT the hospital an hour ago. When Scott walked out to make a phone call to reschedule the week's appointments, I saw a window and snuck out the back door. We've been here for two days with no change, and Scott has no plans to leave until Walter wakes up again. So, I left, at least for a bit.

I'm taking a short detour, a necessary one, before I lose my nerve.

I find him at work, same as always, his routine never wavering except for the occasional ribbon cutting or political event that might garner headlines. Ben Ratliff loves nothing more than the spot-light, even when the event has nothing to do with him. Case in point: our engagement reception the Ratliffs hosted at the country club only a few short weeks ago. Thoughts of that day momentarily stop me in my tracks. Despite Bryant's shortcomings, he's a good guy. Too protective and loyal to his mother, perhaps. Too eager for his father's approval, abso-lutely. But I loved him for a long time, and that doesn't just disappear overnight, even if it wasn't enough. Above all, I've learned love is a choice. And even though I've chosen to end my relationship with him, go a different direction, and save myself from a lifetime of being my future husband's forever second choice, that doesn't mean I've grown cold. Bryant doesn't deserve any of this, not the stigma, humilia-tion, or guilt by association. You can't help the family you're born into, but you sure can keep the patriarch of that family from ruining anyone else's life.

I walk into Ben Ratliff's office without bothering to knock. Startled, he looks up with a question in his eyes, one that is quickly replaced by disdain.

"You already called off your engagement to my son, Piper. What could you possibly want with me?"

"My apologies, sir," his assistant rushes in behind me before I can answer, apologizing on my behalf even though I'm not one bit sorry. "I told her you were very busy, but she came in anyway..."

"I see that. Anita, please escort Ms. Moore out of the building. And please make certain

that—"

"I'm not going anywhere," I say. My words are firm, my determination delivered on a threat. *Have me escorted out, and you'll regret it.* Ben must sense a problem, must hear my hidden meaning because he pauses and leans back in his chair to study me. I've never challenged him, not once in more than a decade of eating dinner with him across the table, attending his many fundraisers and social events, listening to his lame dad jokes on repeat, laughing next to Bryant at every unfunny thing. I can almost see the scales tipping in his brain as he weighs my sudden anger and assesses it against his options. Not a smart move considering I'm madder than I've ever been, and he's fresh out of them. "Tell your secretary to leave," I say with a nod to the woman still wringing her hands inside the doorway, never once taking my eyes off Ben.

He visibly swallows. I wish I could enjoy his discomfort more, but I can't. "That'll be all, Anita," he finally says. "Please close the door behind you." When she leaves, Ben sets the pen down on his desk and strikes a casual pose, his forearms resting in front of him. "What can I help you with, Piper? Do you need money? A recommendation letter? Me to smooth things over with my son, perhaps?" I nearly laugh because, of course, he thinks I'm here to beg for some service I'm desperate for him to provide. Then again, maybe I am. Suddenly, I'm hit with an idea. I take a deep breath. My list of demands has nothing to do with begging. Or Bryant.

"Actually, yes, I do need money. I need a big, fat check donated to Walter Lorry's antique store, and I need a press release telling the whole tri-state area why they should shop there and only there. Then I need you to make every piece of artwork inside his personal collection available at your next fundraiser with a minimum bid that he decides, assuming there are any at all. And then I'm going to need another check made out to Silver Bell Memorial Hospital for the entire amount of Walter Lorry's ongoing hospital bills. I'm sure I'll have more demands later, but that should cover it for now."

Ben laughs, outraged. "That crazy old man? Why in God's name would I ever do any of that?"

I inch closer to his desk and look down at him. So powerful in his Italian leather chair. So polished and well-dressed, from his silk suit to his professional manicure to the Botox, I'm one-hundred percent certain he gets four times a year to obliterate any trace of frown lines. What a sad, sad man. I lean forward, both palms flat on the mahogany desk and look him straight in the eye.

"You'll do that because of Sarah Jones and her

son Scott who looks strikingly similar to your son Bryant—I can't believe I'm just now seeing it. You'll do that for Walter Lorry because of everything you did to his wife and child. You'll do that because if you don't, I'll go to the police. You'll do that because after I go to the police, I'll go to Bryant, Julia, and your entire board at Ratliff Masonry. You'll do that because if you don't, you'll regret *not* doing it for the rest of your life." Walter was right when he told Scott that some decisions made in haste are decisions you regret forever. For me, this isn't one of them. "And just so you know," I continue, "I'm not the only one who knows what you've done, so don't try to mess with Walter or run me out of town or...try to come after me or *hurt me* in any way." I say that last part on a hunch, and he flinches. "Do you understand what I'm telling you?"

Ben's face drains of color, and that's when reality hits. He did it. He did all of it. He ruined a young girl's life, traumatized, and possibly harmed her, and never even hesitated to feel bad about it.

Ben Ratliff sniffs. "Is there anything else?" The words come out on a bite, angry. But he's also scared. He's backed into a corner with no way out, and we both know it. But there is one more thing, even if I did only just now think of it.

"Yes, there is. I'm going to need you to resign from Ratliff Masonry, effective immediately."

He scoffs. "That's too far. You're out of your mind if you think I'm going to do that."

I tilt my head. "Am I, though? From my estimation, none of this is going far enough."

"And who is supposed to run the business if I don't? I created this company. No one knows this job like I do."

I stare at him, placing random puzzle pieces together in my brain until I find the perfect fit. I shrug. "Bryant does, and if not, he can learn. Give the job to him. He'll figure all this out in no time." It's the least I can do after calling off the wedding, an offering of sorts for publicly walking out of his life. "And Ben?" I say, my back to him as I head for the door. I'm done here, hopefully for good.

"What?" The word is a sharp, steel blade pressed to my neck, but it doesn't cut me. Mentally, I run a finger down the blade and dare it to draw blood. It doesn't.

"I want everything done by tonight."

"I didn't push her off that ladder, you know. She fell, plain and simple."

I turn then. The words should make me feel a modicum better, but they don't.

"Did you do anything to help her, or did you just watch her lay there and bleed?"

When he doesn't respond, I know that's exactly what he did. Nothing. He saw a way out and took it, damning anyone in his wake. Damning Sarah to her slow and torturous fate. Damning Scott to a life he didn't ask for.

"Just because you didn't push her doesn't mean you weren't the cause of her death."

My words hit their mark. Bullseye in the center of his chest. I turn and walk out of the office, leaving Ben to sit among the wreckage he's created in his own life. Fitting since he already blew up Walter's. And Sarah's.

And Scott's.

I don't look back.

Honestly, I don't expect I'll ever have to.

27

*S*cott

She told me what happened after she came back to the hospital last week. At first, I was angry. This is my story, not hers, and I should decide how it ends. The feeling lasted an hour, and then it vanished. I don't belong to this town, and this town doesn't belong to me—not the people, the memories, or the feelings. They were never mine to deal with in the first place.

After that, I was relieved. Thankful, even. There are some people I want to waste my time on, but a bullish, entitled narcissist who would hurt my birth mother, his own wife and son, and the first real father I ever knew isn't it. Yes, it's wholly possible Ben Ratliff is my biological father, but sometimes, biology is flawed. When that happens, providence

tends to take over. We're all a product of our circumstances—good and bad. Sometimes it takes both to
lead us toward the best outcome.

Outcomes like my adoptive parents. The best I
could ask for, considering how my life spun out of
control. It isn't every day that eight-year-old boys
find love and acceptance from families who take
them in as one of their own. I found that, even if the
origin of my human chess game was controlled by a
man who didn't have my best interest at heart. Providence, God, Fate—call it what you want, but I think
my placement in the Crawford home came straight
from heaven.

Jesus does indeed love the little children.

Outcomes like Walter Lorry. A man who spent
thirty-six months of my formative years teaching me
how to nurture a life I still appreciate today. Nature,
a night sky, constellations, a love for astronomy, even
a career in helping the less fortunate make the best
of their God-given situations—whether physically
handicapped or mentally challenged. I knew I
wanted to work with special needs children from a
young age; it's only now that I know where the desire
came from. Walter himself. I didn't remember much
about him, but I did remember the significant things
in the same way a child forced to ride a bike has a
lasting sense of accomplishment. You might not be

able to pinpoint the reason, but you know it's there all the same.

Outcomes like Piper. She's responsible for every event that's unfolded in the past nine days, and I'm grateful to her for that. Because of her, so many questions I've asked myself for years have now been answered. How can I fault her for defending me? How can I blame her for taking matters into her own hands when in her hands are where I found answers?

I can't, that's how. I won't, that's for certain.

Besides, I kind of like being around her. So much so, I haven't decided when to leave. As for today, that decision is being made for me once again. Turns out I don't mind letting providence take over for a bit longer.

"Please be careful going up the steps," I say to Walter for what must be one too many times, considering how he scoffs at me.

"I might be old, but I can walk." He holds onto Piper's arm in a painfully slow shuffle up a front staircase that might as well be Mount Kilimanjaro for how treacherous it feels. Piper looks over her shoulder at me for help, and I quickly move from overseeing things from behind to hooking an arm around Walter's waist on the other side of him. I have a flash of playing "swing me" while walking between my parents as a kid. The unclear part is which parents are tied to that memory. Life is certainly a cycle.

"We all know you can walk," I say. "It's the 'walking without falling' that we're not so sure about."

Piper snorts at the same time Walter hums at me. I'm quite certain the song in his head is filled with expletives.

"Walter, please be careful. I still have about a million things to do in this shop before I go back to my normal job, and taking care of you isn't one of them." She's kidding, of course. From the moment they discharged him from the hospital an hour ago, we both knew caring for Walter had become a shared full-time job. And considering we both have actual full-time jobs, now we're equally double-employed. Still, the thought of her leaving fills me with dread, even if her home is right across town, even if I know I'll see her again.

"I don't need you to take care of me," Walter says. "I need you to alphabetize the books." Piper smiles at me over Walter's head, but her eyes look sad. According to her, Walter's words are even more slurred than before, like a man numbing a breakup with an all-night bender. Walter sounds like he's a dozen shots in, but he hasn't had a single drink. No one knows if this is a permanent effect of the stroke or something that will get better with time. The hardest part is that we won't know until time passes.

"Joke's on you. I've already alphabetized the books. Tomorrow, I'm renting a dumpster and setting fire to half your merchandise."

"Touch my things, and you're fired."

When Walter's head snaps around to glare at her, I bark out a laugh. Piper is beautiful and sexy, and caring to a fault, but she's also funny as hell. I'm quickly realizing that it might be my favorite thing about her, which is saying a lot, considering I can't stop staring at her backside, her front side, and all parts of her in between.

"You're not paying me as it is, Walter. You can't fire anyone when you don't have a match. Which brings us back to the dumpster, I guess..." She winks at me over Walter's head, making me laugh again. Midway through, I realize my throat has developed a lump, and I'm still staring. This woman is trouble, and I'm falling headfirst into it. I look away and help guide a still-grumbling Walter into his store.

Our original plan was to bring him home to the house next door, but he insisted we come here to the shop instead, claiming a need to be with his things lest someone break in or needs assistance with the merchandise. When I alluded to him not being able to help with much, he grumbled, so we appeased him by having a hospital bed delivered to the back room of the store. The cot was pushed aside, and in came the bed. Starting tomorrow, a nurse will arrive every morning at ten o'clock to assist with showers, administer physical therapy, and start Walter on the road to getting back to normal again...or to whatever version of normal awaits him when this is all over. We never discussed the matter of entering his home again. For some reason, Walter doesn't want to.

I suspect that reason has something to do with me. Maybe it's the bad memories, or maybe it's the good ones. Maybe it's the fact that he doesn't want to revisit any of them in his current state when he doesn't have much strength to face them. Or maybe I'm wrong, and his reluctance doesn't have anything to do with me. No matter. I'm not dense enough to push it for now. Give me a couple weeks, however, and I will.

We shuffle toward the back room and settle him onto the bed. It's a chore, moving a grown man into position when his muscles are too weak to help, even a man as frail as Walter. But I know what I'm doing, and within seconds he's settled in place with a blanket pulled up to his chest to stop the shivering, a common side effect of medicinal withdrawal; in this case, morphine to keep him asleep. Stroke patients need rest, though most are highly agitated at first. In

Walter's case, they stay agitated for their full hospitalization, quite the lucky break for the nurses on call.

"Can I get you anything?" I ask, standing back to look at him lying in bed while Piper fluffs his pillow and pulls at the ends of his blanket. There's so much ground to cover with Walter that I still don't know how far we'll travel. But if all goes well, I'll get my answers. I just hope the rest of my life doesn't blow up in the process. "Water? Ice chips? A book?"

He shakes his head once, and I take a step back. The man needs space, not the in-your-face meddling of a kid he hasn't seen in decades. Feeling lost and a bit useless, I glance at Piper for direction. Thankfully, she's a little further down the road with Walter than me.

"All right, we're going to leave you here so we can get some work done, but I want you to ring this bell if you need anything." Piper picks up the cheap antique hand bell, gives it a shake, and then sets it on the table in front of Walter. He nods and then closes his eyes. Something tells me we'll hear that bell all afternoon after his nap. For now, it's time to help Piper clean up the mess that makes up Walter Lorry's antique store.

~

"WHAT ARE THESE?" I opened a closet a few moments ago only to be hit with a stack of framed photos so high and deep they were impossible to organize. I pull out a black and white litho of Bing Crosby with 'Mr. Christmas' scrawled across the top in red-ink calligraphy, so striking that my heartbeat doubles in speed. This is Walter's work; I remember it from my childhood.

"Write it up there, way at the top!"

The words crawl out of an old memory, one I can't quite reach. But it's there, waiting for me to touch it. The memory fizzles when Piper speaks up.

"Those are Mr. Lorry's from a long time ago. There are dozens more in there just like them," she says, awe lacing her tone. "Wait until you see the one of Madonna. I would have stolen it if I thought Walter wouldn't catch me in the act. Madonna is one of my favorites."

Material Girl blasting through the living room speakers, the three of us dancing in circles while my mother paraded around with purple ring pops and party-store Mardi Gras beads. "Experience has made me rich..."

Madonna was my mother's favorite, too.

The memory hits strong, making about as much sense as the last one. I dig through the frames until I find the one Piper was referring to and pull out the photo. And there they are, the lyrics to Material Girl written in their entirety across her face in calligraphy so beautiful it's hard to reconcile how the man in the hospital bed in the back room could have managed to create the words.

I pull out another and freeze.

It's a stunning photo of a small boy wearing a white t-shirt and navy shorts standing at the edge of the ocean, feet sinking into the sand until his heels are buried. A smile fills his face like the photo was snapped after a joke, and he's deep into a giggle. Unlike the other designs containing intricate letters scrawled across the faces of the subjects in Mr. Lorry's signature style, the words "Tiny Beach Boy" are written in small letters across the bottom of the canvas—as though this photo deserved more reverence because the subject at hand was special. I now know for a fact that he was.

The boy in the picture is me.

"Build a sandcastle with me!"

I remember that day like it happened yesterday, the way I ran back and forth from the ocean to the sand, gathering as much water and seashells as possible to make the castle stand taller. I remember talking with Walter that day, asking a million questions, him ready with answers as though he anticipated them before we came.

"You won't do that, will you Walter?"

"Do what, Scotty?"

"Keep leaving like the ocean, run away scared? My

dad never stayed, so does that mean you'll leave some-
day, too?"

Walter looked at my mom, then at him.

"I'm not going anywhere, Scotty. I already made my
choice."

"And you're staying forever?"

"I'm staying forever."

But he hadn't stayed forever, had he? Walter left
like everyone else, leaving me to forge a new path
alone. No mother, no stepfather, no more singing in
the living room to songs blasting from the old record
player while fake jewelry hung from our limbs and
spun from the ceiling fan above. No one who loved
me until my new parents stepped up to adopt me.

But then I remember it.

I see it clearly.

I peel my eyes off the photo and look at Piper.
Really look at her. She stands in front of me, the
antique store in the background, and it hits me, the
full force of it slamming into my gut like I've been
punched.

I walk toward the front door and throw it open,
then take the steps two at a time until I reach the
bottom. The main house looms ahead, not nearly as
big as it seemed when I was a child, but somehow
bigger than life itself when faced with the prospect
of reentering it now.

"What are you doing?" Piper asks breathlessly, coming to stand next to me.

"I'm going inside," I say.

"But Walter never lets anyone in," she says, adding with resignation and a hefty dose of curiosity, "Fine, I'll go with you."

"Way to stick to your principles." I laugh.

"They aren't my principles; they're Walter's. And if you're going, I'm going too. I've been waiting for this day for weeks."

At this point, Walter can't stop us; honestly, I doubt he would even if he were healthy enough to try. I think this is what people mean when they ask you to save them from themselves. They want it done even when they would rather not witness the moment it happens. I'm here to see it happen, and I guess Piper is along for the ride.

"All right then, let's go in." There's a key under the front mat, a cliché in the worst form, but thankfully creativity doesn't stretch to Walter's hiding spots. I use the key to unlock the door, then gently push it open. The slight scent of my mother is the first thing I notice like an opened bottle of her favorite cologne was left out all these years. Orange leaves and coffee mixed with cinnamon and old paper, an oddly specific scent but immediately recognizable. It comforts even as it hurts.

We step inside. Piper inhales softly next to me, and I reach for her hand.

We see the words at the same time, words I remember him beginning when I was a child. Neither one of us moves out of reverence to his storytelling.

"On June twelve, nineteen ninety-eight, my life changed forever..."

There, right above the fireplace mantle, Walter wrote his first sentence. The one telling the story of the day he met my mother, *"I walked into the bar and straight into a future I'd been dreaming of my entire life."* And then, subsequently, me.

"Write it up there, way at the top!"

My name.

Alexander Scott Lorry.

Written in big, bold letters. Walter added the last name unofficially even though the adoption process wasn't complete. He continued with stories of cross-country moves and ailing grandmothers, Of campfires and front porch campouts. Of ball games and piano lessons. Of new puppies named Jack and surprise Christmas gifts to me. Of court dates and paper filings. Of impending fatherhood and hopes for my growing up years.

Walter's original words—the ones I remember—stopped there on the bottom corner of the living room wall. It ended on a happy note. A promise for the long future ahead, a future that stopped as abruptly as it started.

He continued writing the story after he lost my mother.

After he lost me.

On the kitchen wall, he wrote of sadness and death. Of loneliness and heartbreak. Of time spent searching and nights spent grieving. Of promises made and promises kept, promises broken and hopes dashed forever.

"Please watch over Scotty."

"I promise I'll stay forever."

In the front bedroom, he wrote of hateful townsfolk, and children caught spying. He wrote of a young girl named Piper who showed up to demand his help but wound up staying to help him instead. Words are scrawled everywhere like they've replaced wallpaper, starting with beautifully artistic calligraphy from the early days and ending with the shakiness of age. Piper and I walk from room to room, taking it all in, reading quietly side by side over the hour it takes to finish.

When we reach the last bedroom, I look over to find Piper with tears streaming down her cheeks, using the back of her hand to dry them off. She offers me a sad smile that reflects the way my chest feels. Tight with longing for what might have been, but light with the new reality of what once was.

What is. What has been this whole time, even if none of us were around to witness it.

In the end...Walter kept his word. He stayed forever.

It was the rest of us who left.

WALTER IS asleep when we check on him, hands folded across his chest so gracefully it's difficult to imagine how badly they shake during the day. We stay with him for a long while, quietly watching side by side, me imagining how much he's lived through, his life rising with fame and falling with heartbreak, all in the span of a few short years. The only comforting part is that Walter Lorry has lived in the way most people only dream about—fully and passionately, experiencing nearly every emotion one can feel. We should all take a lesson from him.

I look over at Piper.

"I think I need to read the last journal," I whisper. It's time to wrap it up, lay it on the table, and discover everything there is to know about the man I once called my father. The only way to discover the gift is to open the package. That's the moment we begin to accept the present for what it is. I need to hear the rest of Walter's story to fully write mine, however messy the ending may be. I think of my job.

I think of my adoptive parents. I think of Walter and Piper, and that's when I'm certain.

The ending can't be all that messy when I've been blessed with so much good.

"I'll get it," Piper whispers back, rummaging through a shoebox, finding the journal in question, and handing it to me. "Want to read it in private?"

I shake my head. Piper's been here for all of it, and I want her here now. "I'll read it out loud to you, same as always."

She smiles, and my heart thuds.

Always.

It's a heavy, weighted word. One that I'm happy to carry for as long as I can.

28

TEN YEARS AGO, THE LAST UNOPENED JOURNAL—FINALLY OPENED

W*alter*

Scientists say there are two hundred billion trillion stars in the sky, and I've spent the last fifteen years counting half of them. There isn't a lot to do as a single fatherless man with no parents, no family, no job to speak of, and zero friends, so I wait here for my friends to come back. Or my son to discover what happened and come find me one day. Whichever comes first, even if none of them do.

So, I sleep out here on the porch.

Under the stars is where I feel closest to you. It's where I promised I'd be if we were ever separated. Do you remember that conversation? I've never forgotten it. *"Look up at the night sky, and it'll be like I'm right here with you. Like I never left at all."* So, I'm out here every night, even as I hear the whispers and rumors circulating around me while I'm trying to sleep. I know the town thinks I'm crazy, an eccentric loner who's off in the head, maybe even that I somehow got rid of my family in a sinister way I'll never speak of out loud. I know they think I'm different, not mentally there, odd in mannerisms and speech. I even know the kids think I'm Santa Claus, that I fly around at night in the off-season, biding my time for Christmas Eve.

What they don't know is I wish I were him so that I could fly from house to house until I found you. What they don't know is that it doesn't matter what the town thinks. That it only matters what you think, what your mother thinks. Because when you find a place to belong, the rest of the world fades away into the background, like white noise that you slowly forget to notice. The only thing I ever noticed that deeply was your mother. Was you.

Now that you're both gone, all I care about is keeping my word.

I promised to love you both forever, and I will.

I promised that you could find me out here, so I stayed.

I promised to take care of you forever, so I try to the only way I know how.

Under the stars, night after night, offering up

prayers of safety and comfort to God, I hope He is listening, so He can tell you for me.

You're loved.

You're cared for.

You're my son.

As long as the day is light, the night is dark, and the stars continue to shine through the blackness, I count stars like diamonds as I connect them in the sky. Like art. Like a painting. Like a love story that glows bright, even when the light is out, and you have to squint to see it.

Dear God, keep her with You.

Dear God, keep him safe.

Dear God, keep me strong.

One star...two stars...three stars...four stars...

I never make it to five.

By then, the tears flowing from my eyes make it too hard to see.

EPILOGUE

One Year Later

Piper

It's Christmastime, and the antique store has never been so busy...or so well-organized. Lighted trees flank the front windows, large red and green and gold ornaments hanging so heavily from every branch the tree practically droops. A child's train carrying various antique books circles the room from tracks mounted high along the ceiling. A whistle sounds in thirty-second intervals to the delight of shoppers—albeit to the public annoyance of me. Spend two hours working here and you'll see what I mean. But Walter loves it. Scott loves it. And although you'll never hear me admit it, I love it too.

Funny how pouring a little money into a run-down store can make a very big difference.

And how a lot of money can sometimes change everything.

The day after we found Walter's life story written all over the walls of the house next door, the store had a visitor. One Mrs. Anita Frankel, secretary to Ben Ratliff, too old to be a mistress—thank goodness —but not too old to be unaware that something odd was happening, judging by her fidgety demeanor and nervous expression. Her eyes darted everywhere but rarely landed on me. They did seek out Scott when he walked in from the back, and she froze in place as she watched him. A woman in the know, it seemed, though it floored me how many people in this town were able to participate in the destroying of another man's life so easily. Almost as if they enjoyed it, like kicking a man already down was their collective way to stay in shape.

"Can I help you?" I asked that day, curious but also certain about exactly what she wanted. I smiled to soften the effect of my disdain.

"Y...yes," she said with a shake in her voice. "Could you please give this to Walter Lorry from Ben Ratliff?" My heartbeat pounded painfully in my neck as she handed me an envelope. It's one thing to suspect, but another thing entirely to know.

"Sure. Can I ask what it's regarding?"

The woman sent me a sharp look then. "I'm quite certain you already know what it's regarding. Just give it to Mr. Lorry, please." And with that, she walked out, the door slamming behind her as she left.

"Should I take it to him?" I asked Scott, already anticipating his answer.

"I'll open it," he said, holding out his hand. Ever since reading that last journal, Scott hadn't believed in waiting for time to pass. Or in waiting for permission. "Walter's still asleep." Apart from a single hour the night before and an even shorter window that morning, Walter hadn't been awake much. Doctors expected that to change soon, but it hadn't changed yet. What was different was Scott; a stranger to Walter and me only last week, he had quickly stepped up to care for the man like the son he was once destined to be. To hear Scott say it, two fathers are better than one if the option presents itself. As a woman who would be forever missing her mother, I tended to agree that he was the lucky one between us.

Scott opened the envelope.

Inside it was a check from Ratliff Masonry made out to Walter Coleman Lorry for half a million dollars. Along with it was a copy of a company-wide email and a separate newspaper clipping urging the town to shop at Lorry's antique store now that the Ratliff family were personal investors.

Though we both knew the Ratliff's would never see a dime of Walter's money.

Underneath the email was a press release announcing Ben Ratliff's resignation as President of Ratliff Masonry. The letter explained that Ben had wanted to retire for years, and now he and Mrs. Ratliff were relocating to Florida while Bryant Ratliff took over the family business.

It was only a matter of time before the line of Silver Bell single ladies began to form in front of Bryant. In all likelihood, they already had.

Honestly, good for him.

I FIND Scott on the front porch, where I've found him nearly every night this past year. It's a sobering thing to know someone spent a lifetime waiting for you to catch up, so sobering that it leaves you feeling unstable like you owe a debt you can't possibly repay over a lifetime of trying. But Scott is working hard to repay Walter for all those years, and the only thing I know to do is join him in the pursuit.

I set a mug of hot cocoa on the table in front of him and clutch my own mug in both hands to warm up. The early December night is a cold, almost bitter one. But Scott never skips time on the porch, so I stay here too. Love means sticking things out even when you're uncomfortable. It means staying true to your word and strong in your convictions, never giving up even when you want to. It doesn't mean comparing, neglecting, or criticizing—something that took me years to learn and a lifetime to stop putting up with. It's silly that it took me sitting on a small-town front porch night after night to learn it, but sometimes when you refuse to learn a lesson the easy way, you're forced to learn it by shining a light on your own ridiculousness, and that way is much harder to endure.

I faced my ridiculousness head-on. Got blinded in the process. And then began to see more clearly in the aftermath.

Today, I might be freezing, but I'm happy. I like to think my mother would be happy too if she were here to see me. Her dream for me might look different, but I think we would both agree this life turned out better.

"What are you doing all the way over there?" Scott says, looking across the outdoor sofa at me, patting the spot beside his knee for me to slide over towards. Scott bought the furniture last week, declaring the cot uncomfortable and unacceptable for stargazing. Walter balked at first but reluctantly admitted to liking the sofa cushions better than that thin piece of military fabric he'd used for over a decade. Besides, Walter doesn't sleep outside as much anymore; other than the occasional night he wants to feel closer to Sarah, he no longer has a reason to.

I laugh with an eye roll, and do as I'm told, crawling across the space between us and draping my legs across Scott's thighs like I do every night. His hand comes around my waist to knead my right hip, and warmth travels up me until I'm almost sweltering with want. So much for freezing. I fist his hair with my free hand and bend down to kiss him long, slow, deep, and appreciative. Not for the first time, not for the tenth, but each time more exciting than the last. It turns out that when you find someone who loves you for you—flaws and all—it makes you feel like flying. Scott is the kindest and most caring man I've ever met, and just like Walter felt with Sarah, I'm planning to stay. When you know what you've got, it isn't an option to let go, not if you can help it.

I turn until I'm straddling him on the sofa, my legs on each side of his waist until he sits forward, and I wrap them around him completely. His hands find the strip of skin between my sweater and the waistband of my jeans, and I pull in a breath and press my lips behind his ear, his neck, his shoulder blade. After all, Walter is asleep, and there's no one out here but us.

"Gross. I can't believe you like doing that." At the sound of J.D.'s voice, Scott and I launch apart like we've been doused with a bucket of ice water. I guess, in a way, we have been.

"J.D., what are you doing back here? Didn't you go home an hour ago?" I straighten my shirt, thanking the blessed Lord above that the kid can't see my flaming red face.

"It's Friday night, and I was bored." He says this like it's so obvious, plunking himself down in the middle of us on the sofa. I smile over his head at Scott. To a passerby, we might look like a little family of three. As it stands, we're just three night-watchers enjoying another evening on the porch; a routine, one we learned to appreciate thanks to the influence of a formerly cranky old man. "Can you help me find the Big Dipper?" he asks. "It's kinda hard to see it tonight with the moon being so bright."

Two things about this: J.D. has never quite found the Big Dipper, even though he pretends to. And he's right; it is bright tonight. It's the first clear night with a full moon in months, and the added light to the sky has dimmed the stars a bit. But Scott isn't deterred. He points to the sky, his finger tracing a tiny arc over our heads.

"Can you see it, J.D.? If you relax your eyes a bit and look a little to the left, you'll be able to make it out, the way the stars make a box of four in each corner, then dip and narrow off to the left like they're forming a handle for pouring. Look really hard, and you'll find it."

It doesn't escape my notice that this is how Walter explained it to younger Scott in the journals all those years ago. A lump forms in my throat at the thought of history repeating itself in such a sweet way.

"I see it!" J.D. says. At first, I have my doubts, but then he traces the stars himself. One by one, corner to corner, as the Big Dipper sits proudly in the sky. I study it, marveling at the wondrous creation for a long reverent moment until J.D. speaks again.

"But what's that?" he asks.

I frown, unsure where he's pointing. I look over at Scott and shrug. He's the star expert, so he should be the one to answer, but he seems as clueless as me.

"What's what?" I ask, looking toward the sky again.

"That. There on the ceiling. What *is* that?"

I look at the ceiling. Look closer. Lit up tonight, thanks in part to the full moon and its brightness, and the Christmas tree lights shining from the window.

"Scott, what is that? It looks almost like—"

Scott sits forward at the same time the front door

creaks open behind us, and Walter steps out. I look back at him, my mouth open, but I'm met with a simple smirk.

"Finally discovered my secret, did you?"

But Walter isn't talking to me. He's talking to J.D.

The boy's eyes go wide. So wide they fill most of his face. I shake my head at the absurdity of it all.

"Walter, what did you do?" I ask, barely containing a laugh.

The old man shrugs. "I figured it was time to come clean. So, I drew them in magic ink, which only shows up when the moon hits it right."

J.D. gasps and jumps up with a breathy, "I knew it." He's so awestruck that I almost feel bad he'll grow up someday and learn the truth.

"What am I missing?" Scott says, still studying the ceiling for a clue. It's right there above him, where it's been all along. All of us grownups were just too serious to notice until now. All of us but Walter that is. He has the heart of a child tucked inside the body of an old man. Either that, or he has a sick sense of humor and enjoys pranking little kids who spy on him for fun.

Because right above our heads is a drawing of the house next door.

And eight grazing reindeer all scattered in the front yard.

And a very life-like Walter standing on the roof, overseeing them all.

With giant pair of magnificent wings spread across his back.

The mural is entitled: "Confession," as though this is a testimony, a secret tucked away underneath a porch for only the stealthiest eyes to see. As though Walter was caught, and his only escape was to fly.

Much like J.D. does right now.

While the adults hold back laughter, the boy launches off the porch and runs away to tell his friends.

THE END

ACKNOWLEDGMENTS

The biggest thank you goes to my dad for telling me the story of an old man in his town who looked like Santa Claus...of how he and the other kids in town were enraptured by him...of how no one knew anything about him except that he had remarkable handwriting. From there, this book was born. Stories are all around us, guys. I'm thankful to have a dad who has spent my whole life recounting them.

To my sisters—Tracy Steelman and Emily Mincks— because they've been my true day ones without faltering (much), and also because I got in trouble for forgetting to mention them in my last book. I'll never make that mistake again. I love you to the moon.

To Christy Barritt, Conni Cossette, Nicole Deese, and Tammy Gray for listening to my many, many, story ideas, helping me plot them, and threatening to kick me out of our group if I didn't start writing them. Haha just kidding (mostly). I love you ladies and would never want to write without you.

To the Arkansas town I grew up in for nurturing my imagination. When I was a kid, I couldn't wait to escape. As an adult, I keep coming back. Life, you know?

To Andrew, Matthew, Nikki, Hampton, Ellison, Isaac, Kailey, Ezra, Luke, Hannah, Owen, Jonathan, Emma, and Zac. To Angelia, Bart, Mark, Hali, Stephen, Christian, Ty, Kirsten, and Alek. To Dad, Mom, Kent, and Marsha...Thank you for making my world a brighter place to live.

To my immediate family: Doug, Jackson, Lilly, Landon, Rowan, Naomi, Whitney, and baby Matayo (coming soon!). To my dogs and cats and fish and Guinea pigs and whatever animal I'll face in my future. I love you more than anything.

To my readers. Thanks for staying with me, even though you never know what you're going to get next. I appreciate you a thousand times over for letting me live my dream.

OTHER BOOKS BY AMY MATAYO:

They Call Her Dirty Sally

The Party Planning Committee

Only Time Will Tell

Before Time Runs Out

The Reunion

The Last Shot

The Aftermath

The Waves

Lies We Tell Ourselves

The Whys Have It

The Thirteenth Chance

Christmas at Gate 18

The End of the World

In Tune with Love

Sway

A Painted Summer

Love Gone Wild

The Wedding Game

They Call Her
Dirty Sally

by Amy Matayo

"Sticks and stones may break my bones
but words will never hurt me."

--nursery rhyme, and the first lie we learned in
school

PROLOGUE
OCTOBER 1998

I*s a life defined by circumstances, or do circumstances define a life?*

I've been asking myself that same question this whole drive. Like most men nearing thirty, I like to think I'm the master of my own destiny. More and more lately, I'm finding that belief to be nothing more than a narcissistic pipe dream designed to make slightly self-conscious guys like me feel better about themselves. Especially because all the research I've done lately points in every opposing direction.

How can you be the master of anything when life chops you at the knees every time you try to stand up?

We all hear about the positive scenarios. The one where a third-generational inner-city kid breaks out of the violent gang his father and grandfather, and great-grandfather all belonged to, graduates from college, and then becomes the poster child for the phrase, "if you just put your mind to it, anything is possible."

Or the prom queen who sleeps with her boyfriend once, gets pregnant at sixteen, raises that baby as a single mom and puts her life on hold for two decades, then becomes a nurse and every third person calls her reinvention story "inspiring." You know, the same people who shunned her when she was an unwed teenage mother and had nothing to offer but a bullseye labeled Gossip About Me on her chest.

Or the drug addict who overdoses on heroin, finds God in rehab, and starts over as an evangelical pastor who preaches against the dangers of addiction and sex—both of which suddenly go hand in hand when one makes it his mission to save the world.

The point being, everyone knows a celebratory redemption story, one where the person in question overcomes adversity and becomes the main character in an undeniably remarkable turnaround story.

But there's nothing but ridicule for the ones who never turn things around.

Like the socialite whose ex-husband was arrested

on a money laundering charge and is now an outcast among her former upscale circle. Or the father who abandoned everything for his mistress and now lives an isolated existence in a run-down apartment with no mistress, ex-wife, or kids. Or the bank executive who embezzled money and lost it all only to wind up living under a forty-second street bridge with his close friend Jack Daniels. Or the beauty queen who fell victim to a botched facelift and now curses her existence behind two-inch thick, closed miniblinds.

No one celebrates the fallen and discarded because no one wants to admit it could happen to them. But we're all just one misstep away from living an upside-down life while the rest of the world points out all the ways we deserve it.

And that brings me back to the question. Is life defined by circumstances, or do circumstances define a life? From what I gather, the short answer is this: When you spend your life around rotten people, you wind up in rotten situations. And if you're not careful, the rotten rubs off, sometimes infecting a body that wasn't even standing nearby. Everyone forgets that rotten carries a stench that travels far and worms its way inside the lungs to irritate the whole part.

From all the research I've done in the last two weeks, almost everyone in Sally's world, most of whom disappeared a long time ago, was rotten. Her caregivers, her instructors, her friends. In short, Sally doesn't belong to anyone, and no one belongs to her. She regularly broadcasts that fact by living alone in a rundown shack at the edge of town and daring anyone to cross her property line. The walls around that woman are high, both physically and metaphorically speaking.

It's no wonder everyone thinks she's crazy.

My only question is whether it's all an act.

While rain falls harder, I push down the blinker and make a left turn onto a spottily paved two-lane road, with an abandoned gas station on one side and a partially collapsed barn on the other. I stare at the second-story barn loft, remnants of long-forgotten straw dangling from a decaying windowsill. Useless, abandoned, like so many other things in this backward town. *"Finn, were you born in a barn?"* I can hear the often-spoken words from my mother in my childhood when I left the back door open on my way outside to play a pickup game of basketball in the school yard across the street. What I never said was I wished I had been born in one. Barns hold generational secrets, and I've always been curious about the past. But that sort of response would have earned me a swat.

The barn disappears in the rearview mirror, a cloud of dust obstructing it in my wake. A tiny greeting card store blurs past on my left, followed by a couple farm houses and a large greenhouse with a dilapidated sign that reads "Ford's Country Gardens" dangling from what appears to be a single rusty nail. The sign sways a bit in the breeze; I wouldn't want to be standing nearby during a strong wind.

Right past the sign is her house.

I slow to a crawl as my pulse ratchets up, the woman's reputation preceding my arrival. Billi is supposed to meet me here, but so far, I'm the only one who's arrived. As the clear outsider in this scenario, I don't like being here alone.

While I wait, I roll the passenger window down a few inches to take the structure in—a tiny house that might have been nice at one time but now is nothing more than a shack—wondering how any human could live in those conditions.

A small section of the roof is caved in at the back, a three-foot strip covered in a tattered gray tarp to keep the rain out. In my mind, I picture a row of metal buckets placed side by side on the kitchen floor, quickly filling up with raindrops, gathering the remnants from what a plastic tarp couldn't possibly manage. The front entrance is nothing more than a two-by-six hole. Rough and weathered two-by-fours make up a door that hasn't seen a coat of paint in decades. A cheap screen hung askew and slapped against it in irregular intervals. *Slap bam! Bam! Slap... bam!* I'm mesmerized by the sound, staring straight at it briefly in a trance-like state until movement catches my eye in my peripheral vision and snaps me out of it.

My gaze swings to the source of the movement, and I freeze.

A filthy, wrinkled woman stands in front of my car, naked from the waist up. An old prairie-style skirt hangs from her waist in an ironic juxtaposition; scandalous on top, modest on bottom, leaving only half her body to the most disturbing imagination. Her hair is wiry and gray, tangled in a heavy mass that likely hasn't seen a brush in weeks. If she has teeth, she doesn't show them, not even to snarl. Her chin juts from its lowest point, the only thing that lets me know she's angry. I blink, stunned by what I'm seeing and unable to make sense of it, but also unable to turn away. I've seen this before. Déjà vu with no context.

I come to my senses and avert my eyes, using fumbling hands to roll down my window. To say something. Anything. Topless women aren't supposed to be standing by an open roadway, even one so lightly trafficked. I start to ask her if she's cold. To offer her the sports coat currently folded neatly across the passenger seat of my car. It's Italian silk, but I have another one at home. A car whizzes by in a rush; not Billi like I hoped, but a carload of whistling, taunting high school boys. Ignoring them,

I attempt to forge ahead like the good Samaritan my mom raised me to be.

"Can I..." the words trip from my open mouth, fighting to break free from the shock of the moment not yet worn off. Too late, I realize my mistake. Too late, I notice the gun in her hand.

My reflexes misfire all at once as I rush to shift into reverse, back up, and get the hell out of here. Every intention I have is a split second too slow. Before the gear makes it into position, the old woman lets out a scream, raises her gun...

And shoots me.

PART IV

29

TWO WEEKS EARLIER

F*inn*

The *Chronicle* is unusually quiet for a Monday afternoon, which makes Mr. Bing's bellow all the more startling. His voice rips through the silent office like a foghorn on a deserted lake, making me jump in my seat. Thankfully, this time he isn't directing his yell at me.

"It's the thirtieth anniversary of the fire," he says, slapping a thick file on Richardson's desk next to me, "and you're going to drive there and cover it." I blink over at both men—at Bing with his trademark scowl he wears even when delivering good news, and at Richardson, who's even more confused than me.

"What fire?" he asks. Rookie mistake. The rule is you agree to the assignment first and ask questions second, never the other way around. This is less a journalism rule than a hard-and-fast working-for-Bing rule. The man doesn't like hesitation. He likes being questioned even less. "I'm already writing a feature on the uptick in recent Ebola cases due next week, plus my wife is due to give birth any day now. Not real sure I have any extra time on my plate."

Bing's scowl deepens while the hairs on my neck stand at attention. *Honestly dude, scale back the negative commentary.* I attempt to ward off any impending confrontation with a question of my own.

"The thirtieth anniversary of which fire?" I'm almost positive I already know the answer, but feigning ignorance occasionally works in my favor around here. It's a gamble, and I've been known to play the slots.

Bing's gaze flicks to me, then back to Richardson, then back to me in an indecisive battle on where to focus his irritation. He sighs.

"The hospital fire in Silver Bell, Arkansas." He waves a dismissive hand between us. "You're too young to remember it, but it was a doozy. Eight people died in the accident. A pregnant lady, six babies, and a doctor if I recall correctly. Made the national news for nearly a year afterward."

"It was nine people, and the infant count was seven," I say more to myself than either of the men. Unfortunately, I'm not as young as he thinks.

"Excuse me?" Bing says, and I internally chide

myself. If there's anything the man likes less than questions, it's to be challenged. But in this particular instance, I'm more the expert, and there's no sense in pretending otherwise.

"The death toll. Seven babies died, and the total count was nine."

He blinks, and there's a not-so-subtle raise of an eyebrow. "And you know this how?"

"Because I was born at that same hospital three days before it happened. It's all my parents ever talked about when I was growing up, the fact that we barely escaped being involved. That, and how happy they were that we moved away since apparently that town is about as backwoods as they come." I laugh a bit to myself, but no one cracks a smile. Richardson sits immobile behind his desk, a dumbfounded expression on his face. In the three months he's worked here, I doubt he's heard Bing speak so many words. Our boss communicates in loud barks and unintelligible grunts. As for Bing, his scowl remains in place, perhaps even deepening. His face is lined with so many wrinkles that it's sometimes hard to tell.

"You've been working here for two years and never thought to bring that tidbit of information up?"

I push a paperclip away from the edge of the desk, one precariously close to falling, and lean back in my chair. "You've never asked me about it, and babies dying isn't exactly a conversation starter." Even though my mother used to tell the story at every social event we attended, so often that I once caught someone mouthing the words along with her.

"You work in the news industry, son. Everything is a conversation starter. What else you got in that vault of yours?" It isn't a friendly question. It's more like a threat.

"That's it, other than the fact that my parents grew up in Silver Bell."

Bing tosses his hands in the air with a frustrated growl. "Pack a bag. I want you in a car pointed north first thing in the morning. The memorial service is two weeks from today. You need to interview all the locals who will meet with you beforehand. Once the service is over, the anticipation about the anniversary will dry up too. If you want people to talk, you need to catch them off guard when they want to feel important. That's my motto.

His motto is actually *"write drunk and edit sober"* —he's got the words hanging on a plaque in bold black letters behind his desk right above an ever-present bottle of Jack Daniels—but I say nothing. Monday afternoon is not the best time to argue, much like every other day of the week. And unfortunately for me, I don't have a pregnant wife at home to fall back on.

"Fine. You gonna reimburse me for gas this time?" It's a stupid poke at his stingy bad habit, but I can't help myself. And like every other time my inner child comes out to play, I immediately regret it. Thank God my boss doesn't have a willow switch or a teaspoon of white wine vinegar I'm forced to swallow. The mere thought of my regular childhood punishment turns my tongue sour.

"I'll reimburse you for gas if you get the story. Although you and your Audi are likely just fine without it."

Fine, he's right. I drive an Audi. It isn't my fault my parents were rich or that working for a newspaper is the side job my dad got me to keep me busy learning a work ethic. A funny thing happened on my way to being forced into responsible adulthood: I discovered I liked it. Now I'm ready for my big break. I want to be recognized for excellence in writing—a Pulitzer maybe, one my parents didn't posthumously pay for. Not a respectful way to think of the dead, but it's there all the same. A desire for an accomplishment all my own, or at least a desire to make them proud.

My conscience stings at the same time my eyes begin to burn, so chances are it's the second one. Even now, six years after my mother's death and four months after my father's, the need for their approval has only escalated. Isn't that what every child wants even well into adulthood—the opportunity to look their parents in the eye and see a glimmer of pride shining back at them? Something has me still chasing that look, even if my only chance to catch it is while staring at a patch of aging dirt over a recently double-marked grave.

It's lonely being all alone in the world.

But this is not the time or place to think about it. I sniff, crack a knuckle and then another to get my mind right, and then adjust my attitude to fake-cocky and smirk up at my boss.

"Audi or not, either the *Chronicle* is cheap, or you are." I'm taking a gamble talking smack, but it's worth the risk when Bing laughs. The man laughs twice in a good year, and once is when Christmas bonus checks get passed around.

I've just scored more than I have in months, and the double-entendre is intended.

Another thing I shouldn't be thinking about right now. My love life—or lack thereof. That isn't going to drive me to Arkansas or get this article written. Not to mention the multiple interviews awaiting me. Of all the facets of this job, the interviews are the worst part. Line up ten people for back-to-back questions and answers, and you might get one eager enough—and off their guard enough—to talk. Especially when a tragedy is involved. Two things people don't like to overshare about are their kids and their hometowns. The first might result in a fractured relationship or lack of trust. The second might put you out of work and shunned by people you used to call friends. The only thing folks value above their kids is their bank account, no matter how many might insist otherwise. Money talks. The threat of losing money keeps loose lips closed, for the most part.

I'll find one person who might talk. More if my perception is off, and these small-town folks want their shot at the spotlight.

To keep reading, buy They Call Her Dirty Sally on Amazon:
https://bit.ly/45ITt1P

Made in the USA
Columbia, SC
03 October 2023

23843939R00224